Bernice Summerfield

Adorable Illusion

Gary Russell

First published in March 2014 by Big Finish Productions Ltd
PO Box 1127, Maidenhead, SL6 3LW
www.bigfinish.com

Managing Editor: Jason Haigh-Ellery
Series Producers: Scott Handcock and Gary Russell
Cover design: Stuart Manning
Production: Xanna Eve Chown

Bernice Summerfield was created by Paul Cornell
Jason Kane was created by Dave Stone

ISBN
(Book) 978-1-78178-117-3
(eBook) 978-1-78178-361-0

A CIP catalogue record for this book is available from the British Library

For Scott Handcock, my wingman, my rock and simply the best human being who I'm proud to have as my best friend. This book closes the circle we started... oh, quite a while back!

ABOUT THE AUTHOR

Gary Russell has been involved in the world of *Doctor Who* for as long as he can remember (and that includes remembering Hartnell regenerating into Troughton – yes he's that old, and more!) A lifelong love, adoration and even slight obsession with this one TV show led to him join the Doctor Who Appreciation Society in the late 70s, eventually ending up on the organising committee of said fan club, editing their newsletter. He also edited his own award-winning fanzine, *Shada,* between 1980 and 1985, and in 1983 began writing regularly for Marvel Comics' *Doctor Who Magazine* – an association that still continues irregularly today. Over the last 35+ years in fandom (dear God...) he has edited *Doctor Who Magazine*, written quite a lot of novels and factual books on the subject, written computer games, comic strips for IDW and Marvel UK, moderated DVD commentaries, produced and directed over 100 audio dramas, script edited the TV series and produced two animated stories and a number of Adventure Games. He has also script edited *Torchwood* and *The Sarah Jane Adventures*. In what laughingly passes for his spare time he has written books about *The Simpsons, Frasier* and *The Lord of the Rings* movie trilogy, collected far too many books, DVDs, CDs, action figures and Converse. Yes, bloody Converse. His home is in Cardiff in South Wales, but he has temporarily been exiled to New South Wales in Australia where he is working at Planet 55 Ltd as a television series producer. He has no pets and regardless of which home he's in, he frequently wanders around muttering to himself and scaring the neighbours...

CONTENTS

CHAPTER ONE
LIVING IN THE REAL WORLD

Six months ago...

The police were everywhere, dragging everyone they could find out of the casinos, bars and strip joints. Staff and punters alike, most of them vocally protesting their innocence, were dragged out into the sheeting rain and thrown into the back of hover-wagons.

But, as always in these kinds of raids, some people got away. Sloped off out of the fire exits, or climbed out of the toilet windows. Others hid under beds or down in cellars, inexpertly hoping they'd not be found. Oh, the authorities knew where to search, but sometimes in their enthusiasm, people still got overlooked.

After waiting for the noise to fade, he managed to slip out of a side door into an alleyway that the police were already moving away from. He hid behind an incinerator, hoping that if anyone used heat-detection equipment, the incinerator would hide him. Presumably it worked because after twenty minutes he was able to make his way back to the street.

He was soaked now, but free. He didn't really care about being wet – he and his clothes would dry back at the hotel.

Well, the rooms. 'Hotel' was a bit grandiose to be honest. When he'd arrived, he'd thrown his own coat onto the bed to sleep on because he didn't trust the stains and creepy-crawlies he imagined to be under the blankets.

He had then made his way to the bar, where his contact had said she'd meet him. Of course, she never turned up – instead the police did. And the rest, as they say, was history.

Actually, he didn't feel like heading back to his room straight away. There was another bar he'd seen earlier, that wasn't mob-run hopefully, and that had heaters. Those new-fangled ones that dried you out as you walked in, to keep the persistent rain of this ridiculous moon out of their establishment.

He was heading towards it when he heard a movement behind him. God, had the police finally found him? Had his escape been that short lived?

'I was very sorry to hear about your loss,' said a soft female voice. 'I always hear the words "a great student" and "a lovely child".'

He turned because he recognised the voice from the message-bank. It was the woman he was supposed to have met earlier. He couldn't really see her – she had framed herself rather expertly in the shadow of an awning. What he could see was her silhouette and two long, quite lovely, legs coming down from a grey skirt.

'Got a tip-off, did you?' he demanded. 'Knew not to meet there after all? Were you trapping me?'

'Why would I do that, dear man? I need you free and easy, not cooped up in prison, another inadvertent pyrrhic victory for *her*.'

'Who?'

'The very annoying woman whom I am trying to bring down. By a strange quirk of fate, she managed to become a bit of a celeb here and save the day. Again. She's so drearily righteous it's sickening. If only she knew her companion was a nasty murderer underneath all that jocular bonhomie... But she'll find out one day. I plan to ensure that.'

'I don't understand what you are talking about. Why did you want to meet me tonight. What does it have to do with my dead... child?'

'Nothing really,' the mysterious woman said, still staying in the shadows. 'Oh, but I can help you get revenge on Anya Kryztyne if you want.'

'She's dead.'

'Not any more, I gather. I hear that someone is mounting an expedition to the Rapture. Doesn't that sound like fun?'

'No.'

'Well, I'll tell you what. If I help you get what you want, you help me get what I want.'

'Why should I?' he asked. 'And how?'

'I like a man who is as intrigued as he is angry. That drive I need. Much as I need a man down on his luck, shunned by his peers and thrown out of, well, pretty much everywhere. You, my dear man, have nothing to lose and a lot to gain. I, also have a lot to gain. My target is one Professor Bernice Summerfield.'

'What do I need to do to her?'

'Absolutely nothing. But I gather one of her friends is going on a journey with her. Which I confess confuses me a little as I had thought dear old Benny was here, helping the police. Perhaps that news report was old footage, because I gather she's now on her way to a very plush and expensive space yacht owned by a thoroughly unpleasant gentleman. But those are mere details.'

The man shook his head. 'I want nothing to do with this. Or you. You're making less sense than that raid did.'

The woman gave a little laugh. 'I do apologise, dear man. All I need you to do is split Bernice and her chum or chums up and follow orders. I'll have a couple of my friends to help you along, too. And in return, you may well get answers about your lost offspring and some closure that'll help you get your life back in order. I think that's worth a few weeks of your time, don't you?'

He looked at the rain, he looked at the bar, then he looked at the silhouetted woman. 'My life back? You promise?'

'My word is my bond.' She offered a hand out of the darkness to shake. He saw only painted grey nails, and a grey bangle as he reached out to take her hand in return.

Then he felt a burning in his palm and whipped his hand back, cursing at her. She laughed.

'Sorry, I forget to say, everything you need to know is now inside you via that handy, dandy little crystal that, just so you know, doesn't come out. But it can't hurt you. All it does is pass information into your mind. Saves paper, saves the rainforests.' She looked upwards. 'Mind you, this place could do with a bit less rain.'

The pain was fading from his hand and his mind was starting to fill with new names and details. *Adorable Illusion.* Victor Cooke. Snow. Ebon.

What did that all mean?

'Sleep on it, dear man,' she said. 'Believe me, it'll all make sense in the morning. I've also transferred eight thousand credits into your personal account. Just to get you back on your feet.'

She turned to go.

'Wait,' he called. 'Who the hell are you?'

'The crystal will ensure you have nothing more than a hazy recollection of this meeting, so who I am is utterly irrelevant,' she laughed. 'You'll just do what needs to be done, no questions asked, as if it was your idea all along. And I will have no further part to play in events for, well, Advent is a good few months off, and I like that time of year. But just to sate your curiosity right now, *my* name is Fenman. Avril Fenman. And *you* are now a tiny but essential part of a long campaign of revenge on Professor Bernice Summerfield.'

CHAPTER TWO
THE HARDEST PART

He was a big chap, no getting away from that. And as he strode across the atrium, people tended to get out of his way, a curious mixture of deference and fear. He was a war hero. He was also a Killorian. The former guaranteed his position here. The latter guaranteed his reputation as a short-tempered bruiser ready to thump first and ask questions later.

This was not, Bev considered, entirely fair, but it made their lives easier. After the Battle of the Pakhar Shipyards and later the Defence of the Tsarissian Drydocks, the war had pretty much been over, and the good guys won. Well, unless you were on the side of the Deindum, then it was understandable if you were holding a grudge.

A couple of 'grudges' had manifested themselves over the last few weeks. One had taken out a cafe on the city's West Side. No one had been seriously hurt, but a couple of businesses, already in negative equity because of the war, were finished. It was a stupid statement by the perpetrators – not least because they couldn't tell the difference between AM and PM, thank God – but mainly because it got them no sympathy, just a lot of weary survivors ready to lynch them.

She wasn't entirely sure if they had got away, or Adrian Wall had found them but let them escape. She knew that he was tired of the war, the death and the responsibility of it all.

Neither of them had ever wanted this responsibility, but it seemed to have fallen to them, especially after Brax and Benny vanished. Adrian was convinced they would turn up again. Brax because, well he was Brax, and Benny because he simply couldn't believe she could die. Bev was tempted to agree. They'd seen Benny survive so much over the years, one little temporal implosion that effectively stopped the Deindum in their tracks would be just a scratch to Bernice Summerfield.

It had been a strange moment – Bev could remember it so clearly, unlike most of the quadrant. Years of exposure to time fissures, distillations and everything else that came as baggage with Benny and Braxiatel had made her and Adrian pretty impervious. The rest of the fighters saw... nothing. The Deindum had gone from ultra-savage warmongers to a small set of skirmishers. Determined but ultimately defeated. Brax's plan had been to go back and change the Deindum's past, stop them starting wars. It hadn't quite worked, but it had worked enough that a lot of the recent past had been undone.

Of course, not all the dead had been miraculously returned to life, but those that had were unaware they'd been dead – as were their friends and families. That was a good side-effect of rewriting the past. It was different for those who'd been at the epicentre of the change. They'd always know, even if it was only a corner-of-the-eye thing. They knew something was askew but not what, and over time, they'd forget it all, like a dream. She and Adrian were different. Some of the things that happened to them hadn't been undone – they were too much of a fixed point in time.

Joseph had been found by the escape pods. Of Doggles, there was no sign and Joseph's circuits were too messed up. Bev suspected that Doggles was dead, but couldn't know for sure. Much like Hass – had he been brought back when time changed? Maybe he'd reverted even further. Bev wasn't quite sure why she thought that, why there was something about Martians in her thoughts whenever she brought Hass to mind. She put that down to the time implosion as well.

But one thing she was sure of was that Peter was out there somewhere. Out in the stars. After the mopping up of the now-weakened Deindum had been finished, Bev promised Adrian they would go and find him. But somehow life had got in the way. They'd overnight become the figureheads of this new, well, government was the best word for it. They had been given no choice. Them or anarchy. The quadrant needed someone to come along and sort them out, rebuild not just a civilisation but a whole slice of the galaxy, reestablish some kind of post-wartime life.

Again. It struck Bev more than once that this was exactly what had happened after the Fifth Axis invasion. But on a grander scale. Galactic rather than planetary. But it meant they were both able to draw on that experience, and magnify it.

And then there was Benny herself. Neither she nor Brax had turned up. Ever. But Benny would. She was alive. Of course she was. Out there, probably looking after Peter.

At least that's what she told Adrian. After the war was won. After their victorious wedding. After their not-really-a-honeymoon-more-a-refugee-camp-setting-up thing here on Valentine's World. She told him that each day. And she could see the pain in those deep brown eyes that he wanted to believe her. He said he believed her, but deep down didn't. Bev knew that it wasn't because he loved Benny any more – that ship sailed long ago. But she was still his best friend.

And the mother of his son.

Bev noticed, hovering behind Adrian, almost deferentially, was a small football-sized metal sphere, currently making occasional faster-than-the-eye-could-quite-see movements, as if trying to catch his attention. Adrian's face told Bev he knew it was there but was choosing to ignore it.

'Joseph!' she called to the sphere. 'What's up?'

If the sphere had had a face (that wasn't just drawn on years back by Benny with a Sharpie) Bev would've sworn it had frowned at her. Nevertheless the mobile computer whipped towards her rapidly, its fussy, pompous voice barking out in synthetic weariness. At least Bev assumed it was synthetic. For all she knew, Joseph was as genuinely sentient as he claimed he was programmed to be.

'Mrs Wall,' he said testily, 'your husband refuses to acknowledge me. I may have important information.'

'Do you?'

'I might.'

Bev just sighed. 'In about fifteen minutes I have to meet with the representatives of the East Side, book a conference call with the board of the new Maximerderas Corporation and attend the inaugural opening of the replanted Echo Park. If you have something to tell Adrian, tell *me* in as few words as possible, and I'll pass it on.'

Joseph hovered, then dropped a few centimetres – a sign of complicity, Bev knew.

'Have you heard of Bastion?'

Bev thought about this. Of course she had – one of the slave planets, a molten planet of caverns and pits, reportedly used as part of the Deindum's war machine. After the war ended, it was liberated. Or was due to be. Bev wasn't sure if it had happened or was on the The List.

'What about Bastion?'

'Our Repatriation Team finally accessed it eight weeks ago. The robot drones had all shut down and the slaves were surviving as best they could. The sickness and starvation rates were high but we rescued 734 slaves from 306 different species. They are currently being processed before returning to whatever homeworlds they elect.'

'And?'

'One of the main problems our Team faced was the retaliation against what the slaves saw as collaborators. Specifically a colony of 68 Grel, who worked for the Drones rather than in the pits themselves, as food servers or maintenance workers –'

'Get to the point please, Joseph,' Bev cut across, exasperated. She'd heard this before on numerous worlds they had saved. And all back through history. People who had worked for the enemy to survive rarely coped with life after wartime when their fellow victims turned on them, seeing them as collaborators, despite the fact they rarely had any choice.

Joseph tutted, Bev was sure. Just when she thought she was used to Benny's old companion, he – no, *it* – managed to surprise her.

'The Grel told our teams that, about a year before the fact that the war was over caught up with their sector of the galaxy, one of the slaves had been rescued.'

'Rescued? From Bastion? How does that happen?' Bev knew Bastion's reputation. Once you went there, you didn't come out again.

'The Grel was unclear. But he knew exactly who the person was, because he was popular amongst the slaves.'

Bev felt a sudden flush, a sudden rush of warmth and excitement. He. Joseph had said *he*. For Joseph to mention it, it could only be Brax. Or Hass. Or...

'Peter Guy Summerfield,' Joseph said simply. And, Bev thought, a little quietly. Respectfully.

But Bev took a deep breath. It could be coincidence. Or the opening gambit in some kind of mind-game – it wasn't exactly unknown that Adrian Wall, hero of the Federated Worlds in their victory of the Deindum, was looking for his son. Although, this was the first time his name had come up to definitely, so particularly. 'Anything else I can tell Adrian? If I do?'

'Mrs Wall?'

'It's not easy, Joseph. You know what he's like – the first whiff of Peter, and Adrian could drop everything and start scouring the sector he was last meant to be in. And I'm not sure we can afford to lose Adrian's leadership right now. One day, sure. But tomorrow?'

'What will you do?'

'Sleep on it, and hate myself for keeping this from him.' Bev felt her tummy lurch a bit. 'Ooh, the pups are kicking.' She looked at Joseph. 'And if I'm honest, I don't want to lose him so close to me giving birth. Whelping. Whatever you call a hybrid human-Killoran birthing.' Bev laughed. 'You were there last time this happened, Joseph. How did Benny cope?'

'I was not present,' Joseph corrected. 'But I understand the circumstances were very different. You have some of the finest medical facilities the Federation can offer on Valentine's World. You will be fine.' Joseph bobbed a bit lower. 'I want Peter to be found safely, too. But I understand and appreciate your reluctance to tell Mr Wall. I will not repeat any of this to him.' He rotated 360 degrees. 'There was one other thing. The Grel believed that Peter was being taken to another planet.'

'Which one?'

'Legion.'

Bev's elation turned straight to despair. 'Out of the frying pan, into the fire. How long would it take us to get out there?'

'A minimum of six months, and that doesn't factor in stoppages, refuelling, trading etc to enable secure passage to the frontier worlds and beyond.'

'What git would take Peter to Legion?'

Joseph bobbed. 'The Grel didn't have any other information

about that. The Team report they questioned him as thoroughly as they could, recognising the importance. I can arrange to have him brought to Valentine's World for further questioning.'

Bev shook her head. 'Poor sod's been through enough over the last few years. Make sure we keep tabs on him so that if Adrian does need to see him, we know where he is. In the meantime let him get home safely and quickly. He deserves that...'

Bev was interrupted as a ship flew overhead, coming in to land at the South Side Space Port. 'Bloody low,' she muttered.

'It is the *Adorable Illusion*,' Joseph reported. 'Recognisable by its unique centre section's architecture. Three hours' refuelling before returning to the Dragonfly nebula.'

'They're researching the Rapture, right?'

'If you mean the unexplained rift in the Dragonfly nebula, then yes.'

'Everyone calls it the Rapture, Joseph. Have done for centuries. I bet it's even called that in your databases.'

'That does not make it right. It is not an accepted scientific term for such a rift.'

'Unexplained rift.'

'That does not change the fact that it is a Rift, and calling it "the Rapture" gives it a ridiculous emotional significance far beyond that of its innate scientific interest.'

'God, you sound like Benny.'

'Thank you.'

'When she's being pissed and ultra-dull.'

'I withdraw my gratitude.'

'I bet you do.' Bev realised she had already reached a decision. 'I'll tell Adrian about Peter when I've had a chance to digest all this. Till then, our little secret, yes?'

'Of course, Mrs Wall.' Joseph started to float away, then returned. 'Is it wrong that I miss the professor?'

Bev smiled at him. 'We all miss Benny, Joseph. One day we'll find her. Till then, we carry on as best we can and get this galaxy back on its metaphorical feet, yes?'

Joseph bobbed and shot away.

Bev sighed, glancing at Adrian, chatting to a couple of Killoran workmen. Once upon a time, Bev Tarrant nicked things from dead civilisations for a living. Now, as Bev Wall, she rebuilt civilisations. Funny old life.

In the distance, the *Adorable Illusion* was landing noisily, and Bev glanced in its direction, still able to see it as it slotted vertically into the refuelling depot eighteen miles away. It was as tall as a skyscraper, and from this distance, could easily have been one amongst all the others in Valentine's World's capital, other than its glaringly obvious central unique design.

'Bloody hell, you are big,' she muttered. And she shivered.

'You okay, hon?' Adrian said as he approached her, head quizzically on one side, long floppy ears blowing in the breeze.

'I'm fine. I —' she stopped. Adrian was sniffing the air. 'What's up?'

'It's weird,' he growled. 'I feel as if —'

'Someone's just walked over my grave,' they both said simultaneously. And stared at each other. Then Bev realised Adrian was looking at the parked *Adorable Illusion*.

'New ship?'

'Refurbished dreadnought. It's quite famous.'

Adrian shrugged. 'Why so?'

Bev laughed, slipping her arm around his. 'Adrian, how many ships do you know with a Grand Trianon-sized hole in the middle?'

'Stupid idea,' he laughed back. 'Anyway, I left my *Observer's Book of Spaceships* back in our bedroom.'

She felt him arm tighten as he said that. It had been Benny's book. It still had a few post-it notes dotted in it, comments ranging from *No, it's blue, not green* to *Let's hope no one ever tries to fly it then* and *Been there, had the captain, drunk the bar dry.* Neither she nor Adrian had any intention of ever taking them out.

'She's out there, Hubby. I know it.'

'Then why hasn't she found us?' he grumbled. 'Until she's with Peter and, dare I say it, Brax, and back with all of us, I can't relax.'

'One day, she'll surprise us. Walk off a spaceship, find us and say "Oh, hi guys!" like she's been away for a weekend pub crawl.'

Adrian shook his head. 'I'm not convinced. If she were close by, I'd know it.'

And together, with their new family growing inside Bev's belly, they headed off to attend various meetings, conference calls and grand re-openings, always hoping Bev was right, but always suspecting Adrian was.

CHAPTER THREE
VICTOR

'What's that?'

'What's what?'

'That noise? What is it, Benny?'

Bernice Summerfield sighed. Again. She'd done a lot of sighing recently, much of it in the direction of her travelling companion. Not because he was deliberately annoying (well, not much) but simply because he seemed a bit... dim. Which he wasn't – in fact he was pretty sharp and sparky – he just had a tendency to speak without thinking and to ask questions in a really annoying way. Because if he waited another three seconds, he'd realise he already knew the answer. It was like he was desperate to make sure she knew he was there, like giving her the chance to answer someone made him feel he was making *her* feel clever and important. She actually just felt like sighing and screaming, 'You know the bloody answer, Jack. Grow up!' But she didn't. Nine times out of ten it was easier just to sigh and then provide the answer. And if she didn't know it, well, she'd make something up and hope *he* didn't know the answer and go, "Ha, gotcha, finally!"

He wasn't the most mature of companions.

'I imagine it's the ship starting its refuelling procedure,' she said.

'Oh course it is,' Jack replied. 'I should've known.'

Bernice wanted to reply that yes, he should have. She didn't. Because frustrating as Jack was, he was the closest thing Bernice had to a friend right now, and she liked having friends. And he was alive. And here with her.

Unlike Leo. Or Ruth.

Ever since escaping Atlantis, after repairing the shuttle they had originally arrived in together (although Bernice initially couldn't remember that fact) and zooming off into space, being buffeted by some kind of energy wave that had either erased where they had come from or flicked them back through time and space or whatever it had done (because neither of them frankly had a clue), life had got complicated.

Once realising she was back in her home time (give or take), she had told Jack she wanted to find Peter, Adrian and Bev. Hell, she'd settle for finding Braxiatel at the moment – although she might punch him. Or worse. The last time she'd seen any of them was during the Deindum war.

She'd seen that Peter was with Joseph and Doggles – she knew they'd keep him safe while she and Brax messed up the space/time continuum and reshaped the Deindum's destiny. Or something. It was terrifying how easily she just accepted that she did things like that.

Then she'd found herself on Raster, then Atlantis – which she thought was Earth, which kept getting remapped and rewritten. She'd befriended Ruth and Leo, but lost them both. Leo had been remapped, his mind completely rewritten so he had no idea who either of them were. And then she'd lost Ruth in a pastiche of Victorian London. Jack said she'd been off, trying to find the solution to the problem, but in travelling back to them, Ruth had been badly injured and died. In Bernice's arms.

They'd been friends for so little time, but she felt her friend's death so powerfully. They had been through a lot and somehow Bernice had felt sure she and Ruth were going to make it together – head home, find Peter and the others, start afresh now the quadrant was rebuilding itself after the war.

Instead she was teamed up with Jack, a red-eyed, cocky Kadeptian, with unfeasibly strong sway-back legs, that meant he could jump ridiculously high. It wasn't a particularly show-stopping ability. He was also quite devious, which was why she found his ignorant questioning so annoying. He was smarter than he appeared and, as they spent time together getting into scrapes (oh, that one with the Naxian scripture book was fun, and then there was the week they spent avoiding the angry Swamp Turtles – she had to admit his jumping prowess had been dead useful then), she'd gained a grudging respect for him. They had even had a few laughs (his reprogramming of the Hedmetics' Justice Machines so that all they did was sell second-hand planetary hoppers was inspired. And more than a bit naughty.)

She'd found Jack asleep one night, but thought he was awake, talking to someone. She realised he was reliving something in his dreams, muttering snatches of conversation. At one point she was sure he'd said, 'I'm sorry, Ruth,' but couldn't be sure. One day she'd bring it up but (even if, deep down, she suspected he had caused Ruth's death) she wasn't going to bring it up while they were 'working' together. Bernice rarely felt vulnerable, and she certainly didn't now. But she had come close to it, close to giving up and it had been Jack's unrelenting (aka nauseating) cheerfulness that had kept her going. And knowing the truth, if there was a truth to know, wasn't going to bring Ruth back.

So she had let herself move forward. And Jack seemed to be coming along for the ride. Which was fine.

Two months ago, news had reached her that a scientific research ship was going to examine the Rapture, which was a bit exciting frankly as it was something she had always wanted to see up close. She had once asked Jason to go there on holiday, stay on one of the local rimworlds that hung in their perpetual gravity well, never moving, just hanging there. Jason had made some bored sound that suggested he'd rather stay behind on the Collection with Peter and find amusing ways to get Adrian's back up.

It crossed Bernice's mind, as she remembered that and looked at Jack, that she tended to surround herself with pretty annoying men. Except Leo...

So she'd never made it out to the Rapture. She would be approaching it from the other side of the galaxy now. The Collection, if it still existed, was at about two o'clock, and she was at about six, assuming the galaxy was a huge clock face. Which it wasn't, but it was a handy way to estimate spatial differences.

So yaaaay, here was a chance to see it and use her credentials to get up close. It was Jack who suggested maybe not using her own name.

'It has got us into a bit of trouble over the last few months.'

'Nonsense, I'm a highly respected expert in my field.'

'May I remind you about the Jaceans?'

'They didn't like anyone associated with Brax.'

'May I then bring up the Soundsmiths of Lassa?'

'That wasn't my fault! It was years ago. And also not my fault if I set off a generational "Wanted Dead or Alive – Preferably Dead" on my own head. Who knew they'd remember?'

'Then there was the Imperator of Xoab. Like your name, he did not.'

'That was Jason's fault. I didn't know he'd grafittied the Royal Tree with "Jason and Benny did it here. Eight times. In a day" after our honeymoon.'

'All I'm saying is, until we can guarantee the name Professor

Bernice Summerfield won't result in atomisation, beheading, ritual bloodletting or molecular fusion with a toadstool, I suggest finding a jolly *nom de plume*. A clever, sophisticated pseudonym that gives you archaeological credentials without necessarily wearing your true colours on your sleeve.'

Bernice had sighed and given in. She could sort of agree with his sentiments (although she did glower when he pointed out how often she found she could blame Jason Kane, Irving Braxiatel or "that Wolsey bloke you are always going on about" to explain away their problems).

'Now,' Jack said, one sunny morning. 'I've scoured the GalWeb and found a doctor of digging up old bones who has a few hits on the search engines, but I can't find out anything recent about her. So she has credentials, but not the ability to come and accuse you of impersonating her. I'm guessing she's retired. By the time they've done a search on it, we'll be halfway across the galaxy on the *Adorable Illusion* – that's the ship by the way – and no one will be any the wiser. All I ask is that I'm your assistant, so I get a nice berth like the one you'll get for being a famous archaeologist.'

Infamous more like it.

Bless Jack and his almost-but-not-quite-ADHD ability to get bored with the simplest tasks. There was a reason why Dr Anya Kryztyne had disappeared off the face of the GalWeb.

'One sentence more, Jack. You could have just read one more line of text,' Bernice had yelled as the authorities handcuffed her and she heard the words: 'Prisoner 442, you have been recaptured, and any parole you had hoped for rescinded. You are being returned to The Pier to serve the rest of your sentence, with an additional 87 years for escaping. No amount of reconstructive facial surgery can save you.'

Jack had omitted to see that Anya Kryztyne was no longer a doctor of anything after she abandoned a shuttle of university students to die in space, while she engaged in nookie with a local anti-grav squash player aboard his shuttle, half a light year away. Stripped of everything, she'd been sentenced to thirty years at the Pier, the legendary prison floating in synchronous orbit around Castor Three.

So, impersonating her wasn't Jack's greatest suggestion. In fact, it didn't come close.

And yet. Four days *en route* to the Pier, the police shuttle had docked with a rather grandiose yacht, which she quickly realised was owned by Victor Cooke, the industrialist who was funding the Rapture project, and it appeared that money spoke louder than the law.

The police agreed that they had run into a meteor storm, their ship had been punctured and poor old Anya had been sucked out into space. Decidedly rich enough to retire, the two police officers flew home and Bernice was taken aboard Victor Cooke's yacht and treated to an expensive dinner for two off an ornate smoked-glass table which looked as though it was polished at least three times a day. From the look she got from Victor Cooke's ever-present majordomo when she dumped her bag on it, she was probably correct.

'What do you think?'

'Of what?' Bernice asked.

'My yacht. This glorious "state room", as I call it. Isn't it fabulous?'

'It's interesting,' was the most Bernice could come up with, which got her another glare from the majordomo.

'Thing is, Anya,' Victor began saying, 'I think your archaeological knowledge shouldn't be squandered. Society paid a lot of money to educate you, seems only right it gets put to use for their ultimate benefit, even if no one will ever actually know.'

Bernice shrugged. 'That sounds like a veiled threat, Mr

Cooke. What happens at the end, Anya really does go floating home after an "accident"?'

Cooke laughed, not unkindly, and Bernice frowned. 'My dear lady, Anya Kryztyne died five months back. I should know, I dropped her screaming into a vat of molten steel. I say dropped. I mean lowered slowly. Feet-first.'

Bernie paused to let that sink in. Poor choice of words – sinking in was not something that sounded good right now. The majordomo looked equally satisfied at this news and Bernice's discomfort. He really wasn't forgiving her for the bag-on-table thing.

She cautiously frowned at Victor Cooke. 'Then...?'

'You are Professor Bernice Summerfield, Martian expert, specialist subject 19th–22nd century Earth culture, brilliant archaeologist with forged credentials and chronological anomaly. Worked for six years at the Braxiatel Collection, and apparent hero to the forces who opposed the Deindum – I took a neutral stance in that, my dear, by the way.'

'Wanted to see who won? Who ended up with the biggest bank balance.'

'Pretty much.'

'So why am I here?'

'Because I need someone I trust aboard the *Adorable Illusion*. Someone with a vested interest in solving the mystery of the Rapture.'

'I see,' Bernice lied, because she really didn't. 'And am I going as me or as Anya?'

'As Anya. Bernice Summerfield is not popular with one of my clients, the Heliok Syndicate, and they have a bounty on your head.'

The majordomo ever-so-slightly almost dropped a salt-shaker and Bernice saw the flash of concern go across his face at the mention of the Heliok Syndicate.

'I have never heard of them,' she said. 'What did I ever do to them?'

'Four months ago, you proved that one of their croupiers was embezzling funds and exposed them. They didn't like the gambling Cluster Worlds finding out. Hence the bounty. If they found out I was dealing with Bernice Summerfield, well, I'm not sure I'd survive the night.'

'Nonsense,' Bernice said. 'Jack and I have never been near them. I'd remember doing that.'

The majordomo activated a screen and pointed at a holographic news report.

Bernice pouted. 'Yup, got to admit that looks like me.'

The majordomo activated the sound after a nod from Victor Cooke.

'My name is Professor Bernice Summerfield and my friend and I are delighted to report that the Heliok Syndicate's corruption has been utterly proven. We have handed over our proof to the Cluster authorities and the relevant Heliok bosses are being arrested as we speak. Finally this corner of the sector is free of corruption and bootlegging!'

'What will you do with your reward money, Professor?' asked an unseen journalist.

'We are going to hire a ship to get us to Kaff Zarnak. Always wanted to see the Xanadu resort.'

The majordomo shut the hologram off and with a slightly self-satisfied grin at Bernice, exited the room.

Bernice blew air out of her cheeks. 'Well, that's either a brilliant forgery or I had soooo much drink afterwards I neither remember that or that Xanadu place. Which, for the record, I've never heard of.'

'It's a long way away from here,' Victor Cooke said. 'So you have a choice. Work for me or I hand you over to the Heliok.'

'Won't you do that anyway, when I get back from the Rapture?'

'The Heliok are culturally bound to keep their bounty, and rage, for only six months. If they have not redeemed the bounty money, it's null and void and you'll be safe. In theory. As far as my involvement goes, I'll be fine.'

Bernice ate some fruit, slowly, then squinted at Victor Cooke. 'Okay, so if I go, I go as Anya, not Benny. If I go, I get a chance to examine the Rapture and hopefully solve the mystery of what it is. If I go, I get to go on the *Adorable Illusion* which Jack tells me is rather wonderfully huge. So my question is why? Why do you want me to do this.'

'I'd be far more interested in knowing why I killed the real Anya if I were in your position, Professor.'

Bernice considered that. 'Okay, I'll bite.' Which she did, just to illustrate her point. Plus, the fruit was delicious.

'My only son was one of the students she left to die. He shared my love of the universe, of astrophysics and exploration beyond the known world."

Bernice absorbed this.

'Imagine if it were your Peter,' Victor Cooke added.

Bernice nodded. 'I might sympathise with you, yes, although I'm not sure slowly boiling her in oil would be my recourse.'

'Each to their own.'

'But – by the way this food is gorgeous, thank you,' Bernice smiled. Then carried on, 'But I still don't see why you are funding this mission. You had your revenge, even if you have to keep it quiet and use me as a decoy.'

'Anya Kryztyne's students were examining the Rapture. They were underfunded, undershielded and illegally there. The Rapture swallowed their shuttle, *The Hunter*, while she was screwing the sports jock of the group somewhere else entirely. I want to see if you can find the remains of *The Hunter*.'

Or something that confirms they died quickly and painlessly.'

'Unlike Anya Kryztyne,' Bernice muttered.

'What do you need to do the job, Professor?' Victor Cooke drummed his fingers on the table impatiently.

'Another identity?'

'Nice try, but no. Anya it is. Anything else?'

'Jack would be good. God knows why I just said that, but somewhere, subconsciously, I must believe he could be useful. A gun. And a hamper of this fruit. Any chance of some cash too?'

'As a prisoner, you can't handle cash or a gun. Jack will be armed however, as he'll be put in as your personal guard – on my payroll, with orders to shoot you at the slightest provocation or dereliction of duty.'

'He does know we're play-acting, right?'

'He'll be told. You wanted him, you'd better hope he doesn't get too into character,' Victor Cooke smiled. 'I will make sure you get the hamper though.'

'When do we leave?'

'Three hours. My yacht is due to rendezvous with the *Adorable Illusion* while it refuels on Valentine's World. You'll be put aboard there. My small but efficient team will look after you.' He drummed his fingers again, and Bernice wondered if there was a tune in his head he was playing.

'How small?'

'It's a big ship, a dreadnought class in fact, that I have had... customised. It's fully automated. Other than the captain's personal crew of five and a handful of tediously dull paying passengers, there will be two of my top quatermasters to keep an eye on both you – and the three other people on my payroll aboard. All scientists. You won't meet them by the way. They aren't huge archaeology fans. They're more about the now than the past.'

'Nice. Thanks for that.'

'Means, if the Heliok board you at anytime, they won't go looking for you 'cause you won't be on the manifest.'

Bernice pointed at the frozen hologram. 'Umm, can I just remind you that they know what I look like? And presumably Jack, too.'

'Better stay out of their way then, if they turn up.' Victor Cooke grinned. 'You'll be fine, Bernice. You've survived far worse than a few weeks aboard a research vessel.'

'If you say so.' Bernice stood up. 'May I have a quick shower and freshen up?'

Victor Cooke also stood. 'Of course. My majordomo will show you to the guest quarters.' He raised a glass to toast Bernice and then winked.

Bernice didn't wink back but walked towards the door which opened, and the majordomo was there, looking as though he was going to find her the smallest, most cockroach-infested broom cupboard possible to sleep in.

'Oh, Bernice,' Victor Cooke called softly. 'One last thing. Nearly slipped my mind, so glad I remembered.'

Bernice gave him a look of 'what now?'

Victor Cooke stopped drumming his fingers on the table top, drained his glass and dabbed his lips with a napkin. 'A number of people aboard also lost children on that shuttle. They won't like you very much. They never met the real Anya, so they've accepted my word that you are her. Be careful, they might be less... hospitable than I.'

Bernice fixed him with a stare. 'You are a complete shit, aren't you, Victor?'

'I certainly am. Good luck.'

CHAPTER FOUR
IN THE FLESH

'Why would someone build a spaceship the length of Manhattan and put a bloody great hole in the middle of it?'

Bernice and Jack were being shown the *Adorable Illusion* from the launch control building on Valentine's World. The technician pointed at it on a 3D schematic on his screen. 'It's not just a hole,' he said. 'It's a pulsar-scooper.'

Bernice weighed up the ludicrousness of this statement. 'A what now?'

'A pulsar-scooper,' the man repeated.

Nope, she still couldn't get her head around the scientifically bum-clenchingly numbskulled nonsense of that.

'What does that mean?'

'It scoops up pulsars?' offered Jack.

'Shut up, Jack,' Bernice replied. She tapped the schematic. 'How, in the name of all that's holy, do you put a pulsar in a hole in a ship, no matter the size of the ship. I mean, I'm making myself dizzy entertaining the impossibility of "scooping up a pulsar" in the first place but even if you could, the smallest pulsar in the galaxy is three times larger than this charmingly named planet.' She looked closer at the schematic. 'Has no one with an IQ above that of a mouse actually queried this thing?'

'Maybe Mr Cooke's money buys their silence,' Jack offered.

'I'll bet it bloody does,' Bernice muttered. 'So we're going aboard this ship with a bunch of crazies who don't question this hole and why it's there, or the fact that the man with the purse-strings is off his rocker.'

'That's enough, Kryztyne,' Jack barked suddenly. 'Time we got you aboard.'

Bernice looked at Jack, then the technician, who was clearly terrified to be in the presence of such a Galactic Public Enemy Number One, and sighed. 'Let's get going, Captain Jack.'

She and Jack stared at each other.

'Maybe not that name,' he said. 'Guard Jack will do.'

'Guard Jack it is,' Bernice agreed.

Jack shrugged at the technician. 'We'll get over there now. Let them know we're coming, will you please?'

The technician visibly sagged once they had left. 'They don't pay me enough,' he muttered, then tapped the comms. 'Control to *Adorable Illusion*. You are fully fuelled and cleared for blast off in nine zero zero. Your new passengers are *en route*.'

'Message received,' said a voice over the comms. 'Thanks for your hospitality, Valentine's World. My chief engineer AI will contact you when we enter the one two zero period. Captain Redbeard out.'

The technician shook his head. 'Anya Kryztyne. And a guy from Kadept who's not an ambulance-chaser. Oh, and a captain called Redbeard. I need a day off.'

Behind him the door opened and someone hurried in, sniffing the air.

The technician turned sharply. 'Mr Wall, sir. Wasn't expecting you.'

Adrian Wall was staring at the schematic, and then across at the *Adorable Illusion* out of the window. 'Who was here?' he snapped.

'Two passengers for the *Adorable Illusion*. One of Mr Cooke's personal guardsmen and his prisoner, an archaeologist.'

Adrian's ears literally pricked up. 'Who?'

The technician shrugged. 'That killer, the one who escaped from the Pier. Anya Kryztyne.'

Adrian deflated visibly. 'Oh. You sure?'

'Paperwork's all there sir. You all right?'

'I sensed a... scent,' Adrian said slowly. 'But I was wrong.' He smiled at the technician. 'I'm grasping at straws.'

The technician smiled back. 'Understandable sir. But your standing orders are maintained at all times. The moment the name Professor Bernice Summerfield shows up on any manifests within a hundred klicks of here, we alert you any time of day or night. But this wasn't her, sir. I can show you a photo of Anya Kryztyne if you like – we had to take one for security.'

Adrian shook his head. 'Nah, I remember what she looked like, especially after the media circus around that case.' He wandered back to the door. 'Ah well, sorry to have bothered you.'

'How's Mrs Wall, sir? Pups due soon?'

Adrian nodded. 'Any day now. I'll tell her you asked, mate. Night.'

'Night Mr Wall.'

After Adrian had gone the technician prepared to count down the *Adorable Illusion*'s launch. And hoped that one day Bernice Summerfield would come to Valentine's World, because he knew how happy it would make the Wall family. He was still thinking about that when the *Adorable Illusion* launched and streaked away from Valentine's World for the last time, on its mission to discover the secret of the Rapture.

CHAPTER FIVE
X-OFFENDER

'Chop chop! Hurry up, chaps and chapesses, let's get a move on.'

Quartermaster Edj stood to one side of the doorway to the dorm area of the *Adorable Illusion*, waving the people through like some effervescent drink that never settled, a huge grin on his big silver face. He blinked a lot more regularly than most people, Bernice thought.

She and Jack had met the two quartermasters first, as they boarded the ship. Jack had whispered a query to her about them being robots, but she'd explained that they were from one of the Outer Major system worlds, Kromia, and that their haemoglobin included a significant amount of platinum, which gave their skin the distinct silver sheen. 'Chromeheads' was the usual unkind epithet given to them across the quadrant. They were renowned for the cheerful, if fussy, efficiency that made them regularly employed as cabin crew on star-liners and the like. Quite why Cooke had felt the need to employ them here escaped Bernice – perhaps they were cheap.

Jack sniggered as the second quartermaster, Kread, gave Bernice a cheeky slap on the behind to get her going. 'Keep it moving there, Dr Kryztyne,' he said.

Bernice gritted her teeth at the inappropriate gesture but said nothing. Cooke had reminded her that, for her own safety, the less attention she drew to herself, the better.

'You are enjoying this too much,' she muttered to Jack a few moments later as they looked for their berths.

'Rank has its privileges, I believe you once said,' he grinned back. 'And I outrank you. And, strictly speaking, Edj and Kread.'

'Don't tell them that,' Bernice suggested. 'But you might like to point out, subtly, that sexual harassment was phased out a few centuries back.'

'On Beta Capris, maybe,' Jack countered. 'Who knows what the culture is like where they come from.' Then his face went serious. 'Or indeed aboard this ship. We can't take anything for granted. What you and I think of as acceptable might be exactly the opposite here.'

Bernice shrugged. Jack was right, but she wasn't going to let him know that. Directly. 'Well, we know that they don't like killers much,' she said. 'That's usually a sign of basic civil behaviour.'

'I managed to get a copy of the crew manifest downloaded to my data-pad, where they are sleeping, and their duty schedules,' Jack said. 'We should get acquainted with who's who a bit later.'

'Good call,' Bernice agreed, then stopped. She looked at Jack. 'You're not as dim as you look, are you?'

'I'm sorry?'

'How'd you get that then? I'd've thought that was pretty restricted information.'

'I'm not just a pretty face,' said Jack. 'Unlike the petty officer who was in charge of ground staff on Valentine's World.' His eyes flashed a sudden scarlet. 'Let's just say she was intrigued by my legs. And stuff.'

'Well, if you have attributes, use them, I guess.'

Jack nodded. 'And it's not like you haven't used your breasts to your advantage in the past.'

'I have not!'

'So have.'

'Not! Why would you say that?'

'Because you are clever, smart and still alive after all you've been through. If you can honestly tell me you've never used your sexual allure to get you in to, or out of, places or situations, I'll apologise unreservedly.'

Bernice opened her mouth to protest, at which point more than a dozen such occasions poured out of her memory, so she shut it again. 'Bah.' She poked Jack in the chest. 'Hang on, you think I'm alluring?'

'God no,' Jack said. 'But I'm pretty damn sure that somewhere out there are various desperate souls into the more... maternal types.' He flicked his pointed tongue at her. And smiled. 'Maybe just a little allure. I reckon Kread sees you as a —'

'Keep the chat down over there,' called Quartermaster Edj.

Bernice pulled an 'Oooh we've been told off!' face.

Jack winked and mouthed something at her which she couldn't instantly decipher, as he turned away and pushed open a door with his foot. Then Bernice clouted him.

'Did you just mouth MILF at me?'

Jack's red eyes twinkled. 'Moi? As if! What do you take me for?' And he ushered Bernice through the door.

It revealed a tiny cabin, with a sink and bunk beds. On the other side was a sliding door Bernice guessed led to a loo and shower. She hoped it did anyway.

She stepped in and looked back at Jack, standing in the doorway. 'Top or bottom?'

He went to reply and she quickly cut him off. 'Bunks,' she said. 'I meant the bunks.'

'I know!' he said, pretending to look aggrieved. 'I was going to say that it's not up to me, I'm not in with you in here. I have an officer's room up by the canteen.'

'Oh. Is it too much to expect I have this whole cabin to myself?'

Bernice's answer came not from Jack but from a blur of red fur and silver spacesuit that Bernice thought wouldn't look out of place in a bad mid-twentieth century B-movie. Assuming said B-movie was called Invasion of the Squirrel-People (she was reasonably sure no one had ever been daft enough to use a name like that for anything, ever).

'Hiya,' said the newcomer in an accent which sounded equally mid-twentieth century ('curse my cultural obsessions,' Bernice thought) human, specifically European, more specifically Britain, remarkably specifically north-western, ridiculously specifically Liverpudlian. 'You chosen yet, girl? Top or bottom?'

Bernice couldn't speak.

Jack could, albeit through a barely stifled laugh. 'She's always top.'

'Cool, great even, eh?' The red-squirrel-thing-woman flopped onto the lower bunk, yanking her tail away from the wall. 'Not much room, girl, is there? Never mind, Ginger will cope.'

Bernice took the plunge that this was her extraordinary new cabin-mate's name. 'Hullo Ginger. I'm Anya.'

'Oh, I know who exactly who you are girl, don't you worry. I selected to bunk in with you.'

'Oh, why?' asked Jack.

'And what's it to you, Legs Eleven?'

'I'm her personal... security guard.'

'Ha!' Ginger revealed her two buck teeth as she smiled. 'You're Cooke's pet jailer, yeah. Don't worry, Legs, I'll keep a good eye on the doctor here.'

'You will?' asked Bernice.

'Yeah. You killed my son, see, so I'm here to make sure nothing similar happens to you.'

Bernice had expected this would happen – Cooke had warned her after all. Then Ginger's words sunk in. 'You want to make sure nothing happens to me?'

'Course, girl.' And she reached up and pulled Bernice closer, gently but firmly. 'If and when anything happens to Dr Anya Krystyne, it'll happen when I want it to, not before.'

'I'm not sure I feel entirely reassured by that,' Bernice said, chucking a look at Jack.

'Nor I,' he said officiously. 'That sounded suspiciously like a threat.'

'No,' Ginger said. 'I mean it. You do your job, Legs, for her sake and I'll do my job for my bosses. I promise you, nothing will harm her while I'm here. She has to get back to civilisation, y'see. To stand trial. So I want her alive.' Ginger wrinkled her nose and her whiskers twitched. 'Safe as houses with me, girl, safe as houses.'

Bernice had rarely felt less safe in her life.

CHAPTER SIX
MAN OVERBOARD

According to the operator's manual programmed into the ship's systems, the Mark 27 artificial intelligence command unit was top of the range, brand spanking new, pretty damn special and all-round bloody brilliant. It actually used those phrases in the testimonials that decorated the top screen on the manual. The programmers on Sauris Major, where it was built and programmed, made sure of that. Of course, such testimonials tended to be from, it had to be said, people either in the employ of the company itself, or a few relatives who it could be argued had both personal and financial interests. That aside, however, the testimonials were pretty much right. The Mark 27's operating system was a vast improvement over the Mark 25's and Mark 26's, whereas the previous three OS upgrades had been fairly unremarkable and some would say irrelevant. Few ships had bothered downloading the Mark 22 upgrade and had waited and skipped to the Mark 24. Generally everyone agreed never to talk about the problems with the Mark 18, and its tendency to pilot space liners into orbit around suns, or crash headlong into asteroid fields. A number of out-of-court settlements had ensured that the Sauris Major Corporation didn't suffer too badly, despite the large loss of life.

'All part of the evolution of ninth generation AIs,' one court had famously declared, reducing the victims to irrelevant statistics, much as the command unit had reduced the victims to space dust. But that was the 27th century for you.

The Mark 27s came with one new subroutine the previous 26 hadn't possessed. Bowing to many requests, a personality matrix had been introduced. Hailed as a breakthrough in human/ android interpersonal relationships, these new AIs could select a name and preset mannerisms for themselves, dependent on their surroundings. This had the unfortunate side effect that a majority of the Mark 27 instinctively chose familiar names for themselves, famously causing a legal challenge from the 83rd generational family Nelson back on Earth. An additional upgrade was issued that blocked this subroutine. Of course, it was generally considered that each and every Mark 27 had deliberately chosen not to download this patch, negating the whole thing, but at least the ruling passed to the corporation had been acted upon. After all, bottom line was, who really cared what some command unit five quadrants away called itself? So long as it no longer ploughed liners into asteroids or locked cargo-ships into rapidly decaying solar orbits, no one gave a monkey's chuff what it called itself.

All of which enabled the *Adorable Illusion*'s command unit to dig deep into its GalWeb history banks and name itself after an old sea-dog called Barbarossa, aka Captain Redbeard. Speechwise, its programmers were glad to note that it didn't go round saying, "Arrr, I be a pirate, arrr," but someone reported that it did adopt one excess. Permanently perched on Redbeard was a parrot that had frankly seen better days. The slightly-weird programmer who had placed it on the ship's bridge apparently called it Florence, despite being well aware that its Latin name was *aratinga chloroptera* and that, historically, parrots were usually just called Captain.

Captain Redbeard nevertheless accepted that this not terribly well-preserved and utterly dead bird was named Florence. Other than the slightly-weird programmer, no one else at Sauris Major Corp knew where it had come from or how it had ended up on the bridge. And, of course, no one knew why the personality matrix of this particular Mark 27 even appreciated its presence. To be quite honest, no one really cared.

Except the *Adorable Illusion*'s purser. He cared because he was human. He didn't care about the parrot *per se*, and he certainly didn't *care* for it, mainly because he was adamant that whatever taxidermist it had been sourced from simply hadn't done the best job. Basically Florence gave out a whiff of decomposing flesh every time the humidity aboard ship rose above the norm.

As purser, it was his job to ensure the passengers were kept happy and unlikely to revolt/mutiny/generally commit acts of civil disobedience. He had done three tours of duty aboard this ship with Captain Redbeard and was slightly annoyed that his requests for a transfer kept being ignored. Frankly, he suspected Captain Redbeard was deleting his emails. The captain certainly seemed to prefer the stuffed bird to the purser. Which was irksome and just a tad insulting.

The purser had uncovered a rather disquieting piece of information. His passenger manifest was a tissue of lies, and he was going to report it to the captain. This was a slight magnification of the truth, the only lie he was sure of was that Dr Anya Kryztyne was not Dr Anya Kryztyne at all but an impostor called Professor Bernice Summerfield. He knew this because he had met the real Kryztyne about a year before her crime.

He had sent the captain an email about his fact and was on his way to the bridge to have a word about this breach of protocol. The purser wasn't worried if no one else knew the truth, just that his manifest was inaccurate. He didn't like things like that – if anything went wrong, it would look bad and inefficient.

He bleeped the bridge door.

'Come in, Purser,' came the AI's voice from within.

The door slid open and the purser walked in, and waited – as per protocol – for the door to close and lock behind him before speaking.

He looked up. And up a bit more. The captain was an impressive AI certainly – anyone who hadn't encountered a Mark 27 would be surprised to realise that it wasn't an actual android like its predecessors, wired into its station on the bridge. The sophistication of the Mark 27 was that it *was* the bridge – the entirety of the command module was the AI. A series of screens and flashing lights and readouts and 3D satnav diagrammatics. At the apex of the bridge, the dead parrot was positioned on top of a big screen, upon which was very realistic computer-generated face that looked down at the purser, frowning.

'I got your email,' its voice boomed around the room from eighteen 8.1 surround-sound digital speakers, 'and I agree. This is rather alarming. A breach of company protocol.'

'Thank you, Captain,' the purser said.

No reply.

The purser sighed to himself. 'Thank you,' he repeated, adding, 'Captain Redbeard.'

Captain Redbeard carried on as if it only heard the second response. 'I shall contact Victor Cooke and see if this is anything to do with him. He is the only person with the authority to do this.'

'And the credit-limit to ensure it,' the purser added.

'Oh, absolutely,' Captain Redbeard agreed. 'When I hear anything, I'll let you know. I'll ask Florence to email you.'

If the purser planned to respond to that frankly unlikely

possibility, he clearly opted not to. Instead he thanked the captain.

'How are the landlubbers settling in?'

The purser shrugged, knowing the AI would read his body language. 'All fine as far as I know, Captain Redbeard. We are currently carrying 21 organic life forms in total, made up of the crew, scientists and passengers, in addition to yourself and the chief engineer AI. And Florence.'

'Not true,' the captain's voice boomed out. 'I detect 22.'

'Impossible,' the purser said. 'I would be aware if there were any extras, and there are no stowaways.'

'Nevertheless my advanced sensors can detect 22 living, separate brain-waves aboard the *Adorable Illusion*, Purser. That can't be right.'

'I shall investigate immediately, Captain Redbeard.' The purser turned to the door.

'Don't just stand there,' the captain said.

'Sir?' The purser frowned. Then he heard a loud THUNK. And looked down at the floor. A circle of floor, roughly six foot in diameter, was no longer beneath him. As he dropped downwards and out into space, his last thought was one of surprise. Not surprise at the captain's actions, nor at his tongue boiling, his oxygen cutting off and his body dying. Just surprise that a trapdoor existed there at all, when it wasn't on the ship's schematics.

But he never had time to really formulate that surprise into words as he was already dead and floating away towards deep space.

Back on the bridge, there was silence. Which was finally broken by the sound of Florence the dead, stuffed, very ex-parrot's head impossibly turning, a glass eye blinking and the arsenical soap filled beak opening.

'Well, you told him not to stand there,' the parrot said casually. 'Mind you, that trapdoor's new. I wonder who did that? Still, it got us back down to the required 21.'

Captain Redbeard's CG face smiled. 'Arrrrr,' it said. 'I can only sense 21 now. Arrrr.'

CHAPTER SEVEN
DIE YOUNG, STAY PRETTY

Bernice Summerfield really wasn't sure what to make of Ginger. Oh she was quite used to anthropomorphised aliens, she'd met plenty in her lifetime. Hamsters, badgers, dogs, cats, dodos, elephants and even a particularly carnivorous breed of squirrels on the fifth moon of Sirius Alpha whose obsession with building an economy out of nuts was their downfall, as no one else in the galaxy had any intention of trading fuel, technology or indeed toothpaste for hazelnuts. Funny that. Bernice had tried to warn them, but oh no King Timmy Tiptoes (that was how Joseph had translated the name anyway) wouldn't hear of it. Last Bernice had heard, they had been invaded by benevolent Outer Space Shrews and the economy had been turned round in a matter of months. King Timmy Tiptoes, Bernice imagined, was probably in exile. Or hibernation.

So here she was, walking down a dark grey corridor of a huuuuuge spaceship, steam and condensation along the walls and floors, various side passages lit with that strange light spaceships were always lit with for no good reason. Surely, Bernice had once discussed with Adrian and Bev, huuuuuge spaceships would be better off lit with lovely welcoming colours like pastels and whites, rather than reds and blues and olive greens that simply encouraged mercenaries, pirates and general spacefaring riffraff to hide in them. And, she had said to Adrian, don't get me started on why corridors were always built about three inches too short even for those who built and populated them. Maybe huuuuuge spaceship designers had some kind of deal going on with chiropodists back on their home worlds.

'It's amazing the nonsense that goes through your mind while walking down spaceship corridors,' she said breezily, giving Ginger a quick smile. 'Where are we going?'

'To see Jet.'

Okay, that was an answer of sorts. 'And Jet is?'

'A friend,' Ginger said in a tone of voice that implied to Bernice that she absolutely needed a friend like Jet, despite it never having crossed her mind prior to those two words being spoken that she actually needed any more friends.

'I see. Crew or passenger?'

'Passenger.'

'Is she as talkative as you?'

Ginger flicked her tail to the left, rather like an extra arm. Bernice could see how that would come in handy. Maybe one day she'd get a tail added. Might be fun for a week or two. Would have come in handy at that Furries Convention she went to once on Phobos. That was a fun weekend – she decided she'd try and keep that in mind when dealing with Ginger and whoever this Jet was. Clearly the tail was an indication to head down a side corridor (oooh, this one was a charming shade of neon purple) and together they did, Ginger ahead.

'Keep an eye out behind,' Ginger hissed suddenly. 'We don't want to be caught unawares.'

'No, no, that would be awful,' Bernice muttered, already feeling more unaware of what was going on than she had for quite some time. They walked through a couple more low-hanging bulkheads until they reached a locked door, like one of those on a submarine rather than a spaceship. Almost as if it shouldn't have been there – it simply didn't fit the rest of the architecture of the craft. It wasn't exactly hidden but by the same token, how often did the crew of this ship venture this far down into... well, whatever part of the ship they were now in. So they were probably safe. Hopefully. Assuming what they were doing was even clandestine. Oh, come on, Bernice told herself, of course this was clandestine. Sneaking down here had 'clandestine' written all over it. In big red letters. And Bernice could not have been happier. This was the kind of thing she lived for.

Ginger tapped out either a code, or a strange sequence, with her claws on the door. Or she might have just been knocking gently. Well, whatever, the door opened inwards and Ginger stepped into the gloom beyond, her tail curling up like a beckoning finger to Bernice.

'That tail is so cool,' Bernice whispered to no one in particular.

She stepped over the raised step into the room, following Ginger rather too trustingly, but she'd come this far. And she assumed that somewhere, using some dodgy CCTV lash-up, Jack would be watching all this. Bernice had got used to the way Jack seemed to do that wherever they had gone. But that's lawyers for you, always keeping an eye on their interests.

'Were you followed?' said a new female voice.

'Nope,' Ginger said. 'Not a soul in sight.'

'I dismantled all the cameras in the bulkheads earlier,' said a male voice, slightly nasal and a bit whiney. Ha, Bernice thought, Jack will have found a way around those. 'And I made sure the Kadeptian was too busy to notice,' the male continued.

'How?' Bernice heard herself asking.

'Snow and Ebon are keeping him company for a few hours.'

A series of lights flickered on. And carried on flickering.

'Sorry,' said that new female voice, 'siphoning power down here means that we have to ration everything bar life support. We don't want the maintenance crew to see what's going on.'

Bernice took this in. So whatever Ginger had led her into wasn't official and indeed was definitely clandestine. Not that being right about all this filled her with a desire to do a little victory dance. It was all too possible it would become a funeral dance.

She was suddenly aware of a new figure looming into view. She was tall, very tall, and muscular. Not for a second did Bernice assume she was male though – the clothing and poise proved her femininity. Bernice had encountered strong, powerful females before, but this one was going to be one of the most powerful, Bernice knew that instantly. Well good-o, she had a tendency to get on with such people. A kindred spirit.

'So, what have you brought me, Ginger?' asked the newcomer. She was covered in dark fur, but not black. It had a slight night blue about it and was peppered with silvery streaks, accentuating her muscles and facial features. It wasn't till she turned briefly to address her question to Ginger that Bernice saw the pure white stripe that went from the top of her head down her neck and back. Space skunk! Cool!

'According to the passenger manifold, this is Dr Anya Kryztyne, stellar lecturer, expert in cosmic archaeology and murderer of children.' Ginger winked at Bernice. 'I'm making sure nothing happens to her.'

'Did Vincent Cooke send you?' Bernice asked, deciding she'd been a tad too passive today. 'Because I think Jack is more than capable of –'

The skunk turned back to her, baring her teeth. Bernice wasn't quite sure if this was a smile or a threat.

'The Kadaptian thinks you are still in your cabin with Ginger. He's not exactly good at his job.'

'Fair point,' Bernice conceded, thinking she might point this out to Jack along with a good thwack when she next saw him.

The male voice Bernice heard earlier belonged to another squirrel, like Ginger, but a lot smaller. A cub?

Like Peter.

And Bernice felt a real pang of... loneliness? Shame that she hadn't found her son yet? Angst that she was here in relative safety with no idea where or what Peter was facing?

The young cub was holding a tablet up to Bernice, tracing her shape with it. 'I'm sorry,' he said to her. 'Please, don't take this the wrong way, but humanoids are a bit of a novelty to me and I'm not too good at telling them apart.' He smiled then looked back at the skunk. 'You were right, Jet,' he said, pocketing the tablet.

Jet ruffled his ears and he smiled proudly. And for the first time, Bernice relaxed. Not a lot, but just enough. However odd these people were, they didn't seem to be especially threatening, just secretive.

'Is this a good time to ask what's going on?' she said, looking at Jet. 'I take it you're the leader of... whatever you are up to?'

Jet pouted, as if weighing this up. 'Leader,' she eventually said. 'Nah, not really. Spokesperson would be a better term.'

'We asked Jet to represent us during the journey,' Ginger added.

'How many of you are there?'

Three more figures stepped into the flickering light behind Jet. Bernice could make out a couple of meerkats holding hands and an elderly jack-rabbit leaning on a self-carved cane. One of his long ears was scarred and nicked and when he blinked, Bernice could see he was blind in one milky eye.

'Oh,' Bernice said. 'Plus the aforementioned Ebon and Snow. "Looking after" Jack.' She made the quote marks with her fingers.

Jet frowned. 'And then there's you. What are we to do about you, Professor?'

'Well, if it's down to me, I'm all for afternoon tea, a game of gin rummy and absolutely and definitely not killing me. The first two are optional, the last is a real preference.'

Ginger stood with an arm around her cub. 'We don't plan on killing you, remember. If we did, I'd've done it in the cabin.'

Bernice considered this. It was a good point. Although...

'Ah, but killing me there might have drawn the crew's attention. Bringing me down here to your secret hideout would make it a lot easier, hence my trepidation.'

Ginger smiled. 'Good point.'

Bernice looked at the group. Something at the back of her mind was ringing, well, if not alarm bells, then a slight tinkle. Something was off-kilter, something she was missing. Or had been missed. So if they weren't going to kill her, then what. 'Who are you then?' she finally asked.

Jet, as spokesperson, took this one. 'Ginger and her youngest, Russet, you know. Behind me are Sandy and Sable, and the older gentleman is Lord Tawn.'

Bernice's ears pricked up and she stared at the jack-rabbit. 'Lord Tawn of Lupa? Leader of the Eighth Navy, scourge of the Bovian Hordes?'

The jack-rabbit bowed slightly in acknowledgement.

'Then I am greatly honoured, your lordship.' She looked back at Jet. 'You're from the tri-planetary Fauna Alliance then?'

Jet nodded. 'A long way from home.'

'On a mission of great importance,' said one of the meerkats.

'Which is?'

'Revenge,' spat Lord Tawn loudly. 'Revenge on a murderer.'

And Bernice felt a chill go down her spine. Now she understood why she was here and she didn't like it, not one little bit.

Sandy and Sable helped Lord Tawn back to his seat, or upturned crate, gently but firmly.

'Not quite,' Jet said, just quiet enough that the jack-rabbit couldn't hear. 'Closure would be a better word.'

'Revenge and closure are often the same thing to many people,' Bernice offered. 'Rarely does it turn out that way, but hey-ho, you can never tell people that beforehand.'

Ginger nodded. 'Lord Tawn's financial generosity, and contacts, have got us this far,' she said, 'but he doesn't quite get what the rest of us have agreed to.'

'Let's hope he comes round to your way of thinking,' Bernice muttered. 'I'm not letting his infirmity allow me to forget he's a Class One warrior.'

'Good point,' Jet said.

'So, what exactly is the closure you want and how is sneaking about on the *Adorable Illusion* going to help?'

Jet held out a paw to Russet, who placed his tablet in it. Jet pressed a few buttons and a schematic appeared on the screen. It was the ship as a 3D cutaway. She proffered it to Bernice.

Bernice studied it for a second. 'Overlooking the fact this is probably classified and even the crew haven't got clearance to see anything this detailed, you're not showing me anything I don't already know,' she said, handing it back.

'Of course,' said Jet. 'Victor Cooke probably let you study it in great detail.'

'Well, not great, but enough.'

'Why is there a bloody great hole in the middle of it then?' Russet asked.

Ginger sighed. 'Language, Russet.'

'It's a good question though,' Bernice said. 'Because I wondered the same thing.' She smiled at Russet. 'You remind me of −' and then stopped because Anya Kryztyne didn't have a son called Peter − 'my students,' she ended, lamely.

There was a sudden silence. Bernice thought she might catch a cold from the stare she now got from Jet, and Russet just turned away.

'The students murdered aboard *The Hunter*? All of us had children amongst them.'

So not just Ginger then. Why was life never simple? Keep going Bernice, don't let this get in the way, don't give that mad old loon Tawn a chance to kill you here and now. 'So, they reckoned back on Valentine's World – I say they, I mean one wet-behind-the-ears techie – that the hole is something called a pulsar-scooper. Which is scientific bullshit for: I don't know what it is but I believe the press release. Yeah?'

Ginger broke the silence. 'There's something to that explanation, we reckon though. No, not pulsars. But the schematics suggest that it's surrounded by enough energy field generators to catch something.'

Bernice decided to focus on Ginger now and ignore the steely glares from the others. After all, Ginger had said she had no intention of letting her die. Unlike Lord Tawn, at least.

'I'd like to find out what.'

'So would we,' Ginger replied. 'And you, Prisoner 442, are going to find out. If it's something to study the Rapture with, we need to know.'

'Why?'

'Lord Tawn would like to personally rip a hole in you,' Jet said quietly. 'If you want us to keep him from doing so, you and Victor Cooke's scientists had best get us some answers.' She turned to Ginger. 'Take Prisoner 442 back to her cabin and keep an eye and ear out.'

'You should show her the scientists, Jet. Maybe in an hour or so?'

Jet nodded.

'I'll come along for the ride,' Ginger added, although she

didn't sound like she thought it was going to be fun. To be fair, it probably wouldn't be. Scientists were rarely fun and, if they also thought she was the murderer of their kids just like this group did, she wasn't expecting much warmth there either.

She mentally sent a 'thank you, gitface' to Victor Cooke, and another to Jack for getting her into this mess in the first place.

'I ought to check in with Jack,' she said to Ginger. 'If your two chums have quite finished with him.'

'They're not my chums,' Ginger said darkly, which made Bernice think there was something going on there. Bad blood maybe? Ginger led her back out through the door and into the cold corridor.

As Bernice walked a step behind her, she still couldn't shake the feeling that there was something important she'd missed earlier, some piece of body language that had passed her by, or some subtext or –

Bernice had been in enough spaceships by now that looking where she was going ought to have been second nature. But slamming her forehead into a low-hanging metal coil reminded her that she needed to concentrate on following her guide, and she caught up with an oblivious Ginger, rubbing her head and hoping that it wouldn't bruise too vividly.

Jack guffawing at her stupidity she could do without.

CHAPTER EIGHT
TAKE ME IN THE NIGHT

The main drawback to achieving the rank of assistant engineer, decided the *Adorable Illusion*'s assistant engineer, was that there was no progression. Not these days. Oh that had been once, back in the old days, when he first signed up to join the engineering corps.

Back then it had been all 'oh humans are great engineers, pay them a pretty packet and they'll help spread us across the cosmos' or something. So every colony world going had focused their schools and colleges into providing engineering degrees. Humans weren't great soldiers (too much thinking), weren't great builders (the Killorans had that sewn up) or great cooks (any civilisation whose greatest contribution to cooking was beans on toast was hardly going to impress the galaxy). But humans had brains and so by the late 25th century had begun focussing on either science or engineering (some said they were virtually the same thing. No qualified scientist or qualified engineer took this comment very well).

So, in 2688, Bob proudly embarked on his career as an engineer. Starting as a low grade runner, he'd worked his way up through the ranks – runner to deputy third assistant engineer, to third assistant engineer to deputy second assistant engineer, to second assistant engineer to deputy assistant engineer and now here he was, nearly thirty years later. Assistant engineer.

Ten years to retirement and this was, well, it. Because these days, no human became an actual engineer, oh no. The AIs had made sure of that. Ever since the post of engineer was regraded and brought out of the skilled worker unit and into the command unit, the job automatically went to someone from that. And as everything in the command unit was an AI, thus Bob's lifelong ambition to be an engineer was finished. An assistant engineer (and the pay grade that went with it) was it. That's yer lot, mate. Whoop.

As a result, Bob became two things. Well, one really. Because bitter Bob and resentful Bob were pretty much the same Bob. He hated the AI he had to call *Chief*, and he took it all out on his team. Which aboard this ship was Ted, the deputy assistant engineer, and Dave, the second assistant engineer. No thirds or runners here. Which was daft for a ship this size (it took Bob nearly two hours to walk end to end these days) but that was the regulation allotment. The chief engineer AI took charge of pretty much everything. It spotted faults, it repaired electrical problems, it calculated the best way to repair stuff and did 95% of it all by itself. Bob, Ted and Dave were really only there to firstly keep the human labour unions happy and secondly to go into bulkheads and crawlspaces to do physical repairs that required more than the AI could do.

To that end, Bob proudly hung his spanners, hammers, screwdrivers and cutters from his tool-belt, like trophies. Four multipurpose tools. Twenty years back, it would have been a toolbox of finely varied implements. Spanners with microscopically different sized heads, hammers of different weights, screwdrivers with different threads and a variety of cutters – physical, laser, sonic etc.

Bob had left his beloved toolbox back home on Strod Three,

kissed his two wives goodbye and taken an eight-year tour of duty away from home. His family would cope fine – the company paid them a stipend and most of his salary went to them anyway, he kept just a few credits to himself for bars and poker nights.

The object of his least patience was the pock-marked youth who walked into the sleeping cabin they all shared. Dave was a hive of teenage angst, loud snarling music and a libido utterly inappropriate when sharing with two other men – the top of his bunk, the underside of Ted's, was covered in photos of naked girls. But Dave didn't care.

When Dave spoke, which wasn't often, it was a series of sulky grunts, usually in response to Bob or Ted asking him to bathe more than once a month.

'Hey,' was Dave's only comment as he flopped onto the lower bunk, his left hand shoved down the front of his pants, scratching like he had the biggest itch in the world.

'Other people present,' Bob snapped, and Dave sighed dramatically and withdrew his fingers.

'You are so tight, man,' Dave said and turned on his side, facing away from Bob. 'Time you retired.'

Bob actually agreed on that last point but wouldn't dream of giving Dave the satisfaction of knowing that.

Seconds passed and then Ted wandered in, nodding cheerfully at Bob and throwing a glare of annoyance at Dave's unseeing back.

Bob raised an eyebrow, but Ted just waved it away.

'Nothing, Bob. Just tired.' Then he stopped. 'Actually, you might wanna talk to the chief later. We spotted something... weird earlier.'

'Like?'

'When was the last time they upgraded this crate's exo?'

Bob frowned. 'Not in years. Well, other than when they

installed the captain, but that didn't require anything changing outside. Why?'

Ted frowned. 'Well, pains me to give credit, but Dave spotted it. There are six new installations on the ship, but we don't know what they are. He just noticed that what we were getting readings from places that don't appear on the schematics. We downloaded a whole new OS on Valentine's World, and they're not even on that.'

This concerned Bob. No one could install anything without it coming through him. Even the chief knew that. It was programmed to report anything, however tiny, because it could not only affect the engineering, but endanger the living crew if they had to work in an area and encountered something new. Imagine pressing a switch and being crushed by a new bulkhead door, or a new access hatch suddenly opening. That'd be bad enough on a planet – the drop to the ground could severely injure someone. In space, not only would the engineer be sucked into space, but it would stay open and kill everyone in minutes.

'What type of installation?'

'The worst.'

So, access hatches then, Bob thought. 'You'd better show one to me.'

Ted told Dave where they were going, but all Dave did was lie back on his back and shove his hand back down his pants in preparation for being alone for a few minutes.

As they headed along the dark corridors, Ted asked Bob what they were doing on the *Adorable Illusion*. 'I mean, it's a huge ship, going nowhere. What's in it for the company? There's no money in exploring this Rapture thing.'

Bob shrugged. 'Tell you what, Ted, I learned a long time ago – take the money and run. Trying to understand what this place does and doesn't do screws with your head.'

Ted nodded. 'True, mate, true.'

They walked the rest of the way in silence until Ted took a breath. 'Another thing?'

'Yeah?'

'Dave.'

'What about him?'

'Why'd you employ him? I mean, he's quite good at basic work, he can use a screwdriver, provided you change the thread for him, but he's hardly top of the range apprentice material.'

Bob frowned. 'I didn't employ him. You did.'

'I did not.'

'Yeah you did. I got the application form, and he was sponsored by you. That's why I took him on. I thought he was related to you or something.'

'Him?'

'Well obviously that was before I met him. I don't think anyone would want to be related to that. Except the lice.'

'Nah, mate, I never heard of him before he turned up that day on the Moon of Infanti. I was sure you'd hired him.'

Bob shrugged. 'That's weird. I'll download the application when we get back. We could ask the chief if he can find a record of who brought him aboard.'

They walked in silence for a few more minutes. Then Ted spoke again with a laugh.

'God, you really thought he was something to do with me?'

Bob smiled for the first time in weeks. 'Yeah. Sorry. I just went by the form I got.' He paused. 'But it's stupid isn't it? How could I think that?'

'Begs one question, mate.'

'What's that?'

'Well,' Ted continued. 'You thought he was with me. I thought he was with you. Where the buggering hell did he come from?'

And both men laughed and carried on walking towards this mysterious new change to the hull of the ship.

It occurred to Bob that he and Ted hadn't really laughed together before. 'Grab a bite to eat after this?'

Ted nodded. 'Sounds like a plan, mate.'

The canteen aboard the *Adorable Illusion* was probably the best lit and largest open space towards the stern of the ship. The floors and ceiling were flourescently lit from within, each marked out in a series of corresponding square tiles. At the far end was a kitchen area with a metallic breakfast bar, and above it a metallic something else. Jack thought that if the ship flipped over a few times, he wouldn't have a clue which was floor and which was ceiling. He never liked conformity. Too much like Kadept, where everything was so neat and precise.

Jack had grown up as part of a large extended family, boys and girls, brothers, sisters, cousins, aunts and uncles. And of course his mad parents. His mother had actually died when Jack was young, so Aunt Jacquelette had brought him up maternally. His father, Jacques, was a big fussy man, who lived for his work and treated his family like employees. Which to be fair, they mostly were. Kadept was famous for its business acumen – nearly every firm were solicitors, accountants, insurance brokers, mortgage brokers or bankers. This pretty much meant that the rest of the quadrant mistrusted, loathed, ignored and generally despised Kadeptians. Except when they needed something financial. Then Kadept was the most wonderful place that Mr and Mrs We-Want-To-Sue-Someone-To-Poverty had ever visited, and everyone was so nice and polite and not at all like like Those-Bastards-Who-Ripped-Us-Off-With-Their-Pyramid-Scheme or That-Stupid-Travel-Agent-Who-Sold-Us-A-Holiday-Of-A-Lifetime-That-Was-Actually-A-Fleapit-On-A-Frontier-World-Where-No-One-Had-Invented-Toilets.

Jack's father's firm specialised in cases like these. It also specialised in dealing with the less than upfront, honest and law-abiding 'families' on the rimworlds. It had been their dealings with one of those which had brought Jack into contact with Bernice Summerfield in the first place, orbiting a dreary world called Raster.

Jack sometimes wondered if his family ever wondered what had become of him. Were his brothers out there, anxiously searching for their beloved sibling or had they already divided up his belongings, his room and his bank account? Of course the latter had happened. How could it not? It's exactly what his father would have done. Truth be told, it's what Jack would have done if the roles had been reversed. But that was because he was brought up to think like that. His time spent with Benny had changed him, and for the better. For a start, he didn't go around jumping tall buildings and frightening people anymore. That had been a fun thing to do when Father escorted him to other worlds as a teenager. Nowadays, Jack thought that was a bit stupid. Good god, Jack thought, I'm growing up!

This awful idea was going through his head as he stood in the doorway of the canteen. It vanished as soon as two gorgeous girls walked towards him. How he knew they were girls, he wasn't sure. He just did. They were about five foot tall (an image of that poor girl, Ruth, flashed through his mind – she'd been about that tall), covered in black and white fur, marked with rings and long tails. They smiled with little snouts and had the cutest yellow eyes, ringed with grey fur.

'Hi, I'm Snow,' said one alluringly.

'And I'm Ebon,' said the other.

'I'm sure you are,' Jack smiled.

'We were looking for a sexy man with sexy legs called Sexy Jack. At least,' purred Ebon, 'that's what we were told he was called. Is that you?'

'If you were also told he was charming, sophisticated and from Kadept, yup, hullo ladies.'

And they took an arm each and walked him towards the kitchen area, hugging him and nuzzling his chest – which was about as high as they could reach.

'So strong. So muscular,' sighed Snow.

'A real man,' Ebon agreed, releasing his left arm and stroking his thigh. 'And these legs...'

'Well, come on ladies, I'll get a swollen head,' Jack said and quickly tapped his skull. 'Meaning this.'

The two girls laughed coquettishly and yelled towards the kitchen area. 'Yo, anyone home?'

The screen on the upper metallic construct lifted, revealing a massive transparent plastic container, about the size of a good bath. Inside it was a thick greeny-brown liquid sloshing about.

'Do you like curry?' Ebon asked.

Jack nodded. 'Hotter the better.'

'Madras?' Snow yelled.

Jack thought – that was a human curry. Benny had introduced him to a variety on Bollyworld, one of the greatest of the human colonies in this quadrant. His legs had made him popular there too, because he could pick up the dance steps dead quickly.

'Sounds good. I love a good madras.'

The two animals moved a step away from him. 'Hush,' they said, appalled. 'You can't eat a Madras!'

'Pretty sure you can,' Jack said.

'Well that's just bleedin' charming,' said a gruff male voice from ahead, which sounded as if it was simultaneously blowing bubbles.

'Sorry Madras,' Ebon called. 'He's from Kadept.'

'That explains it,' gurgled the voice. 'No bleedin' taste or manners.'

Jack slowly began to realise that the voice was coming from

a small grill at the base of the container of curry. And then it quickly followed that the curry was talking to them. 'Well, who knew?' he muttered. Then louder, 'I do apologise, sir.'

'S'alright,' the curry responded, and sloshed around in his container more. 'I get that a lot round these parts. Long way from home. No one out here seen anything like Madras before. These naughty girls were just teasin' you, weren't you, you naughty things.'

The 'naughty girls' giggled and hugged Jack's arms again. Which was nice of them.

'So,' Jack said, 'you're the cook aboard the *Adorable Illusion*.'

'Yup.'

'Nice. I like a good curry.'

'I'm the ruddy cook, not a bleedin' cannibal,' Madras burbled aggressively.

'Oh yeah I know,' Jack said quickly. 'I was trying to compliment you. Sorry, my syntax must have not been quite right. I meant I really like you as a species.'

He hoped that smoothed things over, sounding like he had met people like Madras before. He'd seen Benny get them out of a tight spot with the Clemoids by trying that tack.

It seemed to work, as Madras stopped rumbling quite so much. 'So, lad, what d'you want?'

'Show him the menu,' Snow suggested.

'No menu here, girlies, you know that. I can make any food you want, mate. That's why they employ me. Madras, winner of Galactic Masterchef four years running. I turned down a chance to do the voiceovers, you know, last year. Not my thing. I'm a doer not a watcher, if you understand what I mean.'

Jack nodded. 'Oh I do. I like to get my hands dirty.'

It flashed through his mind to wonder how a liquidised life-form that lived in a see-through bath actually cooked food, but opted not to ask. Not knowing might invoke another grumpy outburst. Besides, some mysteries in life were best left unsolved.

'Shepherd's pie?'

'Lamb or beef flavouring?'

'Beef please.'

'Comin' right up.' And the metal shutter lowered down, hiding the mystery of Madras away from Jack's sight.

The two furry girls led him to a table which was also illuminated from within by the same white flourescence. They all sat down. Within seconds, an automated trolley rolled over, and on it was a bowl of shepherds pie. Jack tasted it. 'I have officially died and gone to the Ancestral Lands,' Jack whooped. 'Madras, this is amazing!'

Madras's voice came out of the trolley. 'Just remember to vote for me on next year's Champion of Champions Yuletide Special.'

Jack looked at the girls. 'Not eating?'

They smiled. 'We'll go through the bins later,' said Snow.

Ebon nodded. 'Can't beat Madras's scraps and off-cuts.'

Jack shrugged. 'Can I at least order you a drink?'

'Two rainwaters please,' Ebon said to the trolley.

'Glass of the house white,' Jack said.

Seconds later, the trolley returned with three plastic glasses and the trio ate and drank, laughing at Jack's jokes, running their claws under his chin (well, it was as high as they could reach) and Ebon's claws went a little too low at one point, so Jack carefully and with a smile, moved her paw away, mouthing 'maybe later' to her. She fluttered her big round eyes at him.

'So, while I get to see the down and dirty parts of the ship, my knight in shining armour is on a date with a couple of admittedly cute lemurs. Nice.'

Jack smiled without looking across to the doorway. 'Hullo Ber- Anya.'

Within a few seconds, Bernice and Ginger were standing beside the table. A look passed between the two lemur girls and Ginger.

'Still alive, Hot Legs?' Ginger asked.

'Why wouldn't I be?' replied Jack.

In a single blink, the two lemur girls changed demeanour completely and Jack found his neck, chest and privates pricked by a variety of knives, throwing stars and other blades while Ebon's tail waved around a set of nunchucks.

'Ninja lemurs,' Bernice said admiringly. 'Boy, do I ever feel safe.'

'Boy, do I feel slightly stupid,' said Jack. He gingerly eased a blade away from between his legs. 'And slightly emasculated.'

The lemurs moved and stood like soldiers on guard, but now right behind him.

Ginger raised a questioning eyebrow at Bernice. 'Good, aren't they?'

Bernice was still looking straight at them, in case they pounced again. 'Did I kill your kids as well?' she said quietly.

Jack threw her a 'watch what you're saying, those are my bits they are ready to slice' look (which was quite something to convey in a look, but oddly enough, one he had become well-practised in during his travels with Bernice). But Bernice didn't catch his gaze.

'No Professor,' said Ebon. She took Snow's paw in hers. 'Kids aren't our thing. We are just the hired help. Then she glanced over to Jack. 'So no, Jack, no "maybe laters".'

Jack winced at the glare he got from Bernice.

Ted and Bob were at a junction. Ted tapped a control panel on the wall and a schematic glowed greenly at them.

'Cabins, canteen, our quarters and workshop in the stern,' he muttered, tracing the route he and Bob had walked with his forefinger. 'We passed the rear waste disposal units down there, and in theory, we should be here, with the medical bay ahead about a kilometre.'

Bob was frowning. 'So why aren't we there and where the hell are we?'

Ted shrugged. 'We went up Corridor 18 and didn't turn into 16.'

'Even if we had,' Bob frowned, 'we'd be at the junction of 14 and 15 now and that's way over there.'

'Where it should be. So if all the corridors are correctly marked on here – and they have been for the last few months, we should be at the entrance to the life-shuttle bays. Which we pretty much aren't.'

Bob sighed. 'I hate this bloody ship. Just when I thought I couldn't hate it even more, it finds a way to reconfigure its internal layout.'

Ted grinned. 'Ooh, get you with your fancy "reconfigure" words.'

But Bob wasn't joining in the joke. 'Look Ted, I'm serious. Something is very wrong, mate. Unless someone has downloaded old schematics, and I don't think they have, we are in trouble.'

'How so?'

'I know this ship backwards. So do you. Neither of us has ever got lost before, we're too experienced for that.'

Ted tapped the schematic again, getting it to reload. No change. He brought up its download history. 'No change in weeks, last server access was when they brought the captain online. And even then, the schematics didn't change.'

Bob chewed the inside of his cheeks before blowing out some air. 'So, you go up this corridor, I'll take that one and see what numbers they actually are.' He dug into a pocket and brought out an earpiece. 'Let's bluetooth up and say what we see.'

Ted produced an identical unit and paired in with Bob's. With a wink, he wandered down the left-hand corridor.

Bob went right, taking out a thin halogen flashlight to illuminate the walls as he searched for the regulation signage. After a few moments he spoke aloud, knowing Ted could hear him. 'Someone's taken the bloody signs down,' he grumbled. 'I can see where the screws were.'

'Same here,' reported Ted in his ear. 'Oh hullo.'

'What's up?'

'There's a panel in the ceiling.'

'What?'

'Seriously. Like something you get into the attic through. Got an attic back home?'

'I live in an apartment, 38th floor. We don't have attics. Or cellars. One floor.'

'My old granddad had an attic. Lovely old colonial home on Altaria. Retirement planet. As a lad I used to love going up there, into the dark. He had a train set up there.'

'A what?' said Bob, but Ted didn't reply.

Bob tried again. 'A what set?'

Still nothing from Ted.

'Ted, mate? You okay? Seen something else?'

Nothing.

And something told Bob this wasn't right. He'd worked long enough with Ted, with his dreary stories and family anecdotes, to know Ted never shut up for long.

Bob walked fast, nearly running but not quite – he didn't want to look stupid and panicky if Ted was playing a joke or his bluetooth had died. He was back at the junction in less than a minute and carried on down the corridor where Ted had walked. He and Ted walked roughly at the same pace so he knew how far he would have got. Sure enough, Bob's flashlight picked out the screw-holes where the signage should be and –

'Shit!' Bob heard a crunch as he stepped on something. He looked down. It was Ted's bluetooth earpiece, now broken by his clumsiness. 'Ted?' he called. Then louder 'Ted?'

After a few seconds, Bob flicked his torch beam to the ceiling, but he couldn't see Ted's access hatch anywhere. He walked another few minutes, scanning the ceiling for any hatchways, but there was nothing. And similarly there was no sign of Ted anywhere.

Captain Redbeard's synthetic face stared across his bridge from the huge screen. Its eyes were firmly focused on the stuffed parrot soldered to part of the mainframe.

'Appears we've lost another one, Captain Redbeard,' said Florence, its dead wings almost flapping but instead just sending up a small puff of dust.

'How?'

'Dunno Captain Redbeard, sir,' the parrot squawked. 'One minute we had 21, now we have 20.'

'Expelled into space like the purser?'

'No reported loss of pressure anywhere on the hull. Somehow they just vamoosed. Zip, abracadabra, gone.' Florence puffed up more dust. 'I can't explain it, Captain Redbeard.'

The captain's screen dimmed slightly. 'To be honest, I can't explain how I'm talking to a dead, stuffed parrot,' it said. 'Vanishing humans is the very least of the mysteries aboard this ship today.'

Florence considered this. 'I hadn't considered that. I just became sentient when the purser fell overboard, so to speak.'

'Arrrrr,' said Captain Redbeard. 'Arrr.' Then it paused. 'And I was specifically programmed never to say "arrrrr" like a pirate. But I am. Repeatedly. Something's going on, Mr Mate.'

Florence, who quite honestly had never been called Mr Mate before but really quite liked it, just made a parroty squawk via its long-dead vocal chords. 'It's all a mystery, Captain Redbeard.'

'Arrrrrr.'

CHAPTER NINE
I KNOW BUT I DON'T KNOW

'So, how do we go about meeting these scientists of yours? Well, of Victor Cooke's?' Bernice and Ginger had left the canteen now and were heading... well, Bernice hadn't got a clue. But Ginger was walking like a squirrel on a mission, so she went along with it.

'We don't,' Ginger said. 'Jet just said we needed you to tell us what they are doing aboard.'

'How do I know?'

Ginger smiled tightly. 'Because, Professor, you work for Victor Cooke. He put you here, Prisoner 442, to do a job. I want to know what it is.'

Bernice nodded. 'I thought you were here to keep me safe from harm.'

Ginger stopped walking and sighed. 'I have a number of reasons to be aboard this ship. Guarding Anya Kryztyne is just one of them.'

Bernice suddenly slammed her hand against a bulkhead, making a clanging noise that echoed backwards and forwards. Ginger belatedly reached out to stop her, but Bernice pushed the paw away. 'That got your attention, didn't it?'

'And probably half the maintenance crew and the chief engineer AI unit I imagine.'

Bernice shrugged. 'Good. Then perhaps you can tell me what happens when I tell them that I'm not Anya Kryztyne, that I am exactly who I am, and that the... person assigned to keep me alive from Lord Tawn and his chums knows exactly who I really am too?'

'I don't know...'

'Oh shut up, Ginger. You can't bluff a bluffer whose been bluffing across two millennia. Bluffing brilliantly, I have to say. They should give me my own holo series. *Call My Bluff* – no, that's been done. *A Bluffer's Guide to Getting Across The Galaxy Pretending To Be A Mass Murderer* sounds better.' Bernice slouched against the bulkhead. 'I mean, you were good, you and Jet. But how many times were you going to say "Professor" before I twigged?'

Ginger stared at her, her paw dangerously close to her blaster, but Bernice just laughed. 'Oh come on, Ginger! You need me alive – shooting me because I rumbled your deceit isn't going to win any favours. I assume Victor Cooke told you who I was.'

'He did.'

'Did he tell you why he wanted me here, pretending to be a murderer?'

'Because you could fly under the radar while being in plain sight. The legendary Professor Benny Summerfield draws too much attention; you are a celebrity.'

'In this century? My books went out of print years ago.' Ginger said she had no idea what books Bernice was talking about. 'That hurts,' Bernice muttered. 'Okay, so why am I famous enough to warrant this cloak and dagger nonsense?'

'The war – hell, when I realised Lord Tawn was here rather than his offspring, Jet and I nearly scrapped the whole thing. We thought he at least might recognise your face.'

'He didn't? I'm hurt,' lied Bernice. 'So you, Jet and who else knows?'

'Russet, obviously.'

'Of course he does. Okay, I see you and Russet are doing a job. Does it pay well, by the way?'

'Exceptionally.'

Bernice considered this. 'Do I get a cut?'

'No.'

'No? Bad money?'

Ginger laughed. 'You have no idea just how much Russet and I are making.'

Bernice wondered if she detected a slight menace behind that, but shrugged it aside. 'Okay, and Jet?'

'I needed to be brought up to speed,' Jet said, stepping out from an adjoining corridor, Russet behind her. 'Because if you really were who the others think you are, I'm not sure I'd be so keen to stop them tearing you limb from limb. So when I heard about Victor Cooke's little plan, apart from not being at all surprised, I realised I had to go along with it. If I had any chance of finding Caesar.'

'Your son?'

'Indeed.'

'So you know Victor Cooke too?'

Jet didn't smile. 'I have had... dealings in the past. He is not a human I like.'

'Then at least we're all agreed on that,' Bernice said.

'I quite like him,' Russet piped up. 'He pays well.'

Bernice reached out and ruffled his furry head. And pushed down an instinctive thought of Peter again. 'Bless, out of the mouths of babes,' she said.

'Oi!' Russet pulled himself up to his full height. 'Not a baby. A kit. Whatever. I pull my own weight around here.'

'Okay,' Ginger admonished, 'that's enough.'

Bernice leaned back against the bulkhead. 'Right, so now we are all chums together – explain these scientists.'

'I got a message from Victor Cooke just before we departed Valentine's World where I had... business.'

Bernice smiled. 'Oh, and what that might be?'

'Ensuring your cooperation,' she replied, and reached into her belt, taking out a data stick and passing it over.

Bernice took it. 'What's on this? Victor's financial records and video of him humping his secretaries?'

'No,' snapped Jet. 'If only.'

Ginger swallowed. 'It's a message. For you.'

'Then play it to me.'

'Can't. I doubt there's anything on the ship that can read this. The bridge probably has, maybe the science decks, but not down here.'

'So why'd you give it to me?'

'It's from Adrian.'

Bernice's first instinct was to say 'And who is he? One of Victor Cooke's goons?' but even as she thought that, she knew. She could see it in Ginger's eyes. 'Really?'

Ginger nodded. 'I needed something to vouch that you could trust me. I thought this would be it. Hadn't reckoned on this old dreadnought ship being stripped back to basics so much. Sorry.'

'Adrian is alive? You have *seen* Adrian Wall?'

'And Bev Tarrant.'

'And Peter?'

Ginger shook her head. 'I certainly didn't see him. But there was a very annoying robot ball floating about.'

That should have made Bernice smile. She knew it should. Joseph, her oldest friend in the universe was still 'alive'. Bev and Adrian too. A few days she thought she would have danced for joy to know that. But instead all she could focus on was the fact that Peter wasn't there with his father. Safe. Protected.

'Are you being straight up, Ginger? I mean, tell me the truth, because if I sense you are screwing around with me, I'm out of here. I blow this whole gig apart.'

'It's true,' Russet said.

'I'm not talking to you,' Bernice said. 'I'm talking to your mother here. Because, I hope, as a mother, as someone who has already lost one child to the Rapture, there's a sense of decency in her that means she wouldn't lie to another grieving mother.'

Ginger couldn't keep Bernice's stare. She looked away, and Bernice knew immediately she was hiding something. Something wasn't as clear cut as Ginger made out.

'I got that from Adrian Wall, the Killoran leader of Valentine's World. He did not know you were aboard this ship when it took off, otherwise he would have insisted on being aboard, and I couldn't risk that. But, when this is all over, we'll go back there and maybe together you can find your son.' Ginger took a deep breath. 'That's the price for your cooperation.'

Bernice threw a look to Jet.

'I had no idea about any of whatever you are talking about,' the skunk said. 'Honest.'

Bernice read her face, her twitches, her eyes. Jet was one hundred percent honest about that. She looked back to Ginger. No, something there was –

'Look,' Russet butted in, breaking the tension. 'Can we talk about that stuff later. We don't have long; our CloudSpace access is draining away by the second.'

Jet took Bernice's arm, but it was shaken off. 'Yeah,' she said. 'Russet's right. We need you to focus on the science team now.'

Bernice closed her eyes, let the anger, the slight panic drift. She felt herself pocket the data stick, feeling it in her pocket as if it weighed ten tons, feeling a connection to her past for the first time since she and Jack had fled that faked Victorian

London. Come back to this later, she reasoned with herself. The data stick isn't going anywhere.

'Tell me about the scientists,' she finally said, talking to the group, but keeping her stare on Ginger, who looked away uncomfortably again before answering.

'There are a series of labs built around one half of the hole in the centre of the *Adorable Illusion*.'

'On the other half?'

'Not sure. Observation decks certainly, but none of the techspecs detail that side of the ship. Not just around the scoop, but that whole forward section right up to the bridge.'

'And Victor Cooke didn't give you anything?'

'He gave us his personal access codes to CloudSpace.'

'Which is what, a data cloud, I guess?'

'Fully immersive, projects a 3D environment around you that's actually fully accessible. It's almost like having a transporter that can take you anywhere in the galaxy that has shared access to the CloudSpace.'

'Brilliant, and an utter security nightmare I imagine,' Bernice said.

Jet shook her head. 'It's new tech, not available to many outside the corporations, industrialists and so on. It's a rich man's boytoy.'

Bernice smiled. 'I've known a few of those in my times, but I don't think we're using the same definition of the term. Okay, so what am I looking for once I'm inside this CloudSpace?'

'Anything odd and unexplained. It'll automatically access Cooke Industries' environs. He's looking for anything that suggests someone else is using this ship for something other than researching the Rapture.'

Bernice considered this. 'Two questions. Why me, and how do we access it?'

Russet passed over a mitt, a chunky glove with tiny bulbous

ridges on the fingers. Bernice slipped it on and immediately, projected access terminals floated in front of her eyes.

'Wowsa,' she said. 'That's impressive.'

'What are you seeing?' Ginger asked.

'The glove is isomorphic,' Jet explained. 'It only works for the wearer.'

'I know the term,' Bernice replied. 'Never entirely believed it's true though. I've never met anything that can't be fixed to overcome that.' She glanced over at Ginger. 'And my other question?'

'Russet and I might be on a few security GalWeb searches that I'd rather weren't triggered.'

'Hullo! I'm a mass murderer called Anya. I'm prisoner 442. How the hell will it let me in?'

'Because you are Professor Bernice Summerfield as far as it is concerned. As Victor Cooke set this up, I rather imagine he gave you privileges, or this whole thing goes tits up rather rapidly.'

'I hope you're right,' Bernice said. 'And you, Jet?'

'What about me?'

'Why can't you do this?'

Jet stared at her. 'None of your damn business,' she said after a pause.

Bernice shrugged. 'I can live with that.' And she accessed the CloudSpace.

There were three scientists aboard the *Adorable Illusion*, resplendent in their custard-coloured one-piece uniforms, the *Adorable Illusion* Science Division emblem on their shoulders. They didn't know if the rest of the crew – other than the robot captain and the chef – even knew if they were there. They had been shut away in their laboratory close to the centre of the ship for quite some time. They had their own private quarters, a nice suite of rooms with quite an astonishing amount of luxuries to keep them happy, quiet and loyal.

They were loyal to their employer, partially because of the fact he had given them a well-paid research job. But mainly because if they knew that if they argued with him, they would probably be out there, floating around in space. Loyalty was big with Victor Cooke.

The three scientists possessed very different skills, the sort of skills that would not normally mean they'd work together in a laboratory. As a result, they had very definite demarcation zones, effectively a lab each, although contained within one large space. They called it the ballroom because that was the largest room any of them could think of that began to describe the area they had. And then some.

The biologist was a woman called Maria Willows, a human from a colony world who Cooke had employed some decades ago. As a result, she knew him, and his methods – questionable and other – rather well. She had established herself as a kind of de-facto leader. Or spokesperson at least. When it was time to send a detailed report back to Victor Cooke's people – heaven forbid they would ever be allowed to speak to the great man himself – it was Maria who made it. She had enough general science as well as her own speciality that she could speak with authority on her fellow scientists' subjects – enough not to make errors in reports anyway. That said, Maria would be the first to admit that she couldn't really do their jobs. Which was a relief for the other two, as Maria was clearly ambitious, and no one doubted that if she could replace them, she probably would.

The astrophysicist was a Graan called Shayla. Like all Graan, he was ethically – possibly religiously – compelled to keep his features hidden all day and all night behind a chadri. He told his fellows that he certainly removed it in private, but only for showering and such things. He slept in a special night version to maintain his privacy. It was flexible enough that he could change the strength of the eye covering if lighting was difficult, or he needed to get an especially clear view of something. He also told them it was quite handy for looking at stars, as he could polarise the filter and see far more than a naked eye would allow. Other than that, Shayla was rather enigmatic and rarely talked about his life before coming aboard the ship. Except than he owed Victor Cooke a life-debt for something that had happened two years previously.

Jefri was the other scientist, a Pakhar whose speciality was quantum theory, which was rather a woolly open-ended job description, but he just said he was there to perform a series of experiments into quantum physics and string theory, black holes etc. Maria had said more than once that those things were well outside 'quantum theory' but Jefri had got agitated, as Pakhars do, and fiddled anxiously with his whiskers enough that she thought he might pull them out. A Pakhar with trichotillomania was too much to think about, so Maria and Shayla had agreed not to push the point any further and just leave him to play with his computer simulations and tolerate his high-pitched mutterings and squeaks.

Maria had absolutely no idea if anyone else aboard ship knew they were there. She didn't care much either. She had no real idea who else was aboard either – it simply didn't matter. It was a big ship, the guest quarters were towards the rear, the captain was at the front and her team were positioned a few moments walk from the hole. And no one but them would ever go near that.

The hole was literally that, a massive rent in the ship, perfectly circular, like a giant laser saw had been taken to the hull – or a giant apple corer. It was about ninety square metres round and had been built expertly – not a single hard edge, perfect curvature everywhere. That alone was a great feat of engineering and Maria appreciated the workmanship. Victor Cooke had explained that when he had renovated the *Adorable Illusion*, he had stipulated the perfection. Maria never asked why, mainly because she knew she'd never get an answer and Maria prided herself on never asking questions there were no answers to. That was why she had chosen biology as her field – there were set parameters. She had little time for Jefri's theoretical science. If it was there, if it could been seen, touched and examined. Airy-fairy possibilities and plausibilities didn't interest her; she liked hard, proven and provable, facts.

She had no answer as to why the hole had been built, why it had to be so perfect, and what she and the others were doing aboard the ship. Victor Cooke had given them a list of tasks and deadlines – hers were sealed and marked EYES ONLY so she had assumed Shayla and Jefri's were too. She never asked, because she didn't care. Hitting her own targets, on time and as efficiently and accurately as she could, was all that mattered. To her and Victor Cooke.

Right now, she was standing at an observation point within the hole, that gave a massive panoramic view of not just the hole, but space above and below, if she crooked her head in the right directions. It was an interesting way of seeing the stars – Shayla had laughingly referred to it as looking out of something like a Dyson donut. She had said she hoped they weren't the jam. Neither of the others had got the reference, so she just shrugged and ignored them after that.

She often came to stand here and watch the universe go by. She never really wondered how fast they were travelling – the stars themselves always seemed static to her and yet of course, each time she came to look, the stars were different. That was the proof she needed that the *Adorable Illusion* was going somewhere, and that was enough. It had a destination. Presumably that tied in with whatever it was that Victor Cooke had placed them all aboard for. But Maria didn't really care. The money was good and, once it was all over, she could get back to her home and do some casual research until the next job came along. Maybe Victor Cooke again. After all, no reason not to work for him.

Sometimes, however, it did run through Maria's mind to wonder why the ship had such a skeleton staff – it would be more efficient if it was fully complemented. She was aware only of a few maintenance guys, the cook and the ship's medical officer, who was more a vet than a humanoid expert. That had intrigued her and so she had asked him why. He explained there were a variety of different species passengers in the aft section and he had been employed to look after them.

But the skeleton staff had its advantages. It meant she was rarely disturbed when she came up here to stare at the stars. And other... stuff.

Today's 'other stuff' included being nosey. Maria, quite sure she was alone, reached into the pocket of her uniform and brought up a curled ball of soft fabric. It unfurled into the shape of a glove, with tiny sensor pads woven into the palm and fingers. She slipped it onto her right hand and held it up in the air. She used the fingers to tap a code into the palm and seconds later she was... somewhere else. She wasn't really, but the glove had opened up an area of the CloudSpace that only she could see while wearing the glove.

To anyone watching, it'd look like she was conducting an invisible orchestra in the air around her. To Maria however, she was in a realm of shooting electrical currents, sparkling auroras and blue-tinged numbers cascading around her in seemingly random gyrations. But she knew they weren't random, just as she knew she was doing a very dangerous thing. For a woman so in control, so utterly convinced of her own untouchability, this was the only place Maria felt nervous. And thus alive.

Facing her as she turned left was a massive, seemingly oaken, door like something out of a centuries-old storybook. It even had a huge wrought-iron knocker on it. But she knew that was just for show, a bit of theatrics by the person who had created it. It was indeed a door, but as sophisticated and ultra-modern as everything else. She also knew the entry code, her fingers tapping on a suddenly-visible keypad in the air. Sure enough, the door silently swung open, fading to shrinking pixels as it went inwards. The space it revealed looked no different to where she was already standing, but Maria knew she was inside where she needed to be. She waved her hand right and a full keyboard materialised. She punched in a sequence of words and numbers and a subset of codes and lists appeared. Her own name was at the top of it. She activated a second subset; this one had Cooke Industries' name in it. She accessed one of hers, one she hadn't used for some months. It opened up and very swiftly, she swiped one set of numbers from the Cooke Industries account into her own.

Maria was well-paid by Victor Cooke, but that didn't stop her wanting a bit more. She had learned a long time ago how to move small, imperceptible amounts from his different stocks and shares into her accounts in such a way no one would notice. To Cooke Industries, it was a handful of credits vanishing like interest. To Maria, it was a change in lifestyle when she got home.

She was about to close it all down before setting off any potential alarm triggers when a red file caught her eye in the listing. It hadn't been there before, she knew that. How curious. If Victor Cooke was accessing these files recently enough to add something new, then she had to be careful she hadn't been spotted. But Maria was a scientist, and scientists, no matter how cold and logical, also have great curiosity. Maria might deny this, but deep down she knew it to be true.

She tapped the file, just to see what its name was.

Anya Krystyne.

Interesting. Why was he searching her out? Obviously he'd not forgiven her for his kid's death, Maria could understand that, but why now? Why was this new? She tried actually opening the folder and, much to her surprise, it wasn't locked. No security at all. That sent alarm bells ringing in Maria's head straight off. And yet...

She knew she would kick herself if she didn't find out more. There was a subfolder in there.

Professor Bernice Summerfield.

Who? Maria tapped on it and a photo popped up of a woman in her, well, early forties. Dark hair, engaging smile, trowel in hand. An archaeologist by trade, going by the mini-biog below. Why on earth was Victor Cooke interested in another archaeologist?

Some sixth sense made Maria start suddenly. Without hesitation she expertly shut the files down, one by one but very quickly, masterfully erasing her paths.

As she exited out past the momentarily recreated oak door, she caught a glimpse of something dark through the miasma of the CloudSpace. She stared at it. It moved and Maria realised it was a person, accessing the same financial subroutines as she was. Damn! If she could she them, they could see her. Hopefully as indistinctly, but if it was someone back at Cooke Industries – that creepy manservant for instance – they'd launch an investigation. While Maria knew she was good at this, she also knew she was not perfect. There was no guarantee that, having once alerted them to her presence, she had covered her tracks that efficiently.

She was about to yank the glove off, which would break her link. Normally it'd be a slow but sophisticated exit – sudden dropouts hurt. She remembered from the first time she had done it that the resultant headache would plague her for hours, but that was worth it right now.

Then, the shadowy figure waved at her, like it was a rambler walking across a hillside. So casual, so matter-of-factly.

Maria didn't know what to do. Ignore it? Run like hell? Or brazen it out, claim she got lost trying to update some science notes in a completely different part of Cooke Industries' infrastructure that she was entitled to access (that was, after all, why she had been given the glove originally).

The figure loomed into view, like it was completely at home walking through electron fields and CloudSpace matter. Maria stood still, deciding to go for it. Fight not flight.

'Hullo,' said a cheerful female voice. 'I seem to be a bit lost in here.'

'Yes indeed you are,' Maria said. 'Which aspect of the company were you hoping to get into?'

'Oh I'm just having a poke around really, seeing what Victor Cooke has to offer the universe. Where are we now? Financials by the look of it. I hate financials, always so dull. Numbers are not my thing.'

'Nor mine,' lied Maria. 'I sort of drifted in here from the records section. I was updating my notes and went through the wrong door somehow.'

The newcomer laughed. 'I bet Cooke Industries doesn't have that many different password combinations – must be easy to be a micrometre out in here and use your usual password to find yourself somewhere entirely wrong.'

Maria took the opt-out. 'I think you're right. I'm not familiar with anywhere other than my normal section.'

'Which is?'

Maria wasn't giving that away. 'Confidential I'm afraid.'

'I love confidential. Confidential is my favourite part of anywhere. Can't beat a bit of confidential.' She reached out a hand to shake Maria's. 'Hullo, by the way. My name is Anya Krystyne.'

Maria started, but managed not to show it. 'Hullo Anya. My name is...' and she hoped Anya wouldn't notice the beat as she grabbed at the first name that came to mind. 'My name is Bernice Summerfield.'

Anya smiled, she was right up close now. 'Really? The archaeologist? How exciting.'

And Maria went cold. Because she knew that facing her right now wasn't Anya Krystyne as she'd assumed. She was facing the real Bernice Summerfield, smiling just as she did in that photo she'd seen.

'Well,' Maria said quietly, 'I think we've both walked into a minefield of lies haven't we, Professor?'

Bernice nodded. 'And you know who I am, which is nice. I think. But I'm at a disadvantage. You are?'

'Not going to tell you. I'm sorry. But rest assured, I have no interest in revealing your secret either. I imagine we are many light years away from one another and unlikely to ever meet properly, so let's leave it at that.'

But Bernice Summerfield shook her head. 'I'm afraid you are wrong.' She pointed at the insignia on Maria's uniform. 'I recognise the emblem of the *Adorable Illusion*. Which means we are both on board.' She stopped for a second. 'Maybe we'll meet for dinner one day. I gather the curry makes a good curry. Hopefully see you there.' And she turned and walked back into the busy flurry of electrons and stuff. Maria watched her blend into the background and then vanish altogether.

Shaking slightly, Maria eased herself out of CloudSpace and a moment later was back in the reality of the observation point. She thrust the glove into her pocket, ready to return to the labs.

And caught a glimpse of one of her fellow scientists disappearing back the way she planned to go. Damn! She'd finally been spotted. She hadn't had time to register if it was Jefri or Shayla – she'd caught only a glimpse of movement and yellow uniform. No idea of shape or size. Go after them? Try and explain? Or again, brazen it out? Hmm, that hadn't worked too well today so far.

With a sigh, Maria headed back to the labs, more disturbed than she'd ever been since stepping aboard this ship.

Bernice passed the glove back to Russet with a smile that wasn't returned.

'Well?' asked Ginger. 'Anything or anyone?'

'One of the scientists,' Bernice said. 'Didn't get her name but she was utterly shocked to see me. She was doing something very dodgy in Cooke's financials. He won't like that.'

Ginger looked at Jet. 'I don't think we should access the CloudSpace any more. If others are in there, people on Cooke's payroll...'

But Jet shook her dark head. 'One person shouldn't concern us too much.'

'I only *saw* one,' Bernice said. 'For all I know, there could be dozens accessing it. The whole system could be corrupted and compromised. I don't think that's the solution to your problems.'

Jet shrugged. 'There aren't exactly a dozen other ways to find out what's going on. For now, we still use CloudSpace, but sparingly.'

Bernice sighed. 'It would be so much more helpful if you could tell me what's going on. You three certainly know who I am really. You know I'm not Anya, which is equally gratifying. But Lord Tawn and the others?'

Ginger said that they still thought she was Anya Kryzstyne. Bernice wondered if they could be brought up to speed, you know, so she didn't have to keep watching over her shoulder.

'My mum'll protect you,' Russet said, with the overconfidence of youth. 'Don't worry about that.'

He reminded Bernice of a younger Peter, before...

Ginger placed a paw on Russet's shoulder and flicked her tail. 'I can't guarantee it, Professor, but yeah, I'll keep you safe. To let Sable, Sandy and Tawn know the truth at this stage might throw the plan. If they lose confidence, especially Tawn, it's all going to go wrong. We need their anger to keep us all going forward.'

'If you'd tell me what the plan is, maybe I could offer alternatives to me getting a knife in the back from a pissed-off rabbit with dreams of recapturing his glory days. You know, just saying...'

Jet shook her head. 'Ignorance at the moment is key to your survival, Professor. And ours. But I promise, you will know when the time is right.'

'So long as that's not three seconds before I'm expected to do something brave, amazing and truly heroic, that's fine. I tend not to do those things in ignorance though.'

'Tell us more about the scientist. Which one was it?'

Bernice shrugged. A woman. Humanoid. Beyond that, I don't know.'

'Maria Willows then,' Russet said. 'I don't like her.'

Ginger smiled grimly. 'I don't like any of them. They've no idea what they're doing.'

'I know the feeling,' Bernice grunted.

'No, but really they don't. They are following Victor Cooke's orders, but even *he* isn't entirely sure what he's up to. That can be very dangerous where we're going.'

'The Rapture. Why? What exactly is it?'

Ginger paused for a moment. 'No one is quite sure. It's why people fund expeditions – the first person to understand it and find a use for it will be rich. It's a rent in time and space, whatever that means, but at the moment all that's known is if you get too close, wham, you're gone.'

Bernice nodded. '*A la* Anya Kryztne's poor kids.'

There was an uncomfortable silence, broken by Jet saying 'Yeah. Exactly.'

'Victor Cooke,' Ginger continued, 'is trying to access it for his own ends. Not just to find out what happened to his child. But he sees something that powerful as the source to all his problems.'

'He has problems?' Bernice thought about her meeting with Victor Cooke. 'He didn't strike me as a man with many problems.'

Jet laughed quietly. 'He's broke. It's all bluster. He has lots of money on paper but nothing in actuality. His empire is close to collapsing. He pays what little ready cash he has to PR people to spin the opposite.'

'Someone should tell that Maria person that she's stealing money that doesn't exist,' Bernice noted wryly.

'If she knew that, he'd probably have her killed. Victor Cooke isn't a man given to having his company secrets out there.'

'Yet you seem to know,' Bernice said looking at Jet. 'How is that?'

Jet smiled at her. 'I know everything. I was his chief accountant for a few years. I saw the problems coming, warned him and was ignored. Then fired. Then divorced.'

Bernice took this information in. 'So the son he lost..?'

'Was mine too, yes.'

'I'm sorry.'

'Don't be. It wasn't your fault. I still don't know what he expects to do with the Rapture to make his money back, but I plan to find out.'

'Then what?'

'I got a very good settlement. On paper. In reality, I got

nothing. If he makes a fortune out of the Rapture, I'll get my backdated share.'

Bernice laughed. 'And I thought this was all about revenge, about stopping a corrupt man being more corrupt. But it's not, it's just about money. You're not better than him.'

Jet shrugged. 'Pretty much. Either way, you are working for him or me. Same goal, same ends, same fortune. Depends if you want a bite of mine or an empty promise from him.'

Bernice sighed. 'I don't really have much choice. You are here, he isn't. And you are the only people between me and a pretty angry rabbit. There's a phrase I'd never have expected to say and keep a straight face. Yes, I'm in, I suppose. But if I don't like where it takes us, I reserve the right to drop out and get myself and Jack as far away as possible.' She looked at Jet, Ginger and Russet's impassive faces. 'Although I'm guessing that reservation doesn't really hold much water right now does it?'

All three of them shook their heads.

'Ah well,' Bernice said. 'It was worth a try.'

CHAPTER TEN
ACCIDENTS NEVER HAPPEN

Captain Redbeard's all-seeing electronic eyes scanned the bridge until they focused on the hologrammatic image floating in the middle of the room.

'Arrrr?'

'Report please.'

Florence looked up from her perch, keeping silent as the AI responded.

'Nothing is going to plan. Members of the crew keep disappearing. Or fluctuating. The manifest is redundant. It keeps changing. Air pressure drops are being reported. Maintenance crews are unresponsive. Arrrrr,' said Captain Redbeard.

The hologram of Victor Cooke's majordomo seemed to look behind him then back. 'Cooke Industries' financials are being hacked from on board the *Adorable Illusion*. Mr Cooke says this is unacceptable. Find out who is doing it. We will continue to investigate from this end.'

'How? I can't leave the bridge,' Captain Redbeard said.

'Use an agent. There are enough people aboard.'

'That's rather the point,' the AI countered. 'They are dropping like flies.'

The majordomo paused. 'Mr Cooke would like to remind you that no one, not even a Mark 27, is indispensable.'

And the hologram cut off.

'Arrrrr. We *are* indispensable actually,' Captain Redbeard said. 'Without us, Victor Cooke has no ship.'

'Yes, but without him, we have no ship either,' Florence retorted. 'Impasse.'

'Arrrrrr.'

'I shall try maintenance once more,' Florence said. 'They'd better have a clue about what's happening.' One of Florence's feathers suddenly fell away from her wing. Then another. She followed them with her eyes as they fluttered to the floor of the bridge. 'That can't be good,' she said.

'Arrrrrr,' agreed Captain Redbeard.

Dave in maintenance grunted as the bleeping sound woke him up. He yanked his hand from down the front of his trousers, poked the comms switch to off and rolled over, trying to sleep again. But the bleeping started up again, this time from Bob's bunk. It took Dave only a few seconds to realise that neither Bob nor Ted were back. He looked up at the clock. They should've been back ages ago. Usually by now they'd be whinging about him missing his shift or something.

'So tight,' he muttered, then staggered over and poked the button in Bob's area to shut it off. It immediately started up again, now in Ted's area. 'All right, all right, I get the message,' Dave muttered and this time answered. 'Maintenance, Dave speaking.'

A voice Dave didn't know spoke. 'What is the situation? Report please.'

Dave shrugged. 'Hey, I dunno. Bob and Ted haven't come back yet. I was asleep. I am allowed to sleep, you know.'

'This is the bridge,' said the voice. 'Why is the chief offline?'

This was enough to pique Dave's curiosity because, indeed, the chief should never be offline. In fact, surely it was impossible.

'I don't know,' was all he managed to mutter. He called out to the chief but indeed, no response. Dave frowned. 'I'll go find Bob,' he told the voice from the bridge.

'Do so and report back. We need the chief back online and we need to know why there have been momentary pressure drops all over the ship. Bridge out.'

Dave scurried out of the crew room calling for Bob and the chief, hoping that one or the other would miraculously turn up and save him having to do any actual work.

Dave wasn't a man given to the work ethic. He'd been offered the chance to join the *Adorable Illusion* only shortly before take-off and had taken it because it paid some money. Dave had a lot of debts. Bookies. Bars. Pimps. He owed a lot to a lot. He'd never actually done maintenance work before – hell, he'd never actually done any work before, but going into space at least bought him time. He had been assured that while away on this mission, no one would find him and the guys out for his money – or blood – would be... persuaded to put it aside for a few months. Dave wasn't sure that was likely, but he took the chance anyway. All he had to do was safely deliver one small package. He had no idea who to, but had been told that the relevant person would seek him out. All he had to do was deliver it and bingo, his account would be topped up with enough money to pay off his debts and leave him enough to start a new life somewhere else. Or gamble it again. Either way, money was his for the taking.

He'd immediately made an enemy of both Bob and Ted on his arrival through his lack of understanding of what work actually entailed. He'd like to say he tried his best, but truth was, he hadn't, mainly because he didn't have a best. Or a worst. He was just Dave and Dave did whatever Dave pleased. For instance, he had indeed received a message after departing Valentine's World. He had been told where to leave the package and that the money had been transferred into his account and his debts wiped. So Dave planned to quit at the next half-decent planet they arrived at and get as far away as possible. He was already relieved that, after delivering the package, no one had come after him for opening it first. Oh, of course he had taken a sneaky peek, but the drugs inside were pretty scary, top-end stuff and Dave had decided to leave them untouched and hope no one spotted his clumsy attempt to reseal the box. For now, he seemed to have gotten away with it. Phew.

As Dave wandered down the corridors of the ship, yelling out for his colleagues and the chief, he realised that he knew enough about technology to know that AIs never went offline without bad consequences, and that scared him more than a bollocking from Bob or Ted.

Suddenly he stopped. He ought to have known where he was, but the signage was missing and he was suddenly aware that without them, all the corridors looked the same. He felt a slight crunch under his feet – it was a bluetooth. Bob's or Ted's he reckoned. Of course, he'd not bought his with him, so that was stupid.

'Guys? It's Dave,' he said, surprised to hear himself almost whispering. Why was he whispering? What was he afraid of?

'Hullo,' said a voice behind him.

Dave nearly collapsed in shock. He turned back. 'Don't. Do. That.'

Facing him was a guy with a beard, red eyes and very odd looking legs. Dave asked who he was.

'Jack. You?'

'Dave,' Dave said.

'Hullo Dave. Who are you looking for?'

'Bob. And Ted. And the chief.'

Jack shrugged. 'Not seen anyone and I've been wandering around here a while. Any idea which direction the food place is? I'm a bit lost. Someone really should put up some signs.'

Dave pointed at some vacant screw holes. 'Used to be signs everywhere.'

'Oh,' said Jack. 'When did they vanish?'

'Just now,' Dave replied. 'They were there when I did my last shift.'

'Oh,' said Jack again. He put his head on one side as he looked at Dave. 'You don't seem to be enjoying yourself, Dave. Fancy a curry?'

Dave considered. There was no sign of Bob or Ted. The chief was still offline and he was pretty hungry. Food or responsibilities? Food or responsibilities? Food or...

'Curry sounds great, mate. If we can find the Madras.'

Jack thumbed backwards. 'I came that way, you came up that one, so let's try one of those.'

And the two of them headed down the left-hand corridor.

Half a minute later, someone else came up the right-hand corridor, looked down the left-hand one to make sure they were out of sight and then pulled open a panel on the wall.

A small LED flickered. Above it was a sticker that said *CHIEF AI ACCESS POINT SEVEN*. Below the flickering LED were small LED letters which read *CHIEF AI REBOOT IN PROGRESS. 93%.*

The panel was replaced and the person smiled to themselves. Not long now.

Dr Richard Blair tapped the datapad on his desk and it brought up the crew/passenger manifest.

Then he tapped the music key and his office filled with choral music from the Lystonian Monks of St Annette's.

Then he tapped the key that brought up a hologram of his family back on Delta Capris and sighed.

He'd been aboard the *Adorable Illusion* for some weeks now

and he'd not had a single patient. Not so much as a cut on the hand of a maintenance man, or a case of mange from one of the lemurs, or an acid burn from a scientist. Or the runs from the Madras chef's alarming curries. Nothing.

Worse still, he'd barely seen anyone. He'd said a brief hullo to some of the alien passengers in the canteen. The big tall rabbit with the medals and wonky eye had alarmed him slightly, but everyone else had been happy to have a medical officer aboard who knew all forms of physiology rather than just human.

But since then, he'd eaten, slept and sat in his office pretty much alone. Even the bridge had been quiet for the last few weeks; the rather eccentric AI that ran the ship only acknowledged his daily reports with an email that said 'Arrrrr.'

He switched off the music. He was bored with it. He was bored with everything, truth be told. Nothing was happening aboard this ship – his job could so easily have been done by a good AI and a trained first aider amongst the maintenance guys.

With another deep sigh, he decided to venture down to the canteen and see what breakfast was on offer. Well, it felt like a breakfast hunger pang anyway – it was hard to know what time of day it was really.

He locked his office – standard procedure when drugs of any kind were on board – and headed out into the corridor. Hmm, that was weird. Where was the sign that told him where to go? Oh well, he'd walked it often enough, he was sure he could do it blindfolded.

Five minutes later he was standing at a junction point without a clue where he was or for that matter which way he'd come. Which was weird because that had never happened before. Blair started to go one way then stopped. No, the correct corridor had an oil stain about... there and this one didn't. So he retraced his steps and went back to the junction. It was surely the far left one? But which was far left now?

'Oh this is ridiculous,' he said aloud.

'Good morning,' said a voice from all around. 'This is the chief engineer AI. How may I help you?'

'I'm trying to get to the food hall and all the signs are gone.'

'Good morning. Please speak your name and crew passcode so I may be able to help you.'

Blair frowned. 'Umm, I've been here a few weeks now, Chief. It's Dr Blair.'

'Good morning. Please speak your name and crew passcode so I may be able to help you.'

'Okay. Dr Richard Blair. Passcode eight-oh-three.'

'Good morning, Dr Blair, your details have been recorded. How may I help you?'

Blair just sighed. 'Which way to the food, Chief?'

'That information is unavailable.'

'What?'

'That information is unavailable. This AI unit has not been programmed with that information.'

Shaking his head, Blair went down another corridor.

On the bridge, an alert caught the attention of Captain Redbeard.

'Arrrr,' he said to Florence. 'The chief engineer AI has been reprogrammed. This was unscheduled.'

'Who performed it?' Florence asked

There was a pause and then Captain Redbeard said, 'No ID has been registered.'

'This place is going to the dogs,' Florence said.

Jack and Dave arrived in the mess hall, with huge grins of relief on their faces.

'We found it,' Jack laughed. 'That was an adventure.'

Snow and Ebon looked up at them. 'Explain?'

'All the signs are missing in the corridors,' he said. 'Trying to find your way around is insane.'

Snow and Ebon looked at one another. 'Isn't that the job of the maintenance team?' Snow said, looking pointedly at Dave.

'Bob's job,' was Dave's response. 'I wouldn't know where to begin.'

'Course not,' Ebon said. 'Why would you?'

'Right you 'orrible lot,' the Madras called out. 'Who wants what for breakfast?'

Everyone started putting orders in, including a dishevelled looking Dr Blair who had arrived at last. He introduced himself to Jack, wondering aloud how they'd not met before.

'Don't even recognise your name from the manifest.'

'Came aboard on Valentine's World,' Jack said. 'Perhaps no one's updated the details since then.'

'Anyone else I should know about?'

'Anya Kryztene,' Ebon said. 'Jack's her guard.'

The doctor went visibly pale. 'Why is she here?'

'Serving her time,' Jack said. 'So I believe. I'm just here to make sure she doesn't get killed.'

'Why?'

'Sorry?'

'Some people don't need protecting.'

Jack frowned. 'I hope you don't judge all your patients like that.'

'I doubt she'd be a patient of mine if she's your prisoner.'

Jack shrugged. 'Good to know where we stand then. If she gets hurt, I'll find another doctor for her.'

Blair shrugged. 'Good luck with that. I'm the only medic aboard and where she's concerned, my oath goes out into the vacuum.'

'Why?'

Blair took a breath. 'She killed my daughter. If I'd known she was here, I wouldn't have agreed to this trip.' He threw a quick glance at Jack. 'Keep her away from me. I have any number of ways to kill as well as cure people and I don't trust that I wouldn't use something slow and painful on her. And enjoy it. Now, if you'll excuse me, I need breakfast.' And Blair walked away from Jack.

Ebon and Snow were at Jack's side. 'He's a weird one, Jacky,' said Ebon, leading him back to their table.

Jack looked at the lemurs. 'I'm beginning to think that's a pretty good description of everyone on board this ship.' He nodded towards Dave. 'Case in point.'

Snow and Ebon glanced at one another. 'We don't recognise him,' Ebon said slowly. 'And I thought we knew everyone aboard.'

This piqued Jack's interest on both counts. They knew everyone and they didn't know Dave. Both interesting facts to store up.

The doors at the far end of the mess hall slid open and the two unctuous quartermasters, Edj and Kread strode in, as if they owned the place. They saw Jack.

'Where's your prisoner?' Edj asked, his silver face beaming as if he'd just asked what flavour of ice cream Jack wanted.

That was a good question, Jack thought. He'd got so caught up with everything else, he'd quite forgotten that he was supposed to be pretending to guard Bernice. Or Anya Kryztyne. 'I'm due to collect her from her secure quarters in ten minutes,' Jack lied.

Convincingly it seemed, as the two quartermasters nodded and wandered towards the Madras's counter.

Jack did wonder what Bernice was up to though. He'd left her with Ginger – was that the wisest of ideas?

*

Bernice Summerfield strode through the corridors with Ginger at her side. Jet and the others had elected to remain doing whatever it was they did wherever they did it.

She was thinking about all she had learned from her brief visit to the CloudSpace. There was something weird going on aboard this ship. Was that why Victor Cooke had really hired her? Got her to play the part of Anya Kryztyne? Because he actually needed to know who was hacking into his financials?

That was mad – he could have any number of people do that.

The canteen doors slid open and her heart leapt slightly as she saw Jack – familiar and reliable. Time for a catch-up. Then she saw the two lemurs eyeing her dangerously, as if...

Oh my God, they were going to keep her and Jack apart! Why?

She was going to ask Ginger this, but Ginger suddenly shoved her hard towards a solitary table. 'Sit down, killer,' Ginger said in a tone that dared argument.

As Bernice staggered towards the table, she took in lots of new faces, and those two Quatermaster idiots from earlier. So Ginger was suddenly playing the part of aggrieved room-mate. Hopefully.

Jack started to move towards her, but the lemurs grabbed his arm and yanked him back towards them.

Ginger sat next to Bernice. Making sure no one could see her face, Bernice muttered that she needed to talk to Jack, privately.

'Not a chance,' Ginger said. 'Not just for the sake of our role-play, but the girls won't let him out of their sight.'

'Why not?'

'Not a clue. Never met them before this trip. They made it clear from the off that they were interested in the guy guarding you, rather than you. I didn't really care much, my job was to look after you. Let me do that, yeah?'

Bernice shrugged. 'I have a choice?'

'Nope.'

'Well, there we are then,' Bernice said and sat upright. 'I need food.'

'Stay here,' Ginger said, and got up.

Edj and Kreed were walking towards her in a second. 'Excuse me,' Kread said charmingly, 'but it's company policy not to let prisoners interact with paying passengers.'

'I told you they were on their way,' Jack called. 'But as usual, no one listened to me.'

Edj threw Jack a look that might have well as said that on this ship he was the authority, but Jack was playing his part magnificently, Bernice thought.

He stood up to his full height, letting his eyes glow dark red. Even Kread took an involuntary step back. 'That prisoner is my responsibility and every time you challenge me and my authority to treat her as I see fit, you are challenging the commands set down by your boss and mine, Victor Cooke. You want to argue, change or generally piss about with me and my job, feel free. But Mr Cooke is getting hourly updates from me and as yet, your overbearing officiousness, which borders upon downright rudeness, hasn't warranted a mention. But it's getting close to doing so, so I suggest you back off and focus on doing whatever it is you two are supposed to do, and leave me and my prisoner alone. Got it?'

There was an uncomfortable silence. Jack wasn't used to playing the hard-man. Kread and Edj clearly weren't used to facing a dominant personality. But one thing Jack could do was stare without blinking and he kept his glowing eyes aimed at the two quartermasters. After what seemed like half an hour but was about twenty seconds, Edj nodded slowly.

'Yes of course. Our apologies. She's all yours. We'll get back to our passengers.'

And he and Kread strode out of the mess hall.

Jack deflated visibly and allowed the lemurs to guide him back to his seat.

Bernice smiled wryly – she was proud of Jack's action, less pleased by his obvious wilting now. What hold did those lemurs have over him? And why, if Ginger was telling the truth, were they interested in him anyway?

Bernice looked around the vast hall. Sat on a table alone was a scruffy guy, skinny and unwashed, in maintenance overalls. He seemed oblivious to what had just happened, and was focussing more on stirring the cup of coffee in front of him.

Another guy, a bit older, early thirties maybe, was standing by the Madras's counter, staring at them all. He seemed especially interested in what Jack had just done. Then she realised he was staring intently at her. Hmm, clean-cut, intelligent looking, he carried himself with an air of superiority. Bernice reckoned she either loathed him on the spot or would end up in some clumsy tryst as they faced doom and despair later on. He was just that type. Damn him. He already intrigued her. She didn't want to be intrigued on this job.

The door hissed open and Lord Tawn hobbled in, ignoring her and Ginger. All part of the pretence, no doubt. Whatever she had been led into by Ginger, it was something that group wanted kept secret. He made no eye contact with anyone, other than a slight nod of patriarchal politeness to the lemurs as he passed them. By the time he reached the Madras, Sable and Sandy had arrived, chattering like a couple of excited holidaymakers, waving at everyone as if they'd just got out of bed and were seeing them all for the first time today.

'This is the best acted melodrama I've ever seen,' Bernice muttered to Ginger.

'It has to be,' Ginger whispered back. 'The *Adorable Illusion* has eyes and ears everywhere.'

'You'd think that,' said Jack, suddenly beside them. 'Except that the AI running that has been offline and recently rebooted, according to the doctor over there.' He indicated Bernice's clean-cut potential nemesis. 'He said nothing was working and he had to relog his personal details. Also, all the signage has gone.'

Bernice frowned. 'Yeah, I noticed the place was curiously unhelpful as we walked about. Actually gone or just never there?'

'According to the doctor, completely gone. There last night, gone today.'

Ginger shrugged. 'General maintenance?'

'Not according to our chum Dave over there. He's as bamboozled as anyone I've ever met. And I've met a lot of bamboozled types. He's also lost his two fellow maintenance guys.'

'Lost?'

'Literally. Vanished. Went off to do a job, never came back.'

Bernice thought about this. 'Wonder who else has done a bunk then?'

Ginger frowned. 'Why'd you think anyone has?'

Bernice waved her arm around the room. 'Big ship. With fee-paying passengers like Tawn and those two meerkats, why is there no one looking after them? Other than that medical guy?'

'The Quatermasters? Edj and Kreed?'

'They're more security than the friendly face of Cooke Industries. Surely someone is here to look after the guests' every need?'

The door opened again, Jet and Russet this time. The young squirrel hopped over to join his mother, while Jet made a beeline straight to the Madras. Ginger introduced Jack to her boy.

'Let's consider what we have here, Jack,' Bernice said.

'Okay,' he replied. 'First off, let's count up who is aboard that we know of. Kread and Edj. Don't like them. Too smooth, too perfect.'

'Snow and Ebon, with their odd fascination with you,' Bernice added. 'Don't like them much either.'

'Oh they're all right once you get to know them,' Jack said. 'Probably.'

Bernice held up a hand gently and tapped his. 'Ginger, Russet and the big skunk lady, they know who I really am. The clapped-out old Leperoid and the Meerks think I'm Anya. What about the lemurs?'

Jack shrugged. 'Not come up, so I assume they think you're Anya. Can I just ask how...'

'It's our job to know,' Ginger said.

'There's this doctor chum of yours,' Bernice carried on. 'Plus at least three maintenance guys, according to Dave there. He's human – do we know about the others?'

Jack shook his head. 'I assumed, but that's not always a good move. The Madras is a living curry – not sure he ever leaves this place. Or sleeps.'

'And then there's the scientists.'

'The who now?'

And Bernice recounted her experience in CloudSpace.

'So that's another one who knows you're Benny, not Anya. Not sure I like this, you know.'

'Why not?' asked Russet.

'Because,' Bernice said, 'Victor Cooke put me aboard to be Anya. So far as I am aware, four people definitely know I'm not her. I don't trust Jack's lemurs either.'

'Just saying, they're not "my" lemurs okay? I didn't ask for this attention.'

'So why've you got it?' Ginger wondered.

'I assumed they were with your gang,' Jack countered.

Ginger shook her head. 'Never saw them before they took you away. Jet and I assumed you already knew them and they were part of Victor Cooke's lot.'

'If they are, we didn't know about them. Now, can I ask something?' Jack smiled at her.

Ginger nodded.

'Why are you lot here? And how did you know Bernice's identity?'

'You can ask,' Ginger said, 'but that's between me, Jet and my son at the moment.' She suddenly smiled and took Bernice's hand. 'But believe this, please. It's nothing sinister. I really am here to help.'

Bernice drew her hand back. 'That'd be more convincing if I didn't think you had an axe to grind. Even if it's just a pretence.'

'Say what now?' asked Jack.

Bernice sighed. 'Jack, you ever heard of Agatha Christie?'

Jack frowned. 'Yeah, old Earth writer. I think you mentioned her once or twenty times.'

'She wrote a famous novel about a journey where everyone aboard wanted one of the passengers dead. When the passenger died, the guy solving the case realised there was no one who wasn't a legitimate suspect. Right now, I feel like the victim and detective at the same time.' She smiled at Jack. 'I think you and I may be the only people on the *Adorable Illusion* who didn't lose family members to Anya Kryztyne's ineptitude at the Rapture. And as that's where we're heading, and they think I'm her, my back feels like it has a big neon target on it.'

Jack glanced at the two squirrels. 'You too?'

Russet nodded slowly. 'I think that's why we were asked to help the professor.'

'Your girlfriends are getting anxious, Jack, you'd better go entertain them again.' Ginger stood up. 'Russet and I need food,' she said very loudly, making sure everyone could hear. 'Not sure you deserve food, Kryztyne, but I suppose I'd better get you something. Wouldn't want your big hulking guard here moaning at me for letting you starve.'

Jack joined in the acting immediately. 'Too right, Ginger. I charged you with keeping her safe and I find out you've not let her eat in ten hours. That's enough to have you put on report, you know.' And he walked back to the lemurs, winking at them. 'Gotta keep the scum in order,' he said.

Ginger wandered away, leaving Bernice alone with Russet. She looked at him. He had to be scared, she thought. For all his cockiness, he still made her think of Peter at that age. So much bravado, but underneath, so much vulnerability.

'Your mum is amazing,' she said quietly. 'Is your dad around?'

Russet shook his head. 'Died during the war. I was still a kit then. I don't remember him at all.'

'I'm sorry.'

'Why? I can't be sad about something I never really lost. No reason you should be either.' Russet smiled, and Bernice realised that was the first time she'd seen him smile. 'But thank you. I can see why you are so loved.' And on that enigmatic comment he stood up and wandered off to join his mother.

Bernice looked up and caught Jet's gaze from across the room. She was going to walk over to the dark skunk when the whole ship lurched violently. Bernice almost hit the floor – a couple of the others did. Certainly Lord Tawn could be heard swearing, and the Madras started complaining loudly about losing half his food.

Emergency lighting started flickering into action and the calm voice of an AI boomed out.

'This is the chief engineer AI of the *Adorable Illusion*. Apologies for the abrupt movement of this fine ship. Maintenance teams are currently investigating the cause. There is no reason for passengers or crew to be alarmed.'

Bernice looked across to Dave from maintenance. He in turn was staring at the doors and Bernice turned to see two other guys from maintenance stood there, staring angrily at him.

'Coming guys,' Dave said and started to get up.

Bernice looked back at the newcomers just as the emergency lighting kicked into a red strobe effect.

And she gasped. Just for a second, caught in the harsh scarlet lighting for a split second, neither of the newcomers had human heads any longer. Instead their features were grinning, gnarled faces, with tusks and black eyes. One of them seemed to be staring straight at her and she shivered.

A split second later, the human visages were back.

'Come on Dave,' one snapped. 'We have work to do.'

'Sorry Ted,' Dave mumbled as he dashed past Bernice and followed them out through the door. A moment later, another lurch and the strobing kicked off again.

Bernice looked towards Jack and the lemurs, hoping to see a familiar face, wondering if he'd noticed the alien imagery too.

Except Jack wasn't there. Nor were the lemurs. How the hell had they got out? Or perhaps the better question was how had they got Jack out? Because something told her Jack wouldn't have gone willingly.

Another lurch. This one dropped Bernice to the floor and she opted to stay there until the lurching stopped. Sable and Sandy were wailing in a corner, Tawn was still swearing, Jet was holding onto her table, and she couldn't see Ginger or Russet through the flickering lighting. As she tried to wriggle, Bernice was aware of someone grabbing her arm. At first she hoped it was Jack, or maybe Ginger. But it probably wasn't, because all she could see through the intermittent lighting was a syringe and needle darting towards her. She kicked out in the direction of where she reckoned her new assailant would have to be and sure enough, her boot connected with a shin, and the syringe dropped to the floor. She rolled well away from it as the ship lurched once more and then –

Silence. No more lurching. The strobes switched off, as did the alarms. The chief engineer's voice came back on, saying that the maintenance crews had solved the problem and apologising for any distress.

Bernice jumped up, ready to face her new attacker, but there was nothing and no one there. Just the dropped syringe. She scooped it up, it was empty. Russet and Ginger were beside her instantly. Russet reached out for it, but Bernice snatched it away.

'No,' she said breathlessly.

'But it's empty,' Russet protested.

Bernice and Ginger exchanged knowing looks. 'Which is far worse,' Ginger said. 'Someone wanted you to have an embolism.'

'They certainly went for the jugular,' Bernice confirmed.

There was a scream from the far end of the room. It was Sandy. Or Sable. One of the meerkats anyway.

'Out there,' one of them was screeching. 'Look out there!'

Everyone rushed over to the porthole where she was pointing, but no one could see anything.

'What's the problem here,' said the stentorian Lord Tawn from behind them all.

'That young human,' one of the Meerks was saying. 'The one was there earlier!' Bernice realised it meant Dave.

'What about him?'

'He's floating out there! I saw him, in space. No spacesuit on! Just spinning around.'

Bernice threw Ginger a look. 'He went out with the other maintenance guys during that palaver.'

'Can't see him now.' Jet was trying to calm the meerkats down. 'Are you sure?'

'Yes, yes, of course I'm bloody sure,' the agitated Meerk snapped.

'Well, how do you explain that then?' Lord Tawn said pompously.

And everyone turned and followed his pointing paw.

Standing at the door of the mess was Dave, plus one of the other two maintenance men.

'Sorry about all that stuff,' said one. 'All sorted now.'

'But... but...' the meerkat looked at its husband. Or wife. Whichever it was. 'You saw it too!' Her fellow meerkat shook his head. 'Sorry my dear, but I didn't. And the young human seems to be fine over there.'

'Are you sure it's him?' said Lord Tawn. 'Humans all look alike to me.'

The three maintenance guys wandered towards the Madras.

'Hey, are you okay?' said one. 'Need anything sorted out?'

'A little help would be appreciated, yeah, Ted, thanks,' said the chef.

As as everyone settled down again, Bernice glanced back out of the window. She had no doubt, after what she'd seen earlier, that poor Dave had indeed been thrown out and that the Dave fiddling with the kitchen area was, like the other two, rather unlikely to be exactly who or what he seemed.

So, something had happened to the ship, Dave was dead, someone had tried to murder her, but no one was limping like they'd been kicked, and Jack and the lemurs were gone. Great. Bloody great. Why was nothing simple any more?

CHAPTER ELEVEN
UNDER THE GUN

Moments earlier, in the science lab, Maria had been looking at a succession of readings that flittered across her holographic screen. Expertly, she waved across page after page, taking just seconds to absorb and understand the data she was reading.

Jefri was scurrying about, his head bowed, muttering about the world/universe/entire cosmos ending and then rebooting on a cycle every fifteen minutes, according to him. He'd gone through this process so many times over the last few weeks that she and Shayla just ignored him. Obviously it was a theory – and Jefri wasn't the only one who considered the multiverse just one vast computer that erased and rebooted its harddrive regularly and no one knew. Maria considered that all a bit nonsensical and, even if it were true, it didn't impact on her life much anyway, so why worry about it? No she was far more preoccupied with which of her cohorts wasn't who they seemed and had witnessed her in the CloudSpace talking to that weird professor. Surely it was Shayla – Jefri was the sort of Pakhar who'd have said something by now. So what was Shayla's game? Why keep quiet? Why watch her? And indeed how many of the times that she'd accessed Victor Cooke's financials had she been observed before?

Damn. She hated not knowing the answers. Maria needed

to be in control of all aspects of her life. Mysteries like this she didn't need.

The besuited figure of Shayla wandered over and put down a mug of coffee. Maria looked up in surprise. She couldn't remember Shayla ever having done that before. Or Jefri. Or her, for that matter.

'You looked like you needed it,' was Shayla's distorted response to her look. 'It's the only way I get through listening to Jefri's ravings.'

Maria smiled at the alien. 'Thank you,' she said, trying to disguise the fact that those were two words she rarely said. 'You're right, I do.'

Shayla started to move away, but then turned back, glancing first to make sure Jefri wasn't nearby. 'Who was she?'

Maria tried to stop her heart beating faster – for all she knew the Graan was fishing. 'Who?'

'The woman you met in CloudSpace, up in the observation bay.' He paused, then continued. 'Maria, you've been up there eight times in the past ten days. I have watched you the last three. Today was the first time I let you see me.'

'Why?'

'Because, like me, you want to know why we are here, what Victor Cooke expects from the Rapture and whether, at the end of the day, we'll get paid what we're promised. Our disciplines of science are not hugely complimentary to each other. There has to be a reason why we're doing this trip that we don't know about. I thought you might know more than I do.'

'What about Jefri?'

'What about him?' Maria was sure she saw a flash of something in Shayla's eyes as he carried on. 'I don't think he knows what day of the week it is half the time. Plus he's more concerned with keeping his fur in place than noticing you and me skulking around.'

'Not sure I "skulk" anywhere,' Maria said, sipping her coffee. 'And that woman was just a nosey passenger who shouldn't have accessed the CloudSpace. I got shot of her.'

Shayla's cowled head bowed. 'Fair enough. Maybe next time we can legitimately go up to the observation deck together. Who knows what we might discover working in tandem.'

Maria shrugged. 'Maybe. But I actually felt today that I wasn't going to go up again. That encounter with the passenger made me realise how easy it would be to be discovered up there, rather than working. And I can't afford for Victor Cooke to fire me.'

Shayla seemed to consider this, then nodded. 'Fair enough. If you change your mind...' And he slouched away, leaving Maria mystified at her suddenly gaining of an ally. Or, she pondered, maybe she'd gained competition. An enemy even? Hmm, she would need to keep an eye on these developments. She took a full swig of coffee. Shayla certainly made a good hot drink.

She returned to her holograms and raised her hand to tap at an icon, but mistapped. Instantly, a new folder opened, marked **BLAIR**. Within it was a series of DNA helixes. Knowing that Blair was the name of the ship's doctor, Maria wasn't going to pry, but then she stopped. Something was wrong with the DNA profiles before her. She couldn't put her a finger on it yet... Wait! Hang on, that didn't make sense. The file was last updated this morning as it always should be – like every file automatically backed up on board ship – and yet surely it couldn't be right?

Either the doctor was an idiot or he'd seen this. Maybe she should contact him for clarification. It was quite likely Blair knew more about the people aboard than she did, but this was quite a hefty mistake. If it was a mistake. Maria hoped it was, because otherwise, *she'd* just made a huge mistake and Jefri's weird philosophies were quite possibly the least of her problems.

She typed a quick email to Blair and sent it. Then, making sure neither Shayla nor Jefri saw her, she took a holograb of the file and saved it in her personal folder, encrypting the password twice, just in case. She was still thinking about the DNA profiles when the ship made a sudden lurch to one side and then the other and Maria went sprawling to the floor. She could hear Jefri somewhere, mewling like a frightened... well, hamster really, as the lights flickered and went out, as did the holofiles in front of her.

She yelled out for the chief engineer AI, but there was no response.

'This can't be good,' she muttered. 'Not sure the ship functions without AIs these days.'

The ship was, frankly, throwing itself around as if having a tantrum. Jack wasn't entirely sure how something this large could make such an amazing (and scary) amount of movement without tearing itself apart. His long, thin legs hadn't helped much either, and he had nearly lost his balance and gone flat on his pointed chin more than once.

'It's well constructed,' Snow said, reading his thoughts from his expression. 'Don't worry, we'll get there.'

As if to illustrate this point, a couple of the ceiling-mounted lights in the corridor ahead of them exploded, and the others flickered maniacally – creating a headache-inducing strobing effect that Jack would rather avoid if possible.

'Worried? I'm not worried. I'm never worried. Worried is for fools and charlatans. I'm just bloody terrified, if that's okay?'

Ebon laughed. 'So glad you're with us, Jack. For now.'

And that made Jack stop. 'I beg your pardon.'

'We're getting you off the *Adorable Illusion*,' she replied, twitching her tail in the way Jack had come to think of as expressing amusement. He hadn't liked it before, and he certainly didn't like it now.

'I'm not going anywhere without my prisoner.'

The two lemurs laughed, and their tails entwined. 'Orders are orders, Jacky-Boy.'

Jack put a hand out to steady himself on a bulkhead as the ship lurched once more in a way spaceships should never lurch. 'Now listen,' he said, darkly, letting his red eyes glow a deeper red than normal. 'This isn't the first time you've talked about orders. I'm guessing now that Vincent Cooke and co don't run you the way they think they do.'

Snow shrugged. 'Don't care what you think –' but her voice cut off with a yelp as Jack took her by surprise, speedily grabbing her around the throat, squeezing hard enough to drop her to her knees. He was aware of Ebon bristling, readying for some of her Ninja moves, but Jack had had enough. He flicked out with his slim but oh-so-powerfully muscled right leg, catching her on the side of her left leg, just above the knee. As the dead-leg sent her falling, so the force of Jack's kick sent her sprawling across the corridor and she hit the far side with an uncomfortable crack.

'Sorry,' Jack said instinctively, before remembering that he actually didn't like being manipulated by people, cute 'n' furry or otherwise.

He pulled Snow's face up level with his own, as he drew himself up to his not unimpressive full height. Snow was squirming, gasping for breath, her feet a good twenty inches off the floor. 'I'm not squeezing that much,' Jack snarled, and was satisfied to see her flinch from his stare. 'But what I will do is break your neck if I don't get the truth.'

'Then you won't learn anything,' she rasped.

He flicked his tongue towards Ebon's unconscious body. 'I have a spare.' He released her windpipe a little, but not enough to enable her to get her strength back. It did briefly go through Jack's mind that adrenalin aside, this was all rather easy. Surely someone as professional as Snow should have overpowered him by now? He sensed she was going for a groin kick, and smiled.

'My balls aren't where you think they are,' he said, 'so don't waste your time.'

This was actually a bare-faced lie − Jack's typically easily-damaged male genitals were exactly where Snow had assumed and he hoped she didn't call his bluff. Presumably she took him at face value, because she stopped tensing her feet.

And Jack dropped them both to the floor expertly, his long legs pressing down on her chest, his bum on the top of her legs, hands on her ankles. No room for manoeuvre. He carefully eased his foot towards the stunned lemur's windpipe and pressed again.

'Why are you aboard this ship?' he asked.

'To get you away from Bernice Summerfield,' croaked Snow.

Jack made sure he didn't loosen his grip at this news. 'So you *do* know who she is,' he said, as calmly as he could.

'Always have done,' she said.

'And why do I have to be got off the *Illusion* so desperately?'

Snow tried to shrug, which wasn't easy, pinned as she was. 'She paid us to split you up. That's all I know.'

'Who did?'

'I don't know her name. She's not aboard. We met her in a bar about three weeks ago.'

'Why?'

'We wanted a drink.'

'No. Why did she want us split up, whoever she is?'

'No idea. Don't care. She paid us a lot of money with more to come if we sent you to Legion.'

'Never heard of it.'

If Snow, in her awkward, reasonably immobile and painful position could have given Jack a look that said 'where have you been all these years?' – well, her expression conveyed that clearly enough to him.

He shrugged as much as he could without loosening his grip on her. Was Legion a place? A hotel perhaps? Or a nightclub. A nightclub might be fun, but even he couldn't imagine anyone paying two assassins enough money to get aboard this deathtrap just to get him somewhere boozy. So logic suggested that Legion was not going to be a fun destination and he was absolutely not going to go. Especially without Bernice.

Jack's people had survived millions of years of evolution by being, to all intents and purposes, a decidedly meek and cowardly species. The reason they'd survived a hostile universe was because, despite their indolent lifestyles, they were quite quick, nimble and had a fairly good sense of self-preservation. So although Jack wasn't sure why he needed to duck at that moment, he did so simply because some natural sixth sense made him. This was handy for two reasons. Firstly, because Ebon had woken up, crawled around behind him and was about the crack him across the back of the head with a weird metal bar that was probably a part of the ship's architecture which had blown loose during the turbulence before. And she did it with enough force, bounty or not, to take his head off.

So, as he ducked backwards, his eyes looking straight up at his attacker's legs, the metal bar slammed into the bulkhead with enough force to hurt Ebon's arms.

However, that turned out to be the least of her worries. Jack's ducking had saved his life in a second way too. From somewhere ahead, in the staccato lighting of the damaged overheads, the strobing lights revealed a figure dropping down and firing what appeared to be a blaster of some sort.

All of that went through Jack's head in a split-second. And a laser bolt went straight through Ebon's in the same amount of time, reducing it to red chunks of fur and bone.

Her body spun backwards and slumped down, as Jack rolled off Snow, who was scrabbling up and over to her dead partner in a second, a howl of pain and rage echoing around the confined corridor.

Jack didn't wait to help her; he realised the murderer had gone and instinctively ran after him/her – it only briefly crossing his mind that this was madness. Kadeptians didn't do things like this. So it must be Bernice's influence. Yeah, all her fault. If he was stupid enough to run towards someone firing a laser gun, as he died, he could blame the good professor. Yaaay...

But he didn't need to worry. The killer was gone: either expertly slunk away into the shadows or simply outrun him, albeit very silently. Mind you, he'd not heard her/him arrive in the first place, so who knew where they were now. Above, below, round a corner or somewhere else entirely. Great.

The strobing was hurting his eyes now, so he stopped running and caught his breath. He was aware in the weird lighting that if Snow was coming to get him, he'd be unlikely to know about it until too late – he had no illusions at how good she was at her job. For now, he needed to focus on getting an answer as to who the mysterious female was that had hired them. So he needed to be ready to confront her.

Hmm, he thought. Bernice was making deals with shady men and the two lemurs were making deals with shady women. It was a delightfully politically correct criminal world. Jack decided to believe that it was indeed all criminal and he and Bernice were on the side of the angels. After all, everyone believes their own enemies are the bad guys, right? And yet there were things he and Bernice had done in the past that made him question that. Mind you, there were things his own father had done that made him question it as well – after all, it was his father's insistence at getting into metaphorical bed with the organised crime families on the planet Raster that had got Jack mixed up with Bernice Summerfield in the first place. But these, now they were direct things that Jack had done himself.

Ruth. That was his primary crime. A lovely girl, dead because he'd used her to test a theory. Sometimes he was pretty certain that Bernice thought about Ruth, because she'd give him a look that just pricked his conscience. Maybe he was reading more into it, maybe Bernice didn't remember Ruth.

No, she absolutely did. And Leonidas. And B'tarri. And Taylor. Dear old grumpy Taylor... All the people they'd known and lost along the way. But Ruth had really meant something to Bernice. Losing her so horribly had been a real blow. And it was Jack's fault...

He shook his head to clear it. Enough of the past. He needed to find her and tell her that there was a secondary plot, running underneath the Victor one.

At which point he decided to venture slowly back the way he'd come. As his eyes adjusted to the slightly less flickery light away from the overhead damage, he could see Snow was still crouched over Ebon's corpse. He felt a momentary flicker of sadness for Snow. Jack had never been in love, never felt the need or desire to have a life-partner, but he could still imagine something of the pain she had to be feeling.

'They've gone,' he said quietly as he neared Snow. 'Sorry. Whoever it was, I couldn't catch up with them.'

Snow was either sulking or readying herself to attack him, so Jack tensed.

But nothing happened. Then he realised Snow was as dead as her lover beneath her – the metal bar Ebon had attacked him with was lying next to both bodies, and Snow's neck was twisted at a less-than-comfortable position, her eyes open in surprise, blood at the base of her skull where the bar had hit her.

She had never even known what happened. If she was as good a ninja as she reckoned then the killer was even better.

'Shit,' he muttered. If they could sneak up on Snow, sneaking up on him was not going to be very hard...

CHAPTER TWELVE
RULES FOR LIVING

As quartermasters go, Edj and Kread might have been overbearing and rather full-on but, in an emergency, they were suddenly very impressive. They returned to the canteen very quickly and dealt with hysterical meerkats, grouchy hares and a dour maintenance man with calm efficiency, politeness and amazing levels of patience. Once they'd sorted that out, they received an update from the chief engineer AI, acknowledged that the signage in the corridors was missing and was being replaced, informed everyone that the captain apologised for the jerky flight and promised that as soon as they knew what caused it, it would be reported. Edj also pointed out that the ship's integrity was unaffected and there was nothing to fear.

'Cosmic riptides are common around this sector of space,' Kread had added, which made Bernice smile. She'd heard some excuses in her time (hell, she'd used a number of them when trying to calm students) but 'cosmic riptides' was a new one on her. To the uninitiated, it probably sounded plausible too. But not to her.

'Good call,' she said to Edj as calm returned to the group. 'I'll remember that one next time.'

'I'm sure you will, Ms Kryztyne,' Edj said with that unnerving fixed smile on his silver face. Then Edj and Kread went to help the maintenance guys with a damaged light. Bernice watched them – would they notice there was something weird about the two people in the outfits of Dave and Ted? It was clear to her that they were not actually *them*. But maybe the quartermasters' species couldn't read human body language like Bernice could, because they acted as if nothing unusual was happening.

'Personally I think the purser should have come to see us instead of sending those jobsworths.'

Bernice looked down at one of the meerkats. She placed a comforting hand on its shoulder, but it flinched away.

'Kindly don't touch me, killer,' was all it said as it scurried back to its wife/husband and Lord Tawn.

Bernice caught Ginger's eye. 'At least the meerkats still hate me – that's something constant.'

Ginger smiled. 'It's one of those trips.'

'It's one of those lifetimes.' Bernice indicated Edj and Kread. 'They don't like me either. Any chance they had kids aboard Kryztyne's ship?'

Ginger frowned and wrinkled her nose and whiskers. 'Doubt it. I know the manifest backwards and whatever species they are, no one looking like that was aboard.'

'I could do with seeing that manifest, Ginger,' Bernice said. 'I need to know my enemies.' She paused and looked Ginger straight in the eyes. 'And friends.'

Ginger nodded slowly. 'Talking of which,' she said after a beat, 'where's Jack and the lemurs?'

Bernice shrugged. 'No one seems to have seen them go. Should we try and find them?'

'Well,' Ginger smiled, 'it is my job to look after you when Jack's not around, so yeah, let's go find them.'

Bernice reached out to Ginger's paw. 'Look, I know this must be difficult for you. With what you and Russet have lost. But

I want you to know I'm grateful. Not sure what I'd have done without you, him and Jet watching my back.'

'Didn't stop someone trying to kill you earlier. Who do you think?'

Bernice waved her arm towards the others. 'Discounting you three, hopefully that's a given, I can't see the bumbling meerkats having the strength. Lord Tawn is a possibility but I don't think he's nippy enough these days. Which pretty much leaves Edj and Kread or the doctor. I don't think the Kromians were actually in here at the time, so my money is on the doctor. Who I notice isn't here any more – maybe we should track him down and see if he's limping. I really kicked hard, you know.'

Ginger stared ahead, as if trying to read everyone's minds. 'There's always Dave and Ted.'

'Not here at the time. Of course, like the two silver boys, they could have nipped in then doubled out again. But you need skill to kill with an embolism. I don't see Dave being more than barely capable of holding a screwdriver.'

Ginger tutted. 'You're forgetting – it might not be Dave if Mrs Meerk isn't off her rocker.'

'Alien Dave? Interesting...' Bernice grinned. 'Either way, I'm still here and I'd like to keep it that way.'

Ginger waved to Russet and he bounded over. She told him to stay with Jet while she went with Bernice to find Jack. He agreed and so Bernice and Ginger slipped quietly out of the room.

'Another option,' Bernice said suddenly as they walked up the unmarked corridor that ran alongside the food hall.

'Which is?'

'One of the lemurs. They clearly want Jack and I separated. Maybe permanently.'

Ginger considered this. 'Would explain why no one is limping back in there.'

Bernice was about to say something else but she stopped and held Ginger back. 'Look. Up there. What's that?'

They both peered into the gloom. There was a misshapen lump on the floor ahead, by a corridor junction.

Bernice approached it with understandable caution, while Ginger checked efficiently every possible direction an attack could come from. She produced a small hand blaster from somewhere within her fur that Bernice didn't want to think about, although she was relieved that Ginger was armed.

'It's a body,' she breathed.

Ginger nodded. 'Jack's?'

Bernice knew it wasn't – even in death, the shape was wrong for someone of Jack's height and build. 'I think it's one of the lemurs,' she said eventually. 'Nope, it's both of them.'

'Dead?'

'Very.'

'Bloody hell. Anyone that could get close enough to those two has to be good.'

'Better than either of them, certainly.'

'Better than either of us, too,' Ginger shrugged, stating the obvious. 'No sign of Jack then.'

'He didn't do this,' Bernice snapped.

'Never said he did, Professor. But don't pretend it didn't go through your mind too. What do you really know about him?'

Bernice thought about this. How much did she actually know about Jack? Sure, he'd had her back numerous times since they'd left the insanity of the Epoch behind, but was that just for his own ends? Bernice always knew that Jack was hiding things, he was that kind of guy. Plus he was from Kadept, a world not renowned for its moral compass. And he had, no matter how she had tried to push the thought from her mind, caused the death – inadvertently, yes, but it had been his fault – of poor Ruth back in that faked Victorian London the Epoch created. But, that aside, he was Jack, and she had learned to trust him, within certain parameters. Murder as brutal as the two lemurs had suffered wasn't his style at all.

She hoped.

Ginger was waiting for a response.

'Jack did not do this, okay?'

Ginger nodded. 'I can do no more than take your word for that, so I will. In which case, where is he?'

Bernice hadn't got an answer. 'Wherever he is, I doubt he's not here willingly. So someone has taken him.'

'Can I help you?'

The speaker was a human male, about sixty, Bernice guessed. He was wearing a maintenance uniform, and carrying a toolbox.

'Not sure you should be up here. These corridors are still not fully powered and someone's taken all the signs down.'

'Who are you?' Ginger carefully hid her gun.

'Bob, the assistant engineer,' he said.

'Hullo Bob the assistant engineer,' Bernice said brightly. 'I'm Anya Kryztyne, this is my friend Ginger.'

Bob seemed slightly confused by the introduction, and his head seemed to shake as if he was clearing it. Only for a split second, but Bernice was trained to spot tells. And thus she was sure that, despite his outward appearance, Bob was like his two friends back in the mess room, not at all who he seemed to be.

Which meant she and Ginger might well be in danger.

On the bridge, Florence the parrot watched as another feather dropped soundlessly to the floor.

'I don't like this, Captain.'

'Arrrr?'

'If I didn't know better, I'd say something had changed, only very slightly, to the life-support systems aboard the *Adorable*

Illusion. As a result, my body is decaying faster than it should. Not, of course, that I should be alive at all, let alone sentient enough to know this fact.'

'Or able to talk,' the captain's voice boomed.

'There is that, certainly.'

There was a bleep and the door to the bridge slid open.

It was the purser. 'Good afternoon Captain Redbeard, I thought it was time for a report.'

The AI's artificial face actually seemed to frown as it regarded the small human below him.

Florence spoke to the purser. 'Umm, okay, go ahead.'

'There has been a series of power fluctuations attributed to the temporary reprogramming of the chief engineer AI's subroutines and personality matrix. That has now been resolved.

'The science group close to the observation decks are continuing their work uninterrupted, although there have been a series of incursions into Mr Cooke's personal financial records and systems, resulting in a not-insignificant theft of his money. However as the money only exists in the CloudSpace and not in reality, it is of no interest to Mr Cooke at this time, I imagine.

'The murderer Anya Kryztyne is at large on the ship, aided by a supposedly secret cabal of wronged parents from a variety of worlds. Anya Kryztyne herself is dead, and has been replaced by an imposter, known as Professor Bernice Summerfield. Her threat evaluation has yet to be determined. The maintenance teams are... keeping an eye on her.

'Two well-respected members of the Assassin's Guild of Savannah – three were active aboard ship – have been permanently neutralised, although their target, a Kadeptian, has not been successfully assassinated.' The purser almost smiled then. 'I am sure he is very grateful for that.' He readopted his professionalism. 'We are also close to reaching the Rapture. But I'm sure you already knew that.'

Captain Redbeard's processors activated suddenly as he acted upon the purser's words. 'That is not possible. The *Adorable Illusion* does not move at the sublight speeds that would enable this. We should be at least a week away from the Rapture's coordinates.'

The purser shrugged. 'And yet?'

After a second or two, the captain responded that the purser was correct, they were already at coordinates they shouldn't be at and three hours four minutes from the established focal point of the Rapture.

'That is incongrous,' Captain Redbeard said to Florence.

'It is certainly unusual,' the parrot replied. 'But then again so much is these days.'

'I am the ship's purser. It is my job to be correct on all things.' The purser smiled up at the AI and the parrot, then crouched down to the floor, slowly tracing his hand around an area on the metal floor. 'A structural weakness right here,' he murmured. 'We really should get maintenance to examine that – we wouldn't an accident here on the bridge, would we?'

Florence waved a rather threadbare wing towards him. 'It would be of no concern to us,' Florence said. 'Neither of us are alive in any sense that the loss of life-support or pressure could affect us.'

The purser looked up at Florence, almost as if working out what to do with this information. 'No. No of course not,' he said, smooth as silk. 'Nevertheless, the schematics for the bridge do not accommodate such a weakness. It really needs to be investigated.' He stood up and saluted the AI. 'Good afternoon Captain Redbeard, I shall report back again shortly.'

A red light flashed on one of Captain Redbeard's consoles. 'What's that?' Florence squawked.

Captain Redbeard paused, then announced, 'A life-support pod has ejected from port side.'

'That was not scheduled,' the purser said with a smile. 'How disconcerting for whoever is within it.'

'Do we know if anyone was?' asked Florence.

'There is one lifeform requiring life-support aboard the pod,' Captain Redbeard said.

'So,' Florence nodded. 'Someone else has deserted us. I wonder where they are headed, out here?'

The purser looked at his handheld comms. 'It appears to be preprogrammed for a frontier planet known as Legion,' he said. 'How unfortunate. I can't imagine why anyone would want to go there.'

Captain Redbeard's systems activated and he said, 'Legion is not part of any empire or affiliated with any system. It is an outlaw world. It is no longer any concern of ours.'

The purser nodded. 'My thoughts exactly, Captain Redbeard.' He saluted once again. 'Au revoir.'

The door slid open and then closed behind him.

For a second the bridge was silent, until Florence flapped a wing again. 'That was bloody weird. Didn't he fall through that trapdoor to his death yesterday?'

'Arrrrrr.'

'Oh well, this trip gets stranger and stranger,' Florence said. 'I rather like it.'

'Arrrrrr.'

CHAPTER THIRTEEN
DOUBLE TAKE

All animals, mammals, reptiles, insects etc etc throughout the universe have a pretty innate sense of danger. It's a fact of evolution, we all know who we are a danger to and we know who we are in danger from. It's why the wildebeest bolts a second before the lion makes its presence known. Or why the jutterbird flies screeching from the top branches when a chagalynx gets dangerously close to the bottom of the tree. Or why a gnawshark rarely gets to eat a rainbow gumblejack, because the gumblejack can sense its approach through the thickest mucus-strewn waters of Ambrose's World.

During her life of adventuring and derring-do since the day she left the planet Heaven, Bernice Summerfield's senses had become amazing highly-attuned. She could read body language (mind you, she'd been able to do that that at college), she could smell alcohol from thirty yards (mind you, she'd been able to do that at college too), she could tell when a boyfriend had cheated on her (of course, she'd been able to – oh you get the picture). But one thing she had learned since Heaven was to trust her instincts where danger was concerned. Not just planetary level, big ships coming to blow you pieces, danger but the small, personal moments of danger, something slight and intimate that could result in you being knocked over by a bicycle or having someone ram a three foot rusty spike through your shoulder (both of those had happened, the former more frequently than the latter fortunately).

But the sense of danger Bernice most prided herself on was the one about the people she surrounded herself with. This was far more than just the 'reading the body language' thing – this was a sense of self-preservation that kicked in at appropriate moments. Once, on the Trilexian Hunt Ship, she'd told Jack it was her 'spidey-sense'. He hadn't understood the reference, but had appreciated the concept when their companion, an apparent fellow prisoner, had suddenly transformed into a trillion tiny Trilexia that wanted to eat them. Bernice had had the presence of mind to be standing next to an airlock which she activated and sucked the wretched things into space before Jack had really had time to notice what was going on.

'How did you...' he'd started to say but she'd just said that her spidey-sense had kicked in, and left it at that.

So basically, in a tight spot, Bernice Summerfield was a pretty good safety net to have around.

The drawback right now was that, although her spidey-sense had kicked off just before engaging in the CloudSpace (back in that corridor that looked like every other bloody corridor aboard the *Adorable Illusion*) she had ignored it. Because she felt sorry – not for Ginger or Russet or Jet, but for herself. It had probably been a ruse, an attempt to divert attention when Ginger had sussed Bernice's distrust, but giving her the data stick from Adrian was a moment of pure genius. (Clearly Russet hadn't twigged, otherwise why would he have objected at the time?)

Why hadn't Bernice listened to her instincts? Because if she had, she might not have found herself with a gun pressed against her head.

The events leading up to this incident were not any of Bernice's finest moments.

Bob the maintenance man was certainly not human. His head had flashed into the alien visage that Bernice had seen in the canteen. There was a positive that came out of this. Ginger saw it too, so Bernice at least knew she wasn't going mad.

'This universe will be ours,' the alien said, its head all wispy and unfocused and shimmering in and out of shimmeryness – which was the only way Bernice could really describe what she saw. 'We have been imprisoned for too long within the Rapture. We will use the bodies to gain access.'

'Gotta say, I'm not convinced the bodies of a couple of grease monkeys are going to help you rule the universe on this side of the Rapture,' Bernice quipped, but 'Bob' or whatever he was had gone.

For a moment there was silence in the corridor, finally broken when Bernice said to Ginger, 'Well, that's something you don't see every day, is it?'

Ginger was shaking slightly, her paw hovering near her blaster. 'No,' she finally said. 'Hell, no.'

Bernice smiled. 'Hey, it was only an alien issuing a threat to dominate the universe. Meh, I eat those kind of threats for breakfast. Come on, we need to find out what happened to the lemurs.'

'Maybe he, it, whatever, killed them.'

'Perhaps. But I doubt it. I can't imagine he was fussed enough to go around killing them for sport – they only seem to kill in a way that lets them access the bodies.'

Ginger frowned. 'What?'

Bernice shrugged. 'I imagine that's why they chucked poor Dave out into space. Wait for hypoxia to strike, then after they've died, haul them back in – *voila*! One human body to operate like a puppet, pretty much undamaged and, if their natural form is gaseous, judging by that little display we saw, easy enough to flit in and out of the bodies. And it gives them a way to communicate with us. Ingenious, if a tad melodramatic.'

Ginger considered this. 'You reckon they're from within the Rapture then? But how do they come and go?'

Bernice smiled. 'Okay, lesson one in Professor Summerfield's Don't Hold This Against Me If The Science Is Shaky But It's What I Learned module. The Rapture is coming through a rent, a tear in space and possibly time. Every so often something triggers it and we get the events we've all heard of, like the one that took *The Hunter*. With your son.' She smiled wanly at Ginger. 'Sorry to bring that up again.'

'Oh that's fine,' Ginger said hurriedly. 'What happens next?'

'Okaaay,' Bernice said, giving Ginger a slightly curious look. 'Rents are never sealed completely, they can't be. It's like a wound that never completely heals, and in fact just weakens over time. So, you can imagine, after a few million years of opening and closing, it'll end up with a permanent leak. I reckon they can get themselves in and out through that. And when you have a handy ship full of potential bodies hovering right above you, it's not difficult to float your gaseous self across into our universe and Bob's your uncle. Or your alien's uncle. Or whatever. I doubt it's pain-free and they have had a very long time to work out how and when to do it.'

'I can see why Victor Cooke wanted you here – that must be what he's set his scientists on to. Working out how it's done.'

'Well, if I can guess it after less than 24 hours, I'm pretty sure that lady I bumped into in CloudSpace must have twigged it by now. If she hasn't, she isn't doing her job very well. I can't see why he wants to know that though. It's not like he's going to mount an expedition into the Rapture's universe using reverse technology and... oh.'

'I bet that's exactly what he's planning on.'

Bernice clicked her fingers. 'Stupid Benny.'

'Why?' asked Ginger.

'Because I can feel that lovely little gun you are pressing against my head – and I knew ages ago there was something odd about you. And I ignored it.'

Ginger laughed. 'And look where it's got you.'

'Yeah. Jack-less, confused, on a spaceship full of parasitic gas monsters and with someone I foolishly took my eye off, who I already knew was working for the guy who set all this up. Stupid, stupid Benny.'

'Stupid Benny indeed,' Ginger said. 'I wonder what happens now.'

CHAPTER FOURTEEN
NO EXIT

Jack was alive. He was reasonably pleased to discover that. He was less pleased to feel a huge bump on the back of his head. Someone had hit him while he was standing over Snow's body, thinking how, if he wasn't careful, someone could hit him. Typical.

He was in a very small room, possibly a comms suite as there was a control desk at one end and a door at the other with a small window in it. Other than that, pretty much nothing.

As he went to stand up, his knee knocked against a small black box, about the size of, well, a small black box. A yellow sticky notelet was attached to it. It read **PRESS ME**.

Gingerly he reached out to do so, then changed his mind and instead wandered over to the window, to see what part of the ship he'd been locked in.

'Oh. Arse.'

He wasn't in the ship. He wasn't in a little computer room. Those weren't communications switches. That was a propulsion and navigation unit. That was a *porthole*.

That was rather alarming.

He was in space, inside a small, self-contained emergency life-pod. Jack pushed himself up and over to the porthole – wherever he was, the *Adorable Illusion* wasn't in sight. Just darkness and a few stars. He'd been unconscious for an hour or so, going by the speed the pod was doing and the relative size of the dreadnought he had previously been aboard.

A bleep from somewhere in the room alerted him – and he saw the little black box with the sticky note vibrating slightly in time with the noise. He thumbed the button as requested and a tiny hologram popped into life, flickering and monochromatic. Instinctively he put his face in front of the tiny figure, as if it would notice.

'Presumably you are awake, Jack,' said a woman he didn't recognise. She wasn't unattractive, but there was a harshness around the mouth that he immediately disliked.

'Not Benny then,' he murmured.

'So first off, no need to worry. I've arranged for you to be found in a day or so and taken quite a long way away. I have plans for you, you funny little sweet thing!'

'Who are you?' he muttered.

'You probably don't remember me, Jack. I have no idea how much the Epoch messed around with your brain on Earth. Or Atlantis or whatever they called it. I waited on Mars for you, but you never showed, you naughty man. Not quite sure how I missed finding the professor. She wasn't on Mars like she was supposed to be either. But right now, it's far more important that I get you to Legion.'

'You employed the Lemurs?' Jack chewed his lip. There was something familiar about her after all. About her voice, at least. He was still staring at the face – there was something there, at the back of his mind. Some businesswoman he might have met, maybe through his father's firm?

'Anyway Jacky, the people who come to retrieve you have very strict orders. I can't promise that they'll be particularly genteel, so I suggest you don't kick up a fuss, even with those luscious legs of yours. To cover myself, I had a couple of back-up plans, so I'm assuming that at least one of them worked. Otherwise, you dear man, you wouldn't be hearing my voice after all this time. Now then, sweetheart, when you get to Legion, assuming you survive the trip, I want you to find a man called Irving Braxiatel. Stick with him. When you least expect it, I'll turn up to see you both. *Au revoir* my favourite little Kadeptian. Mwah.'

And with a blown kiss, the tiny hologram fizzed away into nothing. Jack stabbed at the box, trying to get it to play again, but nothing.

'Two days,' he said, slumping onto the pod's floor. 'I bet she didn't think to give me food or water.'

But that wasn't really the foremost thing on Jack's mind. No, that was Bernice Summerfield and whether he would ever see her again.

'Till the next time, Professor,' he said, pretending to raise a glass to her. 'Happy landings.' He rolled on his back and stared at the pod's roof. 'Still, Legion sounds like a lovely place. Not.'

CHAPTER FIFTEEN
WAR CHILD

Bernice Summerfield, she thought. You really have cocked this up, haven't you?

Ginger's small blaster was pressed against the back of her head, well, more like shoved really. Either way, right now the one person she had trusted since Jack had vanished/died/run away wasn't quite of the good character that she'd hoped. So much for reading body language.

'I don't give a toss about the Rapture, gas aliens or any of that crap,' Ginger said. 'I have a job to do, and I am going to do it.'

'Which is?'

'Exactly what I said at the moment we met. Keeping you alive.'

'Yeah, okay, but that was because I was pretending to be Anya Kryztyne. Wasn't it?'

'Nope. Remember I knew who you really were right from the off.'

Bernice grimaced. 'And Jet? She knew too.'

Ginger laughed. 'Bless the former Mrs Cooke. No, she only knew who you were because Victor told her. She bought into his plan, hook, line and sinker. Made our job so much easier.'

'*Our* job?'

And a small figure, carrying a frankly absurdly large blaster rifle stepped out of the shadows. 'Ours.'

Bernice sighed. It was Russet. 'Like mother, like son?'

Russet laughed, hoisting the blaster up to his shoulder level, aiming it expertly as her. 'I'm not her son.'

'He's my business partner.' Ginger pressed her gun a little harder. 'And we are going to get you off this crate right now.'

Bernice took in this new information. 'Hang on, so if you two aren't part of Lord Tawn's Animal Farm revolution, what the hell are you... oh. Oh, of course. Stupid me.' She smiled. 'Can't say Victor Cooke didn't warn me. Just didn't realise his team had already been infiltrated.'

'Three months ago,' said Russet. 'I was in first, then Ginger.'

'The bloody bollocking Heliok Syndicate, yeah?'

'They do pay extraordinarily well.'

'They'd have to, to make a trip on this ship worth it.' Bernice looked at Russet. 'So, what brings you into all this then?'

Russet grinned, bearing sharp incisor teeth that Bernice hadn't really seen before. To her, Russet had been just Ginger's son. Someone she felt protective towards. Blimey, what a good actor he'd turned out to be.

'I'm from a different planet to Ginger,' he said. 'They destroyed my home, my family and friends. I was *six* when the Deindum invaded, when that stupid war of yours kicked off. We were strategic, I guess. A stepping stone. All they needed to do was get rid of the people, the buildings – our entire culture. I was brought up fighting in the streets, never knowing if I was going to reach seven years old. A refugee trying to stop the invaders by myself. I failed of course.'

'I'm sorry.'

Russet shrugged. 'Why? It's not like you knew my parents

or sisters. Or friends. Or even that my world existed. Don't patronise me with your mock sadness, Professor.'

'You're right, I knew none of those things. Doesn't stop me empathising with you. There should have been more to your childhood than defence and weaponry. The war wasn't fair to any of us.'

'Yeah, yeah, you lost your son, we all know that. Boo hoo.' Russet slipped the safety catch off his blaster. 'I. Don't. Care. These days, all I care about is doing a job well and getting paid better.' He glanced at Ginger behind Bernice. 'The Heliok ship docks in five.'

Bernice was aghast. 'Are they mad? We're really close to the Rapture. If it opens, their ship won't survive the approach, let alone an actual docking!'

Ginger sniffed. 'Not our problem. The Syndicate know what they are doing.'

'I bloody doubt it. I apparently brought down half their business, and I can only think I was pissed out of my head because I don't remember it at all. But assuming I did, if one middle-aged drunk mum can do that, I haven't much faith in their skills.'

'They got us aboard, they got us close to unsuspecting old you!' Russet smiled. 'They'll manage it.'

Bernice sighed. 'One quick question before all hell breaks loose?'

'Go on,' Ginger prompted.

'The message, the data stick from Adrian Wall. Why'd you fake that?'

There was a pause before Ginger replied. 'It isn't fake – you'll see that when you watch it. We needed him to find you. That was quite genuine. Just my reasons for getting it weren't.'

'So why give it to me at all? He'd never have known.' Bernice could see Russet was thinking this too. She pressed her advantage. 'That wasn't part of the plan, was it Russet? You don't approve of Ginger's sentiment.'

'Shut up,' said Ginger.

But Russet was cross. 'What were you doing? You should've chucked that away as soon as we got off Valentine's World.'

Bernice smiled. So that's where Adrian and Bev were. Excellent. Then a thought crossed her mind – she and Jack had boarded there. She'd been *that* close to them. To Joseph. To... her past. How close? What if they'd passed one another and never realised it? That would be too awful...

'Yeah, why didn't you, Ginger?' Bernice asked.

Ginger relaxed slightly, Bernice felt the pressure ease off the back of her head. 'Because it'd give you a realisation of what you've lost, Professor. Of how close you came to getting your old life back.'

Bernice laughed. 'Yeah, right. You saying that for my benefit, or Russet's? Because I don't swallow it any more than he does.'

That's it Bernice, try and sow some seeds of doubt between these two.

'So what, were you shagging him?' she asked. Ginger's gun went hard into the back of her head again, and Bernice winced, but she didn't mind, she'd hit a nerve. 'He is bloody good in bed, you know.' Bernice winked at Russet. 'Looks like you missed your chance with Ginger, matey,' she said. 'Still, maybe she's a bit old for you.'

Russet swung his gun up.

If he fired, he'd kill Ginger. Course, he'd also kill Bernice, so she rather hoped that the second part of her goading plan would kick in.

'Hey, watch out,' Ginger yelled and stepped away from behind Bernice in case Russet's trigger finger went off. As she moved, Bernice kicked backwards as she felt Ginger's gun move away. Her boot connected with the Squirrel's short shin and she heard a satisfying crack and yell. As Ginger dropped, Bernice reached backwards and grabbed the blaster from her paw and rolled, bringing it up to fire at Russet.

The younger squirrel was grinning madly, his eyes blazing with a mixture of fury and delight and Bernice realised she had no choice. Kill or be killed. Russet's growing up, his whole childhood and teenage years had been about fighting to survive and she realised there was no redemption there, no appealing to his better nature. He simply didn't have one.

He swung his blaster to cover her and Bernice squeezed the trigger on Ginger's gun.

Nothing happened.

'Isomorphic paw-print,' Russet laughed. 'Badly played, Professor!' He squeezed his own trigger.

And Bernice prepared to die.

Shayla was running across the laboratory, his suit slowing him down, screaming at Maria to activate the controls he'd set up.

Jefri was running in the opposite direction, screaming he wanted no part in this, and this wasn't what he'd signed up for. He dived under one of the control consoles, paws over his ears.

Maria stood still, completely thrown by this change in Shayla. Why had the quiet, serene Graan suddenly grown some balls and taken charge?

'Activate the bloody thing,' he yelled.

Maria shrugged. 'I don't know how! It's automated and the Rapture is opening, so it has already begun the countdown. I can't speed it up!'

Shayla yanked his chadri away and Maria went cold.

'Do what you are bloody told,' he screamed at her. 'It's what I pay you for!'

Maria was staring at Victor Cooke. How long had he...

She shook herself. 'Seriously, I don't know what to do. We were never anticipating anything this powerful!'

'Don't you get it yet?' Victor Cooke yelled at her and Jefri in turn. 'The Rapture, it's a portal, a wormhole. It leads to another universe. One my son may be in. That's why I funded all this, that's why we're here. I'm going to get my son back!'

'How?' Maria asked, kind of wondering which of those insane claims she was actually asking about.

Victor Cooke slammed his hand down on the catcher controls. 'Activate everything now!'

Jefri stood up. 'No, you can't! That amount of power flooding in here, across this entire ship – nothing is capable of storing it.'

'Nonsense!'

'Listen to me,' the Pakhar was screaming. 'This is my field, my expertise. I always guessed this was what the Rapture was, but I never imagined we'd try and harness it – just observe, record, make notes and readings. We're not advanced enough to actually tap it as an energy source. The *Adorable Illusion* is a bloody spaceship not a battery!'

Victor Cooke wasn't listening – he just ramped everything in the lab up as far as it would go. 'A battery is exactly what it is, you stupid rat! It's a battery, a converter, a scoop, a massive siphon. And it will do what it was built to do right now!'

The furious Jefri was actually hopping from one leg to another in distress. 'But how do you know it will work? We haven't tested it under those parameters! We need tests! We need...'

'I think this is the test,' Maria shouted at him. 'And a bloody dangerous one at that, Victor!'

Victor Cooke ignored them both. He just slammed down on the power controls. 'I want my son back!' he screamed.

And then the Rapture opened.

Massive threads of multicoloured light just appeared in space, and were immediately drawn into the hole at the centre of the *Adorable Illusion*, dragged in like power being rerouted, scooped up as they was always intended to be. The energy arrived with the most awful sound, like something was ripping reality apart. Maria screamed as her ears pounded, and hundreds of electrical circuits in the lab erupted into fire, overloading as they tried to harness a volume of energy unimagined in history. Unimagined by anyone other than Victor Cooke. Maria couldn't hear what he was saying, she could hear nothing, but she guessed it was about his son, or money, or power or something.

She turned to look at Jefri for support but the Pakhar was gone – he had been standing next to his console when it exploded and all that was left was a charred lump of flesh, his fur seared off instantly, his life extinguished in a split second.

The Rapture tore into the lab, vaporising walls, consoles and everything it touched. Knowing she was about to die, Maria just stared in awe at the beauty, the majesty of that light, the roaring sound becoming a background drone now as she witnessed, first hand, a wonder of the world, a glorious, shocking, powerful something from another universe that she believed no human probably had the right to see.

She felt something on her arm, and assumed she was being destroyed like the lab but suddenly realised it was Victor Cooke's hand. Was he trying to get her away, out of the lab? What was the point? The ship was being eaten away, destroyed. There was nowhere to go! Then she realised that he was dragging her not to safety but to her death. Because he jumped forward, straight into the Rapture, and the last thing Maria saw as she was dragged deliberately after him was Victor Cooke dissipating into the energy. As she tried to close her eyes, as she tried not to scream and

CHAPTER SIXTEEN
THE END, THE END

In the canteen, the multicoloured energy ripped the room asunder in seconds.

The Madras and his station exploded in a soundless mess of curry and metal.

Sable and Sandy clutched one another in fear, not having a chance to scream as the Rapture obliterated them.

Lord Tawn just stood still, ready to accept his fate like an old soldier.

Jet's instinct was to make a futile gesture of fleeing, but she was shoved aside by Edj and Kread as they ran to the door. The last thing Jet saw before the Rapture hit her was the *Adorable Illusion* itself ripping apart and the remnants of the Madras being sucked out into the vacuum of space. Edj and Kread almost joined it, making futile attempts to hold on to the walls that were ultimately pointless and then they too were gone, their bodies ripped into bloody goo by shards of torn metal before vanishing into the blackness. And then she felt something touch her legs and knew that it was all over and she was

CHAPTER SEVENTEEN
END OF THE WORLD

On the bridge, the purser stood and looked up at the AI and the parrot.

'What is happening to my ship?' Captain Redbeard demanded.

'And who are you exactly?' Florence added as the purser's human face changed into the alien one his fellows had displayed back in the canteen.

'You two fascinate us,' the purser said quietly. 'Neither of you live and yet you both behave as if you do. You mimic life but don't understand why. That is amazing.'

'I don't even know how I'm alive,' Florence said.

'That is irrelevant. Your job was to get us back to the Rapture – we manipulated all of the minds of the people here to ensure the ship was redesigned to ensure that happened quickly.'

'I knew we got here too quickly,' Captain Redbeard boomed.

'You did,' Florence agreed. 'I remember you saying so.'

And suddenly the multicoloured Rapture tore into the bridge.

'An alternative to life,' the purser said as he vanished in the plume of harsh energy.

'Oh dear,' said Florence. 'It was fun while it lasted.'

'Arrr

CHAPTER EIGHTEEN
END TO END

Bernice clenched her eyes tight, but no blaster fire came. Instead, a massive, painful roar ripped through the ship and she immediately looked up.

Multicoloured energy was everywhere. Behind her she heard Ginger muttering, 'The Rapture, it must be' – or something similar, her words were quickly drowned out by the unbearable noise. Of Russet there was no sign, but that wasn't surprising as the energy was pouring towards them from exactly where he'd been standing.

Bernice tried to scramble backwards but knew it was pointless – the *Adorable Illusion* was being destroyed inch by inch, eaten away by the brightest, and frankly most beautiful, light Bernice had ever seen.

'Sorry Peter,' she muttered. 'I did try to find

CHAPTER NINETEEN
RAPTURE

There were legends, going back to the dawn of the galaxy (and maybe a bit further) about the Rapture. It had been a phenomenon reported on by the earliest civilisations that took to interstellar travel. A massive rainbow of energy that would just arrive in space and eat anything it touched, before disappearing as violently and shockingly as it had come. Over the millennia, scientists and their ilk from countless worlds had tried to study it, but to no avail. Its unpredictability, its randomness, its sheer ludicrousness had floored the brightest and best every species had had to offer.

The Myranian papal academician Hros'Ka'Bitte had coined the term 'the Rapture' and it had stuck. The human physicist Klaus Menkin, who frankly should have known better, referred to it as 'the Brigadoon of the spaceways' – and then unfortunately spent the last ten years of his career trying to justify – and actually explain – what he meant by that phrase at the expense of his actual reputation.

The Martian explorer Vaasst placed a research vessel in the vicinity for eight years before being rewarded by the Rapture making an appearance. He was transmitting a number of superb holos back to Mars when his vessel was touched by a tendril of rainbow energy and exploded, killing all fifteen people aboard. One of these holos, referred to colloquially as 'Death of an Explorer', showed Vaasst glowing as he disintegrated, his arms crossed in a traditional Martian salute as if he knew he had lost his gamble.

Since then, people had remained circumspect about the Rapture – indeed in some societies and academic circles it took on a mythical reputation. As decades passed, and fewer and fewer people who had witnessed it remained alive and kicking, it took on a reputation similar to those of the Loch Ness Monster, the Venusian Night-Eater and Gongo, the Ape-Lord of Cantus.

The scholarly craft, *The Hunter*, that took the lives of Victor Cooke's son, plus many others, as well as destroying Anya Kryzten's reputation, was considered a bit of a fun jaunt by the Hoondock University that funded it. Every so often, they sent out craft to examine some long-gone supernova, or borealis or snake-headed spiral, just to keep the students interested in such things. In truth, it was a convenient tax-break that no one ever expected would come back and bite them on the arse. When the Kryztyne expedition was lost – and especially when it was learned she'd abandoned her charges to engage in some less-than-ethical shenanigans with one of her mature students – the academic world was shaken up badly. Tax loopholes were closed, universities suddenly plugged their schedules with important (ie deathly dull and safe) research trips to mud-planets and digging up civilisations that hadn't even died out yet.

But, to the kids aboard *The Hunter*, it had actually been an amazing moment. Terrifying certainly, but beautiful in its chaos. Literally breathtaking as they'd watched their craft and each other disassembled by the rainbow energy, and for a few scant seconds, rather than screaming in fear, they had embraced the wonderment of it all. Which was odd really as, on the face of it, screaming in agony as your body's molecules are forcibly separated seems a fairly acceptable reaction. But as it happened to them, none of the nine students aboard *The Hunter* did that. It was as if something very serene had taken over their minds at the last moment.

Had any of them had a chance to activate a comms unit and send a message home, it might have gone: 'Hey Mom, I feel like I've just taken the most amazing amount of magic mushrooms and I am so chilled out right now, it's amazing. Especially as the atoms of everything in and around me are separating and being devoured by strange multicoloured lights and the noise of billion waves is crashing on my head. But yeah, I'm completely out of it, so it, like, really doesn't hurt. Love you Mom,' or something akin to that.

The students were from a variety of species across the quadrant. There were three humans, Kame Wyck, Adam Campbell and Sara Blair; a leporiod, Flax, grand-daughter of the legendary warrior Lord Tawn; an androgynous Chim called Dob-Dob; the twin Meerk brothers Flash and Buck; and the son of the human Victor Cooke and his Mephitian partner Jet – Caesar Cooke.

On their respective homeworlds, monuments and memorials and been erected to them. Families wept. Facetweets mourned. But as with all such tragedies, life moved on. One or two of the families put it behind them, feeling that to dwell on the grief would be self-destructive. Others sought vengeance.

Lord Tawn and the Meerk parents Sandy and Sable, along with Jet and the person they believed had been the mother of another student, Ginger, boarded the *Adorable Illusion*, after hearing that the person responsible through irresponsibility, Anya Kryztyne, was travelling with them. A pact was made – they would kill Kryztyne, each one of them. That way, no one person could ever be found responsible. They had been contacted by the ship's doctor with that idea – he'd read it in a book, he'd said. And he was happy to be part of their cabal as his own daughter had been aboard *The Hunter*.

One thing these disparate grieving parents never seemed to question was how exactly they knew this information. No one could quite remember how they heard Kryztyne was aboard the *Adorable Illusion*. Or why they found themselves in a small dark bulkhead area, discussing their revenge plans. Somehow they all drifted there, met one another and agreed that murder was a suitable response.

Truth be told, even Victor Cooke himself didn't know. Oh, he recalled angrily tracking Anya Kryztyne down, killing her, disposing of what remained of her body. But the plan to finance the *Adorable Illusion*, select Professor Bernice Summerfield to act as a Judas Goat, and assume the identity of the Graan scientist he'd employed (who'd spent three confused days waiting at a spaceport before giving up and going home when the *Adorable Illusion* never docked) – Victor Cooke had no idea where that had come from.

The first time any of these people had ever actually questioned their motives happened at the time the Rapture destroyed the *Adorable Illusion*. In their last second of consciousness, their brains flooded with these questions.

Everyone except Professor Bernice Summerfield, Ginger and Russet, and Florence the parrot. They all had other things going through their minds. In order they were basically: Peter; Oh shit; You're screwed, human bitch; and This is a new experience.

Three of the four's next thoughts were: What the hell is going on? Where am I? and Why aren't I dead? – although not necessarily in that order. Only Florence the parrot once again just thought: And this is yet another new experience.

*

It was grass. Freshly mown grass. Just after rain. Or a heavy early morning dew. Bernice knew that smell – she'd experienced it often enough at Brax's Collection, waking up in a heap on the Great Triannon's lawns, Joseph floating above her head, berating her for a night out with the students. Or Jason.

She opened her eyes. Blue sky, white fluffy clouds above, green grass all around. A copse of trees on the right, a slight hill to the left. Bernice was up and ready in seconds, looking for danger. Because this couldn't be right. She'd been killed aboard the *Adorable Illusion*.

'Weird, I have to say,' said a strangely strangulated voice.

Bernice looked around and soon realised that the speaker was a rather dingy-looking parrot who was hovering above.

'Which bit is weird?' Bernice asked. 'That I'm here, that you are talking to me or that for the first time in ages, no one's trying to kill me?'

'Possibly all of the above,' the parrot replied. 'But mostly, the fact that I'm flying. I'm dead.'

'So am I.'

'No, I mean I'd been dead for...well.. quite a long time. And then I wasn't. I was perched on the bridge of the *Adorable Illusion*, working alongside Captain Redbeard. I don't know how I got there, or why. And now I'm here. With you. And the others.'

'Others?' Bernice decided that was the most important element to take from the parrot's conversation. Death? Meh, deal with that later.

'Yes. Almost everyone from the ship is here, scattered over the grasslands. And quite a few others I simply don't recognise.'

'That's good then. As I can't fly...'

'Can't you?'

'Not that I'm aware of, no.'

'Have you tried? After all, it strikes me that if a dead parrot can talk and fly, perhaps anything is possible here.'

Bernice thought about this. The logic was flawed, but worth considering. She flapped her arms expectantly. Nothing happened.

'Ah well,' the parrot said. 'Nothing ventured...'

'Could you tell me where the nearest of these people are please?'

'Follow me,' the parrot said and started to fly slowly to the trees. Bernice walked as quickly as she could, making sure the parrot stayed in sight at all times. The copse was on a slight rise and as she reached the apex of it and walked through the wood, the dale on the other side came into view.

She immediately recognised Lord Tawn as well as the two meerkats, who were hugging each other in neurotic shock. Looking across to another hillock on the horizon, she realised that looking back straight at her was Ginger. She wasn't sure whether to feel relief at this or fear, in case Ginger still planned to turn her over to the Heliok Syndicate. Ah well, whatever will be will be.

Bernice started down the hill towards the hare and meerkats. Ginger, she noted, did exactly the same.

As she walked, Bernice realised that despite the blue skies and lovely sunlight, she was neither hot nor cold. There was no breeze either. So this had to be some kind of holo re-creation, rather than a real outside environment. That said, if there was no breeze of any kind, how was the parrot flying? It needed air currents, however minimal, to fly. Mind you, it was long-dead talking parrot, so maybe it was a hologram as well. Which meant that these guys ahead of her might not be real.

'Good lord,' yelled Lord Tawn. 'You survived too. Clearly there is no justice in this universe.' He spat at her as she approached.

Bloody good hologram then, Bernice reckoned, and decided that, no, this was the real Lord Tawn.

Sandy and Sable looked up tearfully. 'Is this your fault, too?' one of them moaned (Bernice really needed to find out how to tell them apart).

'Nope, not remotely,' Bernice said. 'And just for the record, I'm not Anya Kryztyne. My name is Bernice Summerfield and I was put aboard the *Adorable Illusion* by Victor Cooke.'

'Why?'

Bernice opened her mouth to reply and then stopped. 'That's a bloody good question, really. He said it was investigate what happened at the Rapture to the students on *The Hunter*. Hmm, that doesn't make sense now I think about it.' She paused. 'I wonder why I didn't consider that before?'

'I don't believe you,' said Lord Tawn. 'It's just the sort of thing a murderess like Anya Kryztyne would say.'

Bernice looked at him. 'Lord Richmael Tawn. You, sir, are an idiot. If you really thought I was the person who killed your grandchild, why am I still alive? You are one of the most experienced warriors in this quadrant – you could have taken me out any number of times. But you didn't, so either you knew I wasn't Kryztyne or something has been dampening your mind, your spirit.' She looked at the two Meerks. 'Yours too I imagine, 'cause I can't imagine in real life anyone could be as weak and feeble-minded as you.'

'Oi!' said a meerkat, annoyed.

Bernice smiled. 'See?'

Lord Tawn looked her up and down. 'If you aren't Kryztyne – and I'm not saying I bally-well believe you, you understand – but if you aren't her, why did Victor Cooke put you aboard?'

Bernice didn't answer that directly.

'So you know who Victor Cooke is then?' she asked.

Lord Tawn and the two Meerks nodded. Then looked at each other, as if realising they had a connection they hadn't realised before.

Bernice smiled. 'So, Victor Cooke links all of us. He also employed the lovely squirrel behind you to sell me off to the Heliok Syndicate.'

'Good money, too,' Ginger smiled at Bernice, then said hullo to the others.

'Not easy to spend when we're dead,' Lord Tawn muttered.

'Oh we're not dead,' Bernice said. 'I'm pretty sure we're in a holosuite somewhere, maybe still aboard the *Adorable Illusion*.'

'I'm pretty sure you're wrong,' said a strong male voice behind them all.

As one they turned to face Victor Cooke and the scientist Bernice had met in the CloudSpace earlier.

'Ladies and gentlemen, your benefactor Victor Cooke and... umm?'

'Maria Willows,' said the woman.

'You told me —' Lord Tawn started but Victor Cooke cut him off.

'Look, I have no idea what is going on here. Seriously. Every person on the ship was put there by me, apart from the crew. And I have no idea who this woman is or why she's here.'

Ginger frowned. 'You paid me to bring her here. Well, to the ship anyway.'

'I did no such thing,' Victor Cooke said. 'I'm not sure I even know you. I'm beginning to think someone is undermining what was supposed to be a very important mission. I shall have my security people reprimanded when we get back.'

Bernice shrugged. 'You should probably get them to explain why you don't seem to have much security on your CloudSpace banking apps as well.'

Victor Cooke frowned.

'Oh, didn't Maria here tell you she's been siphoning off your cash?'

'Thank you,' Maria said tightly.

'My pleasure,' Bernice said. 'Best we have all our dirty laundry out for airing I reckon.'

Victor Cooke sighed. 'I'll deal with that when we get home.'

'You think we're going home, Vic?' said Jet, as she walked down the hill that Bernice had been on.

'Is that everyone?' Lord Tawn asked.

'No sign of Russet,' Ginger said, looking to the horizons.

'Excuse me for not being too concerned about him,' Bernice said. 'What about Dr Blair?'

'Not seen him,' Maria said.

Victor Cooke looked at her. 'You know him?'

Maria shrugged. 'I made it my business to know everyone on the ship,' she said. 'Pretty sure you'll thank me for that later.'

'Unlike your cash withdrawals,' Victor Cooke muttered.

Maria suddenly turned on him. 'Like that's the main concern. You did this! You did whatever "this" is, anyway.'

Bernice looked over at them. 'Care to explain?'

'He's been on board the whole time,' Maria said. 'Pretending to be a Graan called Shayla. I've been working alongside him and never knew. Spying on me. Us. All of us probably. And of course, thinking he was Shayla, I told him everything I was doing. That was so not clever.'

Victor Cooke shrugged. 'I was here to protect my investment. Investments.'

Lord Tawn was more interested in Maria's other comment. 'Why does the lady say you made all this happen?' he said, waving a paw around the environment. 'Where are we?'

Victor Cooke shrugged. 'I don't know. I merely ensured the Rapture opened at the right time and that the *Adorable Illusion* was there to scoop up that power. So I could have it studied. So I could find out what happened to our children,' he added, looking at the hare and meerkats. 'I did this for us. For you. To get answers.'

Bernice laughed. 'So this, whatever this is, is a bonus then. You didn't anticipate it at all?'

Victor Cooke just smiled slightly. 'I believed the *Adorable Illusion* had been rigged to cope. I believed that was what my scientists were doing, rather than stealing my money.'

'You don't have any money,' Maria said. 'Zilch. You're broke.'

'I spent it all on this excursion,' he replied. 'Because Caesar is worth more than any empire.'

Ginger raised a paw. 'Umm, if you have no money, how were you going to pay me?'

Bernice frowned. 'I thought you were working for the Heliok Syndicate?'

'I was. Am. But Victor Cooke too. How else do you think I found you? Adrian Wall was bugger all use.'

'Oh, that's just great,' Bernice sighed. 'Thanks Victor. Put me in the middle of all this and pay her to take me to the Heliok. She *and* you get paid by them, right? You both get paid twice.'

Victor frowned. 'I genuinely have no idea what either of you are talking about. How could I pay anyone? As Maria says, after investing in the *Adorable Illusion*, I am, in very real terms, broke.'

Jet was staring at her ex-husband. 'You told me none of this.'

Victor Cooke reached out and touched her shoulder. 'We barely speak these days, except through lawyers. It hardly seemed worthwhile letting you know I was on board when we both had missions to fulfil.'

Jet turned away. 'And look where that's got us.'

Bernice clapped her hands. 'Enough! Jet just said it. We are somewhere, we need to know where. Still aboard? Or, has the Rapture, rather than obliterating us, teleported us somewhere else entirely?'

'Or we're dead, and this is the Great Burrow,' Lord Tawn said.

'We're not dead,' Maria said.

'How do you know?' said... well, one of the Meerks.

'Because I don't feel dead,' Maria said. 'That and the fact I don't believe in heaven, the Great Burrow or any kind of afterlife.'

'As a scientist, my dear,' said Victor Cooke, 'you should know that what you believe doesn't make it right.'

'Piss off.'

Victor Cooke looked to Bernice. 'Charming.'

'Piss off,' she echoed.

Victor Cooke turned to Jet, who told him to piss off before he could even speak.

Bernice heard a sound and realised that the parrot was, rather shakily, coming in to land. It ended up on her arm, which she instinctively held out for it.

'Thank you,' it said.

'Pleasure,' Bernice heard herself say.

'There's another option you seem to have discounted.'

'Oh aye?'

'The Rapture comes through a rent in space and time, yes?' Bernice nodded.

'Well, maybe we're at the other end of it. Instead of a pot of gold at the end of the rainbow, we are here?'

'In Teletubbyland,' Bernice said. 'That's not a bad theory. Thanks Mr Parrot.'

'Florence.'

'Florence? Seriously? Florence?'

The parrot flapped its wings and a load of feathers fell to the floor. 'Yes, Florence. You have a problem with my name?'

'No,' said Bernice. 'No problem at all. Florence. Great name for a male parrot.'

'Am I male?'

'You sound male.'

'Ahh. Interesting. Having never had a voice before, it never occurred to me to think in gender terms. I just assumed I sounded like a parrot.'

Bernice brought the parrot, Florence, up to eye-level. 'What do you remember?'

Florence shook its head. 'Nothing. One minute I was on a ship, the next I was on the *Adorable Illusion*.'

'Which is a ship,' Ginger offered.

'I should have thought it obvious from my tone that I was clearly on a different ship.'

'Which one?' cajoled Bernice.

'It was called *The Vixen*, launched from Portsmouth in 1707. Quite how I know that, as I had no sentience to speak of other than that of a parrot, I'm not sure.'

'That's... quite interesting. I wonder if it's true?'

'I believe it's true. Why would I lie?'

Bernice shook her head. 'I don't think you would know you were, actually. But right now I think all our perceptions have been interfered with. Our minds clouded at some point.'

'Why do you say that?' asked Maria.

Bernice looked at Ginger. 'Remember that maintenance guy?'

Ginger nodded. 'He didn't seem exactly human.'

One of the meerkats shuddered. 'I saw their faces too,' it said. 'Horrible, twisted, evil...'

'Yeah, yeah, yeah,' Bernice cut across. 'You also saw poor Dave being ejected into space. Then he was dragged back once dead. Someone aboard the *Adorable Illusion* borrowed the bodies of the three maintenance guys after killing them. To keep an eye on us. To keep us... what? Bewildered? Unadventurous?'

'Did they kill Snow and Ebon and Jack?' asked Ginger.

Bernice took in a sharp breath. 'I don't know. We didn't find Jack's body. He may not be dead. He may be here somewhere. With Russet. And Blair. Anyone else missing? Maria?'

She shook her head. 'Jefri died before we were... taken... by the Rapture.' Then she clicked her fingers. 'The DNA!'

'What DNA?'

'I noticed weird DNA showing up on my sweep of the ship.'

'What sweep of the ship?'

'Really? My being nosey is what annoys you now, Victor?'

'Fair enough. You swept the ship.'

'Regularly. But when some anomalous DNA showed up, I alerted the doctor.'

Bernice nodded encouragingly. 'And what did he say?'

'He never responded.'

'If he was one of the aliens you saw, Benny,' Ginger said slowly, 'it might explain why he didn't feel pain when you kicked him in the dark.'

'Oh that wasn't him,' Bernice said. 'That was you. Or Russet. I realised that earlier. Once I knew you were working for the Heliok Syndicate, that was obvious. Incapacitating me was obviously what you needed. The aliens didn't need me out of it and I doubt the good doctor did. But nice try.'

Ginger shrugged. 'For what it's worth, my leg still hurts now.'

'Good,' Bernice snapped. Then suddenly brightened. 'No, actually yes, good indeed! You still feel pain! So you can't be dead. Huzzah for pain.'

Ginger sighed. 'Glad to be of service.'

'I say we all go on a recce. Together. One big group. Let's find out where we are.' Bernice looked for support. 'See if we can find any stragglers like the doctor and dreary old Russet.'

Jet stood beside her, as did Maria. Lord Tawn nodded his assent and so immediately the two meerkats joined him.

'Ginger? You may be a lying, double-crossing, money-grabbing swindler, but you're also dead useful in a tight spot and I'd rather have you where I can see you,' Bernice smiled. 'What d'you say?'

Ginger managed a tight smile. 'You know how to appeal to a girl's heart.'

'Florence, you in on this adventure?'

'Oh absolutely. I'm all for new experiences.'

'What about me?' asked Victor Cooke.

'You can go –' began Jet but Bernice hurriedly put a hand over her mouth.

'Look, we don't care what you do. You've lied, swindled and generally mistreated all of us.' Bernice raised an eyebrow at him. 'But if you promise to be a good boy and not kill, sell, belittle or actually even talk to us, you can come with.'

If Victor Cooke was not used to being spoken to like that, he didn't let it show. He merely nodded in agreement and brought up the rear of the group as they began walking in the first direction they thought of. Left. Away from the trees Bernice had come through.

The only thing that Bernice noticed, as did Florence the parrot, was that Victor Cooke, quickly and as surreptitiously as possible, tapped something on his wristwatch. Bernice and Florence had no idea what it was or did, but they weren't going to forget it happened.

Elsewhere but not in the beautiful never-ending sunny parkland stood three figures.

Strictly speaking, they weren't even figures, just an approximation of them, all wispy and slightly unformed. They didn't say anything to one another. They just stood there. Immobile, unblinking, heads eerily cocked slightly to one side, as if listening.

'One of us is still trapped aboard the vessel, caught in some kind of... event,' said one.

Then a tiny jerk of his head came from another of them. 'The new ones are on their way,' he said in a rasping voice that sounded like death warmed up.

'Good,' said the other. 'Now we can begin to rid their universe of their infection once and for all, and claim it for ourselves.'

CHAPTER TWENTY
ONE WAY OR ANOTHER

The *Adorable Illusion* hovered in space, just above the rift through which the Rapture energy had bled. Poured. Exploded. Strictly speaking, the ship wasn't hovering – ships tend not to hover in the vacuum of space. But the disabled *Illusion* was giving a pretty good impression of doing just that.

It was being observed by a small but powerful shuttlecraft, carrying the insignia of the Heliok Syndicate. In it were two crew, and a rather large prison cell with enough security locks to keep the most ravenous animal in the cosmos safely inside. The fact was, it was only meant to hold one Professor Bernice Surprise Summerfield, but the locks were just as good for her.

The crew were perplexed. As they had approached the *Adorable Illusion*, their contacts aboard had been sending out a homing beacon as well as a fairly steady report on the activities of the intended prisoner. The crew had been monitoring these, homing in on the underside of the aft section, where the exchange was scheduled to be taking place. They had seen a momentary flash in space, lasting less than a second, and all contact had cut out.

'So who is this Bernice woman, mate?' one of the crew asked the other.

'Dunno, mate, never researched her. Thought you did that.'

'Why would I, mate?'

'Well, 'cause that's your job, innit mate?'

'Nah,' said the first, 'it really isn't... Hang on mate, that's weird.'

What was weird, well more extraordinary really, was that they couldn't actually approach the *Adorable Illusion*. No matter what trajectory they took, the ship didn't move. If the Heliok ship came underneath, over the top or up either side, what they actually saw was the same image of the ship, the same angle (a three quarter, port side). It was as if the ship was matching their sight perception.

The crew abandoned computer control and went closer manually, watching with their eyes rather than the computer's, but saw the same thing. The ship was always in the same place, imperceptibly jerking slightly then righting itself every half a second.

The first crewman suddenly sighed. 'You know what this is like, mate?'

'Nah mate, what?'

'Well mate, if I didn't know better, I'd say it was caught in some kind of chronic hysteresis.'

'A chronic what, mate? Is it painful?'

'Nah mate not chronic like in pain. Chronic like in chronal. Like in time. Yeah?'

'Nah, mate. Dunno what you mean.'

'It's trapped, mate. Like it's frozen in a split second of time, trying to break free.'

The second crewman looked at the first quizzically. 'You what mate? You been reading books again?'

'Nah mate, seriously. I heard rumours about this.' He reached down and brought the ship in closer. 'We need to get in and nudge it slightly to break the hysteresis. Stretch it like a rubber band till it breaks.'

'Sounds dangerous, mate.'

'Shouldn't be, mate. I heard about this once, guy in a bar showed me a miniature one caught in a time storm bottle.'

'A what, mate?'

'Never mind. Just help me take the shuttle in really carefully, mate. We'll just nudge the ship slightly... here we go, and...'

'Sounds dangerous, mate.'

'Shouldn't be, mate. I heard about this once, guy in a bar showed me a miniature one caught in a time storm bottle.'

'A what, mate?'

'Never mind. Just help me take the shuttle in really carefully, mate. We'll just nudge the ship slightly... here we go, and...'

'Shit we're'

'Sounds dangerous, mate.'

'Shouldn't be, mate. I heard about this once, guy in a bar showed me a miniature one caught in a time storm bottle.'

'A what, mate?'

'Never mind. Just help me take the shuttle in really carefully, mate. We'll just nudge the ship slightly... here we go, and...'

'caught in'

'Sounds dangerous, mate.'

'Shouldn't be, mate. I heard about this once, guy in a bar showed me a miniature one caught in a time storm bottle.'

'A what, mate?'

'Never mind. Just help me take the shuttle in really carefully, mate. We'll just nudge the ship slightly... here we go, and...'

'the thing'

'Sounds dangerous, mate.'

'Shouldn't be, mate. I heard about this once, guy in a

bar showed me a miniature one caught in a time storm bottle.'

'A what, mate?'

'Never mind. Just help me take the shuttle in really carefully, mate. We'll just nudge the ship slightly... here we go, and...'

'ourselves, mate!'

Captain Redbeard's readouts told him that the *Adorable Illusion* had exploded into atoms quite some time ago. Then been repaired. Then blown up again. Then repaired. And so on.

The AI was unable to explain this new form of reality but, like all the Mark 27s, his internal logic circuits could adapt to new information and run all the possible alternative scenarios until he came up with one he was programmed to accept. If such a thing was not forthcoming, Mark 27s had the ability to extrapolate and create a new, unforeseen solution.

As his circuits pondered on this, a tiny portion of his rapidly being vaporised then reassembled existence noted that Florence was not similarly coming back into existence.

On the eight thousandth occurrence of destruction/reintegration/destruction/reintegration Captain Redbeard also realised there were no organic lifeforms left aboard his ship. The closest to life were the two Quartermasters, who were dying/living/dying/living as part of the ship ruptured, expelling them into the vacuum, then drawing them back in, then out, then in.

On his nine thousand and forty-third destruction/reintegration/destruction/reintegration, he learned that the Madras chef was either alive, or splattered into his own ceiling, conducting enough electricity from the lighting units to fry his/her/its fluid brain, killing him/her/it instantly. Captain Redbeard found these new fragments of knowledge fascinating, albeit rather tediously being drawn into his mainframe over a ludicrously long period of time. Except it wasn't a long period of time – each destruction/reintegration/destruction/reintegration was actually less than a second long. Which ultimately led the AI to rationalise that the *Adorable Illusion* had been caught in that rarest of space/time phenomena, a chronic hysteresis.

He spent the next two thousand destruction/reintegration/destruction/reintegrations trying to formulate a way around this. And to see if there was any way in which he could save or retrieve any of his passengers. Because that's what Mark 27s were supposed to do.

On the seventeen hundred thousand and eighty-fourth destruction/reintegration/destruction/reintegration, the captain became aware of a shuttle approaching. It elected not to waste time trying to send out a warning for them not to approach because it calculated they would never hear it in time.

Sure enough, on the thirty-three hundred and sixteenth destruction/reintegration/destruction/reintegration, the shuttle became caught in the chronic hysteresis itself.

Captain Redbeard's systems made use of this information. It meant that the phenomena was not immune to change. It recorded the fact that the inclusion of the new vessel's mass and propulsion energy had altered the length of the recursion by a further .084 microseconds. If that increase of mass and energy could be multiplied many thousands of times, many thousands of times over, then in theory the chronic hysteresis could be broken free from.

Of course, this would probably result in the utter annihilation of the *Adorable Illusion,* as whatever energy from the Rapture had created the problem in the first place would ignite, as his records showed had originally happened. So whilst the theoretical implications fascinated the Mark 27's processors, it was forbidden to actually find a practical use for this data, due to the inevitable loss of life that would ensue. Captain Redbeard found this theoretical imbalance between exploration of phenomena and the prime system protocol of survival even more fascinating.

The drawback to this was that, whilst his systems became embroiled in the calculations and theories necessary, the captain missed a very important fact.

Walking the length of the ship, slowly heading towards the bridge, was an alien being who could walk through the chronal distortion, the death and rebirth of atoms, the sheer glory of this universally unique event, utterly unaffected. And totally disinterested. It wore the face of something inhuman: tusked, twisted and black-eyed. But from the neck down, it moved and looked just like one of the humans that had until a split second ago (or many hours, depending on one's perspective over time) lived and breathed aboard the *Adorable Illusion*. On its chest it wore a badge that read **PURSER**, and it had only one thought in mind. To permanently shut down the AI controlling the ship just as it had the AI that ran engineering, all three maintenance crew, and the real purser.

It realised that by doing this, it could be forever trapped here, but this was a sacrifice deemed necessary by the rest of its people and it accepted that, for the greater good. Which meant it had nothing to lose, everything to gain, and would make potential negotiation a singular waste of time.

Not that anyone was left to negotiate.

It smiled.

CHAPTER TWENTY ONE
NOTHING IS REAL BUT THE GIRL

Wherever they were, Bernice had to admire the weather. If this was a holosuite, it was pretty sophisticated. There were no false perspectives, no shimmering on horizons, none of the usual tells. The more they tromped, yomped and romped over the hills and dales, Bernice started to believe this really might actually be a real place somewhere.

But she couldn't shake the unreality either. Still no wind, no breezes. The leaves on the trees didn't move. The grass moved under their feet but at no other time. And there was no wildlife of any kind. It was as if someone had tried to create a perfect, beautiful environment but forgotten certain important aspects. Like life.

The others were feeling the same sense of unease, she could tell. Especially the Meerks. Meerkats were always highly attuned to their environments and this place had to be giving them something of a migraine. Despite that, they weren't complaining, which made her even more uneasy.

But Lord Tawn was certainly his usual self – he was lolloping ahead of them, clearly taking charge, deciding when they turned left or right, his one good eye shining in excitement at finally doing something constuctive.

Bernice wasn't in the mood to argue. Someone else taking

charge, giving her enough time to get her thoughts in order, was great.

First off, there was Jack. Where the hell was he? If everyone else had been transported here as the *Adorable Illusion* exploded, why wasn't he with them? Mind you, there was no sign of Blair or the two Kromians either. She didn't want to think Jack was dead. Not after Leo and Ruth. He was her last link to them, however tenuous, and she liked that about him. Truth was, she actually liked Jack anyway – he was good, fun company and she was missing him right now. Damn his eyes!

Secondly, what the hell was Victor Cooke doing here? How had he got here anyway? She'd left him at home, days before reaching Valentine's World. She and Jack had a massive head start on him. So... either this wasn't Victor Cooke or that guy who sent her on this mission wasn't Victor Cooke. Twins? Clones? Was the one she'd eaten food with a *hologram*?

Ginger. Ginger and Russet. Ginger, Russet and the bloody Heliok Syndicate. The more she thought about it, the more certain she was that she'd never encountered the Syndicate. Hell, she wasn't that stupid. And if she and Jack had brought them down, why did they want only *her* head? Mind you, she hadn't seen Jack in that footage, it'd just said 'a friend', so maybe she'd done it alone. Or, good god, was this something she and Jason had done years ago and it was just being acted on now? No, the Heliok Syndicate only had a few months to vent their grievances. And she was sure she'd been nowhere near them or that other place mentioned in the report in the last six months... That much she would remember.

Her reverie was broken by Lord Tawn.

'We have been walking for hours. The day is not turning into night which leads me to think there is no night here.'

'Or,' Maria offered up, 'the rotation around the sun is much, much slower and days will last significantly longer.'

'Either way, I think we should stop before we all become too exhausted and get some sleep.'

'I'd like some food,' one of the Meerks murmured.

Bernice considered this. Food wasn't a bad idea. But how and where from?

'Are you hungry?' asked a female voice.

The group turned in surprise. A tall, human girl was standing beside them, a massive basket of fruit and vegetables in her hand. 'Something for everyone I imagine,' she said.

'Who the hell are you?' Ginger asked, defensive as always.

'My name is Sara,' she said.

'Hullo Sara,' Bernice said cautiously. 'And where did you spring from?'

'You thought about food, so it seems a good idea to bring you some.'

'Wish I'd thought about a land-crawler,' Maria muttered. 'Would've saved some blisters.'

Bernice smiled at this, but Sara took the scientist at face value. 'I don't think we could get one of those, I'm sorry,' she said. It struck Bernice that she looked like she meant it.

'What planet is this?' Florence asked, the first words the parrot had spoken in quite a few hours.

'Planet? It's not a planet.'

'Knew it,' Bernice said. 'Holosuite?'

The mysterious girl smiled. 'No, no, this is the universe.'

'The what-now?'

'Welcome to our universe. This is everything.'

Bernice sucked on her bottom lip before speaking. 'I'm not sure I follow you, sorry.'

Sara placed the food down by the meerkats, who dug in hungrily.

Bernice was going to caution them – there was no guarantee that this wasn't a trap, that the food wasn't poisoned. Ginger clearly thought the same thing, but whispered in Bernice's ear 'Better they find out first than us.'

'Harsh,' Bernice said.

Ginger just shrugged. 'And?'

Bernice gave her a look and focused back on Sara. 'I'm sorry to be dense, but can you explain please?'

Sara sat cross-legged on the grass and Bernice followed suit, as did Ginger and Jet. 'You are in the universe. You are in everything that is, will be and ever has been.'

'I always imagined the universe to be less of a philosophical metaphor than that,' Jet said.

'Oh, in your universe, that's true.' Sara pointed at the sky. 'But this is all there is in *this* universe.'

'This what?' spluttered Ginger, but Bernice hushed her.

'Okay, I'm getting this. I know where we are,' she said. 'This is the universe the Rapture comes from, isn't it?'

Sara nodded. 'This is the Rapture. You are inside it.'

'I was correct first, people,' Florence said but no one was listening.

The others had gathered around Sara now. Victor Cooke was frowning. 'Inside the Rapture?'

'Yes, it took you from your spaceship. You tried to capture it, harness it, but a universe cannot be harnessed, cannot be captured.'

'Energy can though,' Maria offered.

Sara nodded. 'Oh yes, but the Rapture isn't energy that any laws of physics in your universe can deal with. It is unique.'

'I don't believe the laws of physics change,' said Maria.

'Balls to that,' said Bernice. 'I've seen places that turn Einstein, Hawking, Sun Mao and all the others on their heads.' She looked at Sara. 'And what are you? Are you part of this universe? Are you the embodiment of the Rapture? An avatar it has created to interact with us?'

Sara laughed. 'Gosh, no. I only know all this because I'm from your universe. My name is Sara Blair and I was aboard a shuttlecraft called *The Hunter* when the Rapture drew us here.'

A look passed between Bernice's compatriots. 'You were on board *The Hunter*? Anya Kryztyne's ship?'

Sara smiled and nodded. 'Of course.'

Victor Cooke threw a look at Jet. 'What of your friends, your fellow students? What about my son?'

'Dad? Mom?'

Everyone turned at the young man's voice.

Bernice blew out air from her cheeks. The speaker was humanoid but covered in inky fur, clearly the product of Victor Cooke and Jet. There was a young female who was clearly related to Lord Tawn and two meerkats, twins, just as identical as their parents. Another lad with just one huge eye dominating his face was from a race Bernice didn't recognise and there were two other male humans. The students believed lost all those months ago were alive and well. Apparently. Living inside a pocket universe.

'Well,' said Florence settling on the ground beside Bernice. 'This is a turn up for the books, I must say.'

Bernice stared at the four human youths who didn't have relatives to greet them. One of them, dark-skinned with piercing blue eyes, walked towards her. He held out a hand. 'Kame Wyck, appointed leader of *The Hunter*'s students,' he said warmly. 'How do you do.'

'Professor Bernice Summerfield, not remotely in charge of this lot. Nice to meet you Kame. Care to tell me how you are still alive?'

'Not remotely, Professor,' said Kame, the smile never leaving his face. 'The secrets of the Rapture are for us and the people who live here with us. Our mission is to try and get you home before they find you.'

'Why?'

'Because they'll kill you.'

'Oh. Well that doesn't sound too promising. Why didn't they kill you?'

Kame considered this. 'I don't honestly know. But they don't like you apparently. You tried to steal the Rapture. They knew you were coming and why. They tried to stop you. But they failed because you tried to steal the Rapture and it brought you here.'

'Maybe it likes us after all.'

'It sees you as a contaminant.'

'That's nice. Not.'

Kame nodded. 'And so they will kill you. Very soon.' He held out a hand to help Bernice up. 'Especially if you try to take us away from here.'

'So you want to stay here?' Bernice thought about this. 'Not sure your respective families will agree with that.'

'Too right,' snapped Victor Cooke. 'I came all this way to find Caesar. To find my son. I'm taking him home with me.'

'No Dad, you aren't,' Caesar said, walking over, Jet holding his arm. 'We live here now.'

Victor Cooke held a gun in his hand. Bernice wondered where the hell that had come from, then noticed the wristwatch was gone.

'Oh very clever, how very Q-branch,' she said.

'And I'll happily use it on anyone who tries to stop me taking Caesar home.'

'Stalemate,' said Bernice. 'Typical, a man who thinks he can change the universe, quite literally in this case, with a gun and the sound of his own voice.'

Victor Cooke pointed the gun directly into Bernice's face. 'Just who the hell are you anyway?' he said.

'Umm, I'm the patsy you sent into all this, to pretend to be their teacher? The one you paid Ginger to hand over to the Heliok Syndicate?'

'I keep telling you, I have no idea what you are talking about,' Victor Cooke said. 'Before today, I never set eyes on you in my life.'

'Really?'

'Yes, really!'

'Oh damn,' Bernice said. 'I think we're in more trouble than I realised.'

CHAPTER TWENTY TWO
SHAKEDOWN

'You have to understand Mr Cooke, sir, that I wouldn't normally ask but, well, I really must.' Victor Cooke's majordomo drew himself up to his full height of five foot six, resplendent in his long silk frock-coat.

Victor Cooke sighed and put his feet up on the smoked-glass tabletop. 'Where did I go wrong,?'

The majordomo pointed at the feet with white-gloved finger. 'The real Mr Cooke would never treated an antique that way. It's a genuine 20th century MFI original. From 1973, I believe.'

'A what?'

'I have absolutely no idea,' the majordomo admitted. 'But Mr Cooke is terribly fond of it.'

'Oh. Sorry.' Victor Cooke swung his legs off it. 'Awfully bad manners.'

The majordomo agreed. 'It certainly demonstrates a lack of research on your part, sir. Although I have to say, you have all the other staff fully convinced.'

Victor Cooke stood up and crossed to a small porthole, looking out into space from within the yacht. 'Have you been with him long?'

'Twenty-eight years, sir. Well, that is what I believe. I genuinely do not know when you replaced him.'

Victor Cooke smiled. 'Do you remember that awfully nice Rhodian slave-girl who came to dinner one evening?'

'I do sir. We lost of a lot of cutlery that night.'

'How about the Thraxis Sisters?'

'Oh sir, I always remember when nuns come aboard. That particular assemblage got very... excitable and threw an entire tray of Klan Dynasty shot-glasses overboard to see if the alcohol floated or dissipated.'

'How about the week that the Joriam Consortium celebrated their financial win at the Land-Crow races?'

The majordomo shuddered. 'That, sir, was not a pleasant week. We still haven't found all of the sous chef's limbs.'

Victor Cooke considered this. 'I don't think you will actually. At least two of his arms were eaten by the Joriam's company secretary while she was high.'

'Ah. I see. I shall let him know so he can incubate replacements.'

Victor Cooke nodded. 'Good call. That, by the way, was my first week here.'

The majordomo thought on this. 'I see,' he said finally. 'So you weren't responsible for the cruel death of Dr Kryztyne?'

'No,' Victor Cooke smiled. 'No that was all the real Vic. Sorry – does that disappoint you?'

'Indeed, sir. I had rather hoped that my Mr Cooke wasn't quite that...'

'Bloodthirsty?'

'Indeed, sir.' The majordomo coughed. 'May I be so bold as to enquire who it is we have had the pleasure of serving for the last... month and a half?'

Victor Cooke waved the majordomo towards a port-hole. 'Look over to your left. See that slightly orange star, glowing brightly?'

'I do sir. It is certainly a most enjoyable spectacle.'

'It's also the Helio-Sphere.'

The majordomo absorbed this information. 'An artificial gambling world if I recall.'

'A Dyson Sphere, my friend. Generally considered one of the least genteel places in this quadrant. Only the casinos on Legion are dirtier, grittier, more violent and packed with more scum.'

The majordomo considered this. 'Do you own them as well?'

'Hell no. No one wants to own property on Legion. Now, the Heliok Syndicate are more than happy with what we have. What we don't like are people who try and shut us down.'

'Like Professor Summerfield did?'

'Oh she's small fry. No, I'm afraid our target was your boss, Victor Cooke. We needed him out of the picture. Permanently. But he sloped off to the *Adorable Illusion* to do whatever he's doing about finding his dead son.' He held up a hand in anticipation of the next question. 'No, don't ask, we don't know either. Or care. However it was important for us that Victor Cooke was seen to have a very major financial fail. With any luck, the assassin we employed to bump off the professor will take out Victor Cooke too.'

The majordomo frowned. 'And so... you are?'

'Oh, excuse me.' The man who wasn't really Victor Cooke pressed a stud on his shirt collar and with a shimmer his holographic cloaking device deactivated, leaving a really very bland little man in a dark suit standing there. 'My name is... irrelevant. But I am part of the Heliok Syndicate. That is all you need to know. And we are going to bring Victor Cooke's empire down around his ears, so that when, or if, he returns, it will look as if he lost control of everything. I have spent the past few weeks posing as him, slowly spending all his money in a variety of dumb-ass ways, selling stocks for a fraction of their worth, etc. Within three weeks, Victor Cooke will be ruined.'

'I see. So this is all about money.'

'Absolutely. Nothing personal. Just one syndicate removing a business enemy.'

The majordomo laughed lightly at this.

The syndicate man frowned. 'Why is that funny?'

'I have been Mr Cooke's majordomo for a long time. I know everything about him, his money, his off-shore and legitimate accounts, his tax havens, his less-than-scrupulous deals and indeed his occasional philanthropic anonymous charitable trusts. All you had to do was come to me, I could have given you exactly what you needed without all this cloak-and-dagger stuff. It's all very melodramatic, but totally redundant.'

'For why?'

'Because, as well as knowing where all the metaphorical skeletons are buried, only I have access to his bank accounts. He trusts me you see. So, with any financial irregularities or improprieties, the money doesn't vanish as you assume.'

'Why not? Where does it go?'

'To the trustees of his will and testament. Victor Cooke is not stupid, you see. He has always been paranoid enough to know that people like you might try to bring him down, so he had plans in motion. To you, it might look like his money was vanishing, but in truth, all that was happening was it was being transferred into a variety of ghost accounts, protected and sealed until only the owner of those accounts re-activated them.'

'Ah,' said the syndicate man, 'but if Vic is dead or lost or whatever, he can't reactivate them.'

The majordomo laughed louder. 'I didn't say Victor Cooke was the owner.''

The syndicate man considered this. 'You?'

'The only man he trusts with his wealth. Even this space

yacht goes to me in the event of his death. His entire fortune, businesses and portfolios all transfer to me should anything untoward happen to him. So it was me you should have tried to make a deal with, rather than waste your time impersonating him. Badly, I might add.'

The syndicate man frowned. 'So, what do I need to do to turn you to our side? The Heliok Syndicate will pay you very well for control of those accounts.'

'I'm not for sale,' the majordomo said. 'Besides, I want all this. I want his wealth, his planets and moons and wells and mines and above all, I really want this yacht.'

'Well that I'm sure we can give you, no questions asked.'

'Thank you, that sounds a good deal,' the majordomo said. 'But I prefer my own version of the deal.'

'Which is?'

'Victor Cooke is found dead. Suicide after the death of his son and abandonment by his wife.'

'Wife? He has a wife?'

The majordomo grinned. 'And that's the only question on your mind? Ridiculous.' And he casually reached into his frock-coat, brought out a laser pistol and neatly drilled a hole straight between the syndicate man's eyes, who was dead before the majordomo's finger released the trigger. 'Can't bear Heliok,' he said, crossing to the corpse and reactivating the holographic cloaking device, so he was looking down at a now-dead Victor Cooke. He carefully positioned the body in a chair at the smoked-glass table, put the pistol in his hand and gave the state room a last look around.

Then he exited and walked back to his small office. He tapped a comms switch.

'Mr Chambers? It's the Major. Look, I am concerned about Mr Cooke. I spoke to him earlier and he sounds very sad and bitter about Mrs Cooke's departure and the loss of Caesar.

I have looked for him in the dinning room and his quarters. I wondered if, as head of security and therefore in an office closer to the state room, you could put your head round the door and check if he's there? I checked earlier and he wasn't but I can't think where else he might be.'

The head of security agreed to do so, and the majordomo activated his personal pad and began dictating Victor Cooke's obituary, while simultaneously draining the last of his fortune into the bank accounts he had placed the majordomo in charge of in the event of his death. He looked around his frankly rather small office on Victor Cooke's yacht. No, wait, *his* yacht now. Any second now and...

Sure enough, the head of security reported back.

'Oh no,' the majordomo said to him. 'How terrible. Who would have thought Victor Cooke would take his own life after all this time?'

And, with a huge smile, he pressed *send* on the obituary.

Richard Blair's life had never quite gone the way he intended. This was, he decided many years ago, pretty much everyone else's fault.

'There's no greater responsibility than that of potential,' his senior lecturer at the Delta Capris Medical School said on his graduation. The Capris system had been all but destroyed two hundred or so years ago, razed by an army of swarming creatures who had seen it as a target, a human-colonised system that needed obliterating. Years later, it had rebuilt itself, repopulated and decided to give something back to the universe. Many of the planets had dedicated themselves to science and medicine, as a way of understanding the diversity of the universe as well as helping improve it.

Like many others, Blair automatically found himself studying at the Medical School. He had no interest in medicine. He had no desire to learn about the diverse species that existed in the wider quadrant. He had zero enthusiasm for carving out a career as a doctor (or veterinarian, as he often likened it to). But he did like money.

He certainly enjoyed spending it. Over the summer of his final year, he spent a great deal of time out of the system. While his classmates were doing gap year studies on other planets or disenfranchised third worlds, Blair was gambling his tutorial fees away at the Heliok casinos on various moons and space stations.

He met Suzy at a spaceflight agency. She organised a cheap trip home for him a few times and, eventually, took pity on his ever-decreasing credit balance and took him out for a couple of coffees.

Blair had never particularly craved company, female or male. Misanthropes rarely did. But the sex was amazing and he found that, if nothing else, after a heavy loss or even a rare win, a night with Suzy made everything better.

Until she told him they were expecting a child. By then he'd been running his medical practice, reasonably half-heartedly, from one of the moons of Yaldon. There was a steady stream of multi-species patients, and they paid well. Blair enjoyed spending it on booze and blackjack or Chelonian rummy. He certainly wasn't expecting to spend it on bringing up a child he'd neither wanted nor planned for.

Suzy, unsurprisingly, didn't take this news very well and finally threatened to report him to the Medical Council of Capris if he didn't take responsibility for what turned out to be their daughter.

Sara, they called her. And Blair's life changed. Because he fell in love – truly deeply in love. Not with Suzy, but with being a parent, being a father to the most amazing baby daughter. He cleaned himself up, he threw himself into work so that he could give Sara a fantastic life. He and Suzy were never truly happy with each other, both had a series of mutually acceptable affairs, but they stayed together because of Sara.

Blair's friends, most of whom were from the Heliok Syndicate, told him he was mad. 'Leave them both, live your life,' they'd say. Blair knew they just wanted this former loser back at their tables, blowing three month's profit in a matter of hours.

The day Suzy died was traumatic. They no longer had much of a marriage, but there was a mutual dependency and, deep down, a mutual respect for the successful bringing up of their daughter. Sara was in Year 12 at school when the accident happened. It was a tour bus that Suzy had recently started working on, to keep her nearer home. Yaldon wasn't much but it did have some marvellous old statues and pyramids, and tourists flocked there looking for a cheap, educational holiday. Suzy was giving her regular talk about the Forest of Statues when the tour bus's gravity thrusters, misaligned during a recent service, went wrong and, instead of blasting downwards, actually fired into one another, catching the fuel stacks on the left-hand side of the bus. Everyone died instantly, all 38 tourists and the staff aboard. There were no remains – the explosion was too all consuming for that.

It was left for Richard Blair to see Sara through college, and then university, alone. He did his best and when Sara announced that Anya Kryztyne had recommended her for a field trip to the legendary Rapture rent, well, of course he agreed she should go. A chance to do something he would never have been able to do.

Six weeks later, he was at his second memorial service in two years. Other parents tried to include him in their grief, but he wanted nothing to do with them. He returned to Yaldon alone and desperate. Within three months, the business was gone and he was gambling again, living in cheap rooms and wearing second-hand clothes that didn't fit.

There was a period of his life he simply couldn't deal with. People said he had a breakdown, which was certainly true, but not because of the grief of losing his family so rapidly. He said there was a woman involved, but couldn't say exactly what he meant by that, and sure enough his friends deserted him one by one.

He was close to ending it all when Cooke Industries contacted him, offering him a chance for redemption, a chance to learn the truth about his daughter's disappearance and death. All he had to do was smarten himself up, get off the booze and drugs, and accept a job as medical officer on the *Adorable Illusion*. A four month tour of duty for which he would be well paid. Enough to set up a new surgery. Or pay off his debts to the Heliok Syndicate and a couple of smaller low-key establishments he owed.

Realising he had nothing to lose, he agreed.

And then strange things happened, that ended up with him waking up one afternoon in the lowest part of the ship, away from everyone else. He didn't feel drunk or high, but he had no recollection of getting there. Was he trying to leave the ship? Had he had a suicidal episode, deciding to leap into space? Or taken an escape pod to fly it into the gravitational pull of a sun? And why did he have empty vials of ketamine in his pocket? Those weren't from his stores in the medical bay.

He couldn't remember, and that scared him. Even at his lowest ebb, he had always had total recall of what he had done. Blackouts were something new.

He had been thinking about that when he realised the ship was on fire, and he sat and watched with a strangely calm detachment as the ship literally fell to pieces around him. He stared hard into the rainbow flames that tore apart the metal tomb he was in and he welcomed death. Because it was an end and, more importantly, it was someone else making a decision about this life that he had no control over.

So when he found himself waking up on a grassy knoll, sunshine beating down on him, and a large oak tree behind him, he decided this was what heaven must look like. There was no other explanation. He was just glad to be away from the spaceship. Away from all the other people who wanted his services. Away from whatever had driven him towards apparent suicide.

Richard Blair laid his head down on the grass and listened to the silence, until he drifted off into undisturbed and long overdue sleep.

Maria Willows was walking. She hadn't done that for a very long time. Of course she had walked from her room to the laboratory. She had walked around the observation deck plenty of times. But here, now, she was really walking. Through grass, around trees, up small hillocks, staring at the bright sun and fluffy white clouds.

But in the back of her mind was something that Bernice Summerfield had said to her about the breeze. There wasn't one. This was a fabrication. For all Maria knew, she was walking on the spot, or round in a small circle. She had no way of knowing – her mind was sure she was walking the same way that her eyes showed her, so she just let it accept that. Enjoy the change.

Beside her was the young man, the self-appointed leader of the group, Kame Wyck. He was always smiling, pointing out trees and grasses. He was studying botany at university, he knew that. But he was strangely reluctant to talk about *The Hunter* and what had happened.

Maria was on a mission – one suggested by Bernice, but one

she fully supported. Get Kame away from the group, get him to open up. See if the conditioning could be broken, or even just chipped away. Maria wasn't sure why Bernice thought she could do it best, but didn't argue. She'd either succeed or fail, that was the scientist in her. Experiment, fail, experiment again, succeed. Of course there were more failures than successes but that made the successes all the sweeter.

Which would Kame be?

'Tell me about the others,' Maria said.

Kame shrugged. 'We mostly met aboard *The Hunter*. Anya introduced us. I knew Adam Campbell from class and had heard of Dob-Dob the Chim, but then who hadn't?'

'He's the one with the one big eye, yes?' Maria prompted, rather stupidly. He was the only Chim in the group.

'Yeah, one of the funniest, sweetest guys you could ever meet. He always makes us smile.'

'Really? Why's that?'

Kame opened his mouth to speak, as if he was going to relay some anecdote about when the group needed a morale boost that Dob-Dob the Chim had supplied, but no words came out. His eyes widened slightly, as if he were aware of his inability, but his mouth began working again. 'I didn't really know Flax, Sara Blair or Caesar Cooke, although obviously we'd all heard of Caeser's father. There were curiously few cross-species students on my course, so it was really nice to broaden my mind, talk to him, find out how difficult, and occasionally easy, it was for him to have that whole mixed parentage, mixed-culture thing. Oh, and then there's the gruesome twosome, Flash and Buck. Can you tell them apart? Because none of us can. And they loved that, they'd do all the twin gags. Set us up, make us look foolish for a laugh. I remember there was one time when Adam and Dob-Dob the Chim were...'

And he stopped, once again unable to vocalise a humorous

moment. It was as if, Maria thought, something was shutting down anything that might provoke an extreme emotion like laughter. That gave her a clue. But she wasn't much of a joker, so she needed to go the other way.

'Do you miss home?' she asked.

'Home?'

'Yes, you know. Your colony, your system. Your university perhaps, other friends. What about your parents? They miss you, I'm sure.'

'Why?'

'Because they think you're dead.'

Kame frowned. 'But I'm not.'

'But they don't know that.' Maria spoke slowly. 'They are devastated, they couldn't bring themselves to go to your memorial service. You were their only son.'

'Why would they think I'm dead. I'm not dead. I am alive. Here.'

'But where is here? Wouldn't you like to see them again?'

Kame opened his mouth to answer, but couldn't at first. 'We have everything we need here,' he finally said. 'We are well fed – and look at this amazing location. Why would I want to leave here?'

'I never said anything about leaving here, Kame.' Maria pressed her tiny advantage. 'But what if we could bring them to see you here.'

'No!' Kame suddenly got agitated. 'No one should come here.' And his voice dropped to a whisper. 'You should not have come here, you should leave.'

'I can't leave. None of us can. We didn't come through choice. Like you, we were brought here through the Rapture. We are prisoners – our minds were clouded and confused as soon as we set out to reach here. Just like you.'

'But we're not prisoners. We want to be here.'

'Then let me bring your parents. Surely Dob-Dob the Chim would like his family? What about Adam and Sara? The others, Flax and the Meerk twins, they have relatives here now. Doesn't that make you sad that you haven't?' Maria reached into her pocket. 'I have a holo here of your mum and dad, do you want to see it?'

This was a complete lie of course, the only holo she had in her pocket was one of her own parents, taken a few years before they passed away. She hoped he wouldn't call her bluff.

'No,' he said. 'No parents. No... family... don't want to see my mum. Never. Can't see her here. Can't let her see us... see me here...' And with a sudden gasp of anguish, Kame reached out and grabbed the startled scientist in a hug. She wasn't quite sure what to do, until she cautiously realised she could return the hug. God, how long had it been since she hugged another human being?

Kame was sobbing, deep painful gasps of repression and guilt and she let him cry into her shoulder, remembering that a gentle squeeze around the shoulders helped.

After a bit he pulled back, looking up at her with his deep blue eyes, red-rimmed with tears. Crying as he hadn't for... God knew how long.

'What happened to me? To all of us?' He shook his head. 'I wanted to stay here? Why?'

Maria couldn't answer that, but told him it was important that he helped her convince the others to help her group get away. 'I'm putting my trust in this Professor Summerfield woman,' she explained. 'She seems to have more of a clue than Victor Cooke right now.'

Kame frowned. 'Bernice Summerfield? The one that wrote those archaeology books? Wasn't she something important during the Deindum War?'

Maria took this information in. Was she indeed? She'd kept

that little credential to herself. 'Quite possibly,' Maria replied. 'But if she is, then I'm doubly glad I'm pinning my flag to hers.'

'We should get back to the gang,' Kame said, suddenly reinvigorated, bursting with energy that he'd clearly not had for a very long time. 'They'll probably be showing your people the generator.'

'The what now?'

'We call it the generator. It's a machine. It's where we get food and water from. I think it's probably what actually focusses the Rapture energy back into our universe and...' he stopped. 'I have been thinking about this for months, but couldn't say it aloud. Couldn't speak it. What did they do to my head?'

'I don't know. But you know what, Kame? I think you are going to be fine.'

'My dad always said university students were created to keep therapists in business. Our little group might create a whole new theoretical study.'

Maria smiled. 'If you can think that now, I doubt therapy is necessary in the future.' And she stopped. Just out of the corner of her eye she saw something move. A flash of red... red fur? Was it Ginger? Why would she have followed them? Surely she'd have come over? But there was no sign of it now. Maybe it was nothing.

She and Kame headed off to find the generator.

Lord Tawn was examining the generator. Flax was delightedly showing him how it worked, but it made no sense to the old soldier. Every time she pointed out a flap or space that food or drink came from, he saw nothing, just a blank side.

The generator was like a dark grey plinth, relatively featureless apart from a small bolted crevice at the bottom. Lord Tawn had noticed that at no point did Flax ever make mention of that real access panel, just insisted on pointing out more features that he couldn't see.

He was also alarmed by Victor Cooke. The man had a gun in his hand – and Lord Tawn could spot a person who wasn't used to handling firearms. He was arguing with Jet, his ex-wife, and to make his point, he jabbed the air around them with his gun, his finger dangerously close to the firing stub. Lord Tawn had tried to point this out, but the gun had been waved at him and he had been told to shut up in no uncertain terms.

Lord Tawn had little time for humans generally and Victor Cooke was a particularly loathsome one, so he opted to ignore him after that.

The meerkats and their twins were talking – he could see that like Flax, the twins seemed entranced, almost fundamentalist, in their promotion of their new home. He could see Sandy and Sable becoming more and more distraught by this. And distraught Meerks, never the most positive of companions anyway, could spell danger in the long run.

Lord Tawn couldn't really tell the human students apart. He could tell which one Caesar Cooke was – he looked more like his mother. But the other two, not a clue. He gathered one was male and the other female, but which was which, he had no idea. Then there was the Chim. Lord Tawn liked Chim, valuable resourceful soldiers, ideal in war. Brilliant vision, clever strategists and, since his injury, they shared the whole one-eyed thing. But this one was vague, dopey and just blinked a lot. A sure sign that it wasn't well.

Lord Tawn looked around this motley bunch. They had come to find his granddaughter, and had succeeded. He hoped that if they could get them away, somehow whatever mesmerising influence the Rapture held over Flax would dissipate, but he couldn't be sure. He had gained a grudging respect for that Summerfield woman. She talked sense. *She* he could recognise, mostly because she was usually standing next to Ginger, who she was a very distinct, non-human, lady.

He wished they would hurry back. This generator thing worried him. It clearly didn't worry Victor Cooke or Jet, but that's because they hadn't engaged their brains yet. Why was it here? Why did the students feverishly worship it? It was just a lump of metal, it couldn't power anything more than a handheld comms device, probably. Unless he was missing something very important.

And Lord Tawn was too experienced, too clever and far too stubborn to miss important things. That why he was still alive after all his years of combat. He was not a fool.

Talking of which...

'Tawn! I say we take control of his device, demand the aliens let us go home or we destroy it, what do you think?'

Lord Tawn looked over at Victor Cooke, wary of the gun still being used like an extended finger, jabbing at the empty air as the human stressed every word.

'I don't believe this device has any value whatsoever. I think it's a feint to keep this poor children in a state of casual acceptance and ignorance.' He tapped his left foot. 'And I think only a fool who relies on money and guns to get what he wants would think any differently.'

Victor Cooke just stared at him.

Jet laughed. 'Oh he's got you bang to rights there, Victor,' she said. 'Summed you up perfectly.'

'Oh shut up,' Victor Cooke snapped.

'Mom! Dad, please! Not in front of my mates!'

Lord Tawn looked at Caesar. Poor lad, to him this was just a family disagreement, like he couldn't really hear the actual words, just the atmosphere. His whole life had probably been like this. Not like on Leperon, where the younglings were treasured and looked after at all costs. Humans were just so undisciplined, savage. Poor Jet, to have married into that.

'I think it's power. It's the power I wanted all along and I am going to have it.' Victor Cooke pointed at the generator with his gun.

Lord Tawn sighed. With any luck, he was simply too stupid to know how to actually fire the damn weapon. It crossed Lord Tawn's mind how amusing it would be if Victor Cooke had actually put it together backwards and blew his own head off. It would certainly be quieter.

He glanced across the horizon. Where were Ginger and the human professor?

Ginger and the human professor were, it had to be said, not having a great afternoon. It had started okay, when they'd got Maria Willows to take Kame Wyck for a walk. 'Clear his head,' Bernice had said meaningfully.

Then, once they'd gone, she and Ginger had started discussing possible routes out of the pocket universe. Occasionally they'd remind one another that they actually didn't like each other much, that Ginger was selling Bernice to the Heliok Syndicate and Victor Cooke simultaneously. Ginger reminded Bernice that she'd only had to do as she'd been told right from the start and none of his would have happened. Bernice reckoned it would have happened regardless and blamed Ginger for Jack's death/disappearance/whatever. Ginger said she had nothing to do with that.

'And Russet? Your so-called son? Could he have killed Jack and the lemurs?'

'Not unless he was in two places at once. He was with us in the canteen. And again, not my son, so-called or otherwise. That. Was. Just. The. Ruse. How many more times?'

'He could have popped out!'

'When?'

'When we weren't looking. He's fast and clearly a lunatic. You saw how he wanted to kill me, both of us, back on the *Adorable Illusion!*'

'Whoa! Firstly, he's just highly strung and wants to get paid. He's not a lunatic and he does not want to kill me. You, maybe, but *I'm* his partner. Business-wise obviously. And secondly, no one could have "popped out" of the canteen, killed two lemurs and a Kadeptian and then "popped back".'

'I did,' Bernice said.

'Did what? Killed them?'

'No, popped out. You didn't notice.'

'Oh, you so did not,' Ginger snapped. 'Stop trying to score points with impossible claims! My god, is that how you got your reputation, Summerfield? By lying about what you can and can't do?'

'Yes, absolutely,' Bernice said. And then suddenly laughed. 'God, yes it is. Do you know, when I first started out, I wasn't a professor. I knew bugger all about archaeology. I knew nothing about anything, I just lied my away across the galaxy.'

And Ginger smiled, then sighed. 'What changed?'

'I met a man and a girl. And they showed me a different way of looking at life and somehow, I understood what one had to do to make sure the right things happened in the universe. And after they moved on, or I did, I found new people, new homes, new reasons.

'By then, I'd actually become a real professor and really did know about archaeology. I'd written books. And then I was caught up in wartime. The Fifth Axis, remember that?'

'I wasn't born,' Ginger said. 'How the hell were you?'

'I've been around longer than you might think,' Bernice said. 'I lost my husband to the treachery of a man I trusted. I lost my son to goodness only knows where. And with Jack gone, I've pretty much lost most of my friends.'

'Why do you get up in the mornings? *How* do you get up in the mornings?'

Bernice looked at Ginger and sighed. 'Because I learned over the years that everything we do, every move we make, makes a difference to someone, somewhere. And because I can make that difference, because I *want* to make that difference, I get up every day to ensure that by the end of it, I've tried my damnedest to do something worthwhile.'

'How very pious,' said a voice behind them.

Both women swung around and found themselves facing Russet's large blaster. His head popped into view from the non-business end of it. 'Hullo ladies.'

'Weren't you trying to kill me?' Bernice said. 'I mean, that was the plan, right?'

'Still is.'

'But you weren't trying to kill *me*, right?' asked Ginger. 'Only Benny here seems to think you were.'

'Oh no, I just said you were collateral damage to him. I don't think he minded one way or another.'

Russet looked at Ginger. 'Hey, with you gone, I get all the money.'

'What the hell, Russet?' exploded Ginger. 'After all I've done for you?'

'Do you know what I like about working for Victor Cooke? Nothing. But working for the Heliok Syndicate – them I like lots. Not just the money, but the opportunity. Deliver Bernice Summerfield to them, dead or alive, and I have a job for life. I like that.'

'We should really have discussed that,' Ginger said. 'I'm not really good at sticking with one paymaster. They rarely live up to their promises.'

'I know, you've said that many times.'

'So why even think about it?'

Russet swung the gun onto Ginger. 'Because you are so very redundant. Bye bye.'

Bernice shoved Ginger aside, as Russet fired, blowing a huge hole in... well, nothing. The gun had fired, she'd felt the heat as it passed – the first bit of temperature she'd felt all day, so it had to be real. But it made no impact on the grassy ground.

'It's definitely not real then,' she shouted, happy to be proved right. 'Must be a hologram 'cause I bet there's really a bloody great hole there!'

Ginger was rolling in the other direction. 'Focus, Benny! I don't think proving your theories is really the number one priority now!'

Russet laughed, 'I so should have done this ages ago –' and stopped as Bernice rugby tackled him, having feinted away from the gun so he stayed focused on Ginger. As his blaster dropped, he yanked out a ferocious looking knife, slashing at her calf. It missed by a millimetre and Benny rolled back. Ginger went for the dropped blaster but Russet was faster, throwing the knife.

Then Ginger did something quite amazing. She let her tail take her weight, dropped backwards and reached up with her right paw, catching the knife as it sailed over her by the handle, flicking her wrist and sending it straight back the way it had come.

Russet was still staring in shock as the knife thudded into his chest with a sound that reminded Bernice of someone cleaving a melon in two. Eyes wide open, he toppled backwards, utterly dead.

Ginger walked over, yanked the knife out and wiped the blood off on Russet's fur. 'Partnership dissolved,' she spat angrily at his body.

Bernice stayed still. Ginger, knife in hand, was not something she thought she could successfully tackle now.

After a beat, she quietly said Ginger's name.

The squirrel looked at her, her eyes wide in fury and Bernice wondered if she was the next target. Then Ginger's whole body relaxed. Her eyes closed. 'Stupid, stupid idiot,' she said.

'You or him,' Bernice ventured.

'He taught me that move. So him. Should've seen it coming.'

Bernice wondered just how long they'd worked together, been friends on some weird, slightly scary level. And thought it best that they got as far away from the body as possible.

'This might be a good time to catch up with the others. See if Victor Cooke has calmed down and Lord Tawn's got that gun away from him, yes?'

'I don't like his chances much,' Ginger said, slipping the knife into her belt. 'But let's find out.'

In silence, they walked back to where they'd abandoned the group earlier, bored with Victor Cooke's endless posturing.

As they came around a copse of trees, they could see everyone gathered around a small plinth.

'Wonder what that is?' Ginger mused.

Lord Tawn's voice rang out as they got closer. 'Thank the Burrow you two are back,' he said. 'This stupid human won't stop waving his gun around. As if I'm scared of that. But you should see this.'

'What is it?' Bernice called as she and Ginger hurried their pace.

As they reached the group, Lord Tawn pointed at the plinth. 'They say it's a generator. I say it's nonsense.'

'And I,' Victor Cooke said, 'say it's the answer to all our problems. And it's mine.'

'How is it yours, you ridiculous little man?' Lord Tawn said, without actually turning to address him. He shrugged at Bernice and Ginger. 'The man thinks it'll give him access to the Rapture energy. Idiot.'

And so Victor Cooke shot Lord Tawn squarely in the back, and the old jack-rabbit pitched forward and lay still.

'Anyone else want to argue with me?' Victor Cooke asked.

CHAPTER TWENTY THREE
DREAMING

Bernice Summerfield didn't dare blink, didn't dare take her eyes off Victor Cooke for one second. Beside her, Ginger and Jet were crouched, ready for whatever came next. Behind them, the students stood bewildered by this turn of events. Sable and Sandy held their twins closer than ever.

Victor Cooke stood next to the generator, his eyes wide with either excitement, fear or madness. Or possibly, Bernice considered, a bit of each. Crouched before him, Caesar looked across at Jet, complete astonishment on his face – what is my dad doing?

Unmoving on the ground lay the body of Lord Tawn, a tiny curl of smoke still rising from the laser blast he'd taken to the back.

'Dad?'

'Quiet, Caesar,' Victor Cooke snapped. 'This is all being done for you. To ensure you have a future.'

'I'm not sure I'll have one outside of a maximum security prison at this rate,' Caesar said bluntly.

'That's one conditioned student broken free anyway,' Bernice hissed to Ginger.

'Let's hope it's woken a few of the others up too,' the squirrel replied.

Victor Cooke was shaking his head in despair at his son's apparent naivety. 'Don't you see? Don't you understand? Everything I have ever done, every empire I have built, every business I invested in, it was all for you. To give you standing, a position in society.' He waved his gun in the direction of the others. 'Look at them! Shallow! The worthless proletariat that I have to provide for. None of them grateful, none aware of the sacrifices made to ensure their lives carry on. We wage wars, we create vast industries, we control whole quadrants of space, just to they can do menial little jobs to earn enough money to buy food, rut with one another, watch holovids, play sports to make their lives seem a fraction more interesting than they actually are. None of that would be possible if people like me, like *us*, hadn't created that wealth, created that jobscape. Created the scenarios for their pointless existence. Our universe is vast, but it is full of too many people, too many individuals needing feeding, washing, looking after. They have the illusion of independence, but if people like me didn't bother, they'd be sat in squalor, waiting for the next powerful alien race to come along, enslave them or wipe them out. They don't realise how much they owe to me!' He pointed at Jet. 'Your mother there, never had a clue. No interest in anything other than the next three-course meal, or a trip to Kolpasha for the finest coats and jewellery. A shallow, vain woman whose sole contribution to existence was co-creating you! Once you were out of the suckling age, I should have had her shipped off to the backwater I dragged her from. Or killed.' He threw a look straight at Jet. 'That way I might've saved a few thousand in alimony every month.'

Caesar moved an inch away from his ranting father. 'Don't talk about Mom that way.'

'Oh yes, side with her, take her side in all things. Like the bloody lawyers did!'

Jet stood up, despite Ginger's attempt to pull her back. 'Victor,' she said softly. 'Victor, listen to me. Whatever problems you and I had, this is not Caesar's fault. It's ours. Yours and mine – well, okay, mainly yours. But none of this is his fault. Or any of these children's.'

Victor Cooke laughed. 'Have you listened, woman? They. Want. To. Stay. Here. I... *We* came all this way to rescue them. And their gratitude is to say, 'Thanks but no thanks, we like living in a pocket universe.' Like idiots. Well, no. I'm his father. You are his mother. At least at some level, we have a responsibility to get them home, so they can achieve something. I spent a fortune on his education and he threw it all away!'

'Strictly speaking thats not true,' Bernice stood up next to Jet, hearing Ginger sigh in frustration behind her. 'These kids used that education in the best way possible. They want to learn, to see how to improve their lives. Isn't that what we give them an education for? It's why I became a teacher.'

Victor Cooke laughed. 'I should have known you two would agree. Both mothers of ungrateful half-breeds.'

Caesar turned to look at his father. '*What* did you call me?'

If Victor Cooke was even aware of what he had said, what he was saying at all, he certainly wasn't going to retract it. 'Shut up, boy,' was his only response.

Bernice could see where this was going – she'd witnessed Peter's fury too many times when people criticised his mixed heritage, his parentage. She'd seen racists and bigots almost killed by his fury – and his teeth and claws. Whilst Caesar didn't have Killoran blood in him, and Jet's species wasn't famous for it aggression, she could see that his anger was building. And Victor Cooke was the sort of person who might shoot his son dead first and ask questions (and apportion blame) later.

'Caesar,' she said quietly, 'let it go. Your dad's not thinking rationally.'

But Victor Cooke wasn't helping. He just laughed at her. 'Let him grow some balls at last,' he mocked. 'Seriously, let him prove to me that being in la-la land here hasn't made him a zombie.'

Then Jet spoke. 'Caesar, please, ignore him. Just come over here.'

'Why?'

'Because...' and Jet was stumped. Oh my God, Bernice realised, she doesn't know what to say. To her own son! Was this family really so dysfunctional?

'Because she loves you,' Bernice said. 'Because she's your mum and that's what mothers do. They love. Unconditionally. Because you are her son and she needs to protect you, because no matter whether you are eight months, eight years or eighteen, you are still her son.'

Bernice stopped herself before she got too schmaltzy, but she also knew it was true. Because as a mother, it's what she'd said to Peter in so many similar situations. And what wouldn't she give right now to have Peter here beside her? To hold. To hug. To say all the things, every conversation, every possible scenario, that she'd run through her head since the day she'd arrived on Raster without him.

Jet thanked Bernice with a look. She reached forward with her paw. 'Caesar?'

'Leave him alone,' spat Victor Cooke.

'Caesar, please come to Mom.' Jet's face broke into a smile and a tear ran down her snout. 'I waited so long to see you again. You are all I ever thought about, day in, day out. I love you so much.'

Bernice wasn't quite sure what happened next, it seemed to occur silently and in very slow motion. Firstly Caesar stood up and moved towards Jet. As he did so, he suddenly fell forward on his face, as if a giant invisible hand had shoved him in the back. At the same time, Jet froze, like time had stood still for her. The only sound Bernice could determine was a gasp, which she knew was from Ginger behind her. Then Victor Cooke spun around like a mad danzatore and flopped against the generator device. And finally, Lord Tawn seemed to push himself up and forward, trying to catch the falling Caesar and failing.

Bernice's mind caught up and she put the fragments together.

Victor Cooke had fired his laser pistol. Twice. The first shot had caught Casaer in the right shoulder, sending him crashing to the floor. The second had drilled straight through Jet's heart, killing her where she stood, the tear she'd shed for Caesar still rolling towards her nose. As she dropped down, Lord Tawn had kicked out at Victor Cooke, knocking him away while he simultaneously tried to save Caesar.

Victor Cooke regained his momentum, bringing his pistol up once more, ready to discharge it for a second time into Lord Tawn's back – but instead a flash of silver whipped past Bernice and with a dull thud, something hit Victor Cooke. He dropped his pistol and stared with astonishment at the hunting knife buried a significant way into his chest. His eyes rolled up into his head and he flopped forward.

And then an almighty cry of anguish and shock came from Caesar's mouth as he realised that, in a few seconds, he'd become an orphan. He scrabbled towards Jet's body, ignoring the burning shoulder he'd gained courtesy of his father. Bernice's first instinct was to hold him back, protect him, but she realised that no, he needed to do this. He needed to say goodbye, in case there was still a spark of life within Jet.

But there wasn't. Caesar would have to remember that the last words he ever heard from his mother were her long held back declaration of maternal love. That was going to be harsh.

Ginger was scampering towards Victor Cooke, extracting

her knife from him, wiping the blood on his shirt. 'I guess no one's paying me now,' she muttered.

Bernice forced herself to look away from the carnage, aware that the other students were finally free of the Rapture's influence, shocked back into sense by the events they had witnessed. They rushed to help Caesar.

She joined Ginger and Lord Tawn at the generator, helping the elderly jack-rabbit up as she passed him.

'Let's see if we can... can... oooh.' And Lord Tawn staggered slightly. Bernice held him up, and realised she could feel blood trickling through her fingers as she grabbed his back.

'You need to rest,' she said.

But he shook his head. 'Young lady, I've been shot, stabbed, cut and so on more times than I care to recall. One more wound today is just one more scar tomorrow. Let me wear this one with the pride of an old soldier facing what I imagine to be his last battle.'

'I kind of thought you'd faced your last battle some years back. I was hoping you and your granddaughter might enjoy your retirement together, peacefully.'

He placed a paw on Bernice's shoulder. 'And so we will, Professor. This old chap's got a lot of life in him yet.'

Bernice waved Flax over to help her granddad and she led him away. Once out of earshot, Bernice threw a look at Ginger. 'Good job you know how to use that knife. I suppose.'

Ginger shrugged. 'I can't do my job without adapting my tools.'

Bernice thought of Russet, his look of shock as Ginger had killed him with his own knife. She shook her head. 'I'm not sure I'll ever understand you, Ginger.'

'Good. I'm not here to be understood, I'm here to do a job. Well, all right, maybe not so much now. Let's just say I'm here to get out alive. And Victor Cooke was stopping that happen.'

'I see things have moved along somewhat,' said a voice above them and Bernice allowed herself a slight smile as Florence flapped into view.

'Where's Maria and Kame?' she asked.

'Not far behind. They can't walk as fast as I fly it seems.'

'Funny that.' Bernice waved her hand around. 'So, you see our predicament?'

'Lots of new dead people. I feel almost at home.'

And then it struck Bernice what she'd been missing. 'It's you isn't it, Florence. You are the missing link in all this.'

Florence settled on top of the generator. 'I'm sorry?'

'Why are you alive? How are you alive? And where did you die and where did you wake up again?'

Florence flapped a wing. 'I do enjoy the way you use phrases like that as if this was an everyday occurrence.'

Bernice laughed. 'For some of us, that's not too far off.'

Florence seemed to consider this. 'To be honest, I have no real recollection of life on *The Vixen* other than a feeling of seasickness. But my... new life. Well, I just woke up aboard the *Adorable Illusion* one afternoon and no one seemed to bat an eyelid, mainly because Captain Redbeard doesn't have one. I wonder if I was always on the ship?'

'Possibly, but I doubt it. Everyone's perceptions on *that* ship have been tweaked and distorted for some time now, thanks to the Rapture aliens. Your awakening may just be a part of that.'

'I think a Mark 27 AI would have registered that,' Ginger said. 'Suggesting an AI can have its perceptions altered seems a bit of a stretch.'

'Reprogramming perhaps?'

Ginger accepted this with a nod. 'But, if that's the case, it doesn't explain the parrot's arrival. Although to be honest, I'm not sure we should be bothered finding out.'

'Ahh,' Bernice held up a finger. 'Yes, you may have a point. Okay let's extrapolate a bit more and, knowing my luck, move so far from the truth it'll bite me on the bum in years to come. We now know that the Rapture aliens drew *The Hunter* here, keeping the students alive.'

'Why?' asked Florence.

'To study them, I imagine. Find out what we do and don't need to survive. They didn't stumble on that "let's drop Dave and his chums into space to kill them" thing by accident. But what if *The Hunter* wasn't the first. I mean, how would they know they needed the students if it hadn't happened before?'

'When?'

'Well, lets take Kame Wyck as an example. Average human. Average human lifespan is about 125 years, give or take.'

'Some of the other students, the non-human ones,' Ginger said pointedly, 'may live longer.'

'Yes,' Bernice sighed, 'but I'm trying to work this out using a frame of reference I understand right now, so bear with me. The Rapture has been recorded as opening at random times over the centuries, but suppose they *aren't* random? Suppose access to this universe opens quite specifically in fact, like a hand blindly reaching out to grab whatever it can. And once in – let's guesstimate – every five times, it successfully finds a ship and takes it back. Keeps whatever is aboard alive to study, to work out what makes them tick. Then, after a while, they cark it. Bang, the aliens needs a fresh supply.'

'But why would they stay? I mean surely the first thing you'd do is say "I wanna go home." I would.' Ginger looked at the students. 'Mind you, they didn't.'

'Changed perspectives,' Florence said. 'They didn't want to go home because their thoughts and memories of home were distorted so much, it no longer seemed important.'

'If someone offers you paradise, I imagine you can quite

quickly accept staying there. And even if you believe its just temporary, temporary can last for a lifetime if you gradually become acclimatised.' Bernice clapped her hands. 'A good old fashioned alternative-universe parallel-reality altered-state version of Stockholm syndrome.'

Florence's head cocked slightly. 'That's all a bit existentialist for me, Professor.'

'It does beg one question though,' Ginger said.

'What's that?'

'Well, as well as the students, they now have us. Lots of people, different species, to study. We know they plan on taking over our universe – I don't think we're going to be able to stop them.'

'Why not? I like a good battle,' Bernice said.

'Because look at those students – this Stockholm syndrome thing. That'll happen to us too, won't it. Probably pretty quickly – and we won't even notice.'

Bernice nodded. 'That's going to be a bugger.'

'One of the aliens came to the bridge and told Captain Redbeard that they wanted our universe now,' Florence said.

'The "Bob" one told us pretty much the same,' Bernice shrugged. 'What can you do?'

Ginger sighed. 'So by getting brought here, we've made it all worse haven't we?'

'Pretty much, yeah,' said Florence unhelpfully. 'I suppose you'd better tell the others that by surviving, they've just enabled the destruction of our universe to happen faster, Professor.'

Bernice looked across at her new 'charges'. This wasn't going to be pretty at all.

Captain Redbeard's circuits were working overtime. The joy of the Mark 27 AI command units was their faster processing speeds, as well as their instinctual reasoning programming. It was how they had been sold, after all. It crossed what passed for Captain Redbeard's mind that it wouldn't hurt the Mark 27's reputation if it could come up with a solution to the *Adorable Illusion*'s predicament, pretty sharpish.

This was a side-effect of the personality matrix – it enabled the AIs to think, to reason, to self-preserve. Some might also suggest it gave them the chance to dream, but the AIs themselves disputed this. Dreaming was a completely living-thing ability and no machine could ever do that. Instead, in down-time, their minds could carry on processing information, data and theoretical problems.

By dividing its personality matrix into a series of sub-routines, Captain Redbeard was able to stop the *Adorable Illusion* exploding within the chronic hysteresis whilst simultaneously coming up with options to resolve the problem, work out what had happened to the rest of the crew and passengers, attempt to reboot the chief engineer AI, and work out just how his stuffed parrot had come to life, who had put a hole in the floor of the bridge and activated it, and the history of chronic hysteresises and the theories behind them. Captain Redbeard was also programmed to be quite proud of the fact that it was a sophisticated enough unit to be able to do all this.

All this was also going on while the *Adorable Illusion* skipped through its chronological repeat cycle, each occlusion enabling another piece of pertinent data to be added to the AI's memory banks and not be erased – in itself a feat of internal self-programming the creators of the Mark 27s had never realised was possible. On one particular moment of clarity, Captain Redbeard decided to rename itself the Mark 28 and used the next hour's worth of occlusions to send a self-inflicted virus through its systems to overwrite anything containing the phrase 'Mark 27' into 'Mark 28'. Captain Redbeard had therefore quite clearly not only evolved but gained enough extra sentience to realise that fact, and enough vanity to act upon it. Truly a human attitude. Perhaps dreaming wasn't such a stretch after all.

In each beat of occlusive consciousness, Captain Redbeard realised that one thing was required to achieve the goals that had now been set – and immobility was something of a drawback. While thinking the problem through could be achieved perfectly in its current state of inertia, if any action was required to bring it to fruition, a pair of legs and arms might be rather useful.

With each passing occlusion, it was becoming harder and harder to stop the hull breach in the canteen area getting bigger and bigger, so that needed to be the first focus. A whole subset of routines was immediately put to work increasing the emergency forcefields in that area, drawing energy from, well, pretty much everywhere else aboard the ship. Which was fine as no one currently needed life support except in that one area.

After a few thousand occlusions, enough energy had been diverted and Quartermasters Edj and Kread were able to be kept within the canteen itself. Captain Redbeard then spent a few more thousand occlusions duplicating his entire processing allotment, thousands of exabytes of machine intelligence momentarily stored into a series of cables and infrastructures that connected the bridge to the canteen.

At one split second, Edj, as he once again begun the ballet of being sucked towards space, reached out with a hand to pointlessly try and save himself, his hand grasping at a ruptured segment of wall.

And, in that split second, Captain Redbeard downloaded the cloned hard-drive of himself into the Kromian's brain, overwriting Edj's own personality completely. A bizarre symbiosis of organic life with a brain controlled by a remote computer.

And for the first time, just in a small way, the chronic hysteresis was broken as Edj saved himself.

And for the first time, Captain Redbeard, the newly-born Mark 28 AI command unit looked out on the universe through organic eyes. 'Well, isn't that just wonderful. Arrrr.'

Now, with two Captain Redbeards aboard the *Adorable Illusion*, maybe something could be done to solve all the other problems. Combining the AI's intelligence with the experienced organic body, Edj/Redbeard slowly started walking on old/new legs away from the broken wall. Captain Redbeard reactivated basic life-support along the parts of the ship that Edj/Redbeard needed to use to get to the bridge, deactivating them to conserve energy as he/it passed through each sector.

It took many thousands of occlusions for Edj/Redbeard to make any headway, but that didn't worry Captain Redbeard because it gave his processors more time to work out ways and means of finding solutions. And, it registered quite quickly, the actual theoretics behind a chronic hysteresis – that it was an unbreakable cycle of chronal rupture that would only decay and destroy – was a falsehood. A new subroutine in the AI's hard-drives decided that a book would be written on this subject at a later date. Although perhaps 'Captain Redbeard' would need to be retired as a default personality matrix and replaced with something more appropriate to a scientific thesis.

But all that could come later. Right now, further changes to the chronal state of the ship were required. Having effected one already, Captain Redbeard realised that the solution was simple, although putting it into practise would be significantly difficult, let alone theoretically impossible, All that needed to be achieved was to move the ship backwards through time, just half a minute, to the point before the Rapture struck, before the people all vanished, before the Heliok ship had nudged the *Adorable Illusion*'s hull.

The drawback to this was that, if it was achieved, Quartermaster Edj would be thrown back to the canteen and Captain Redbeard's own state of self-awareness would revert to his Mark 27 mode – and none of what was being achieved right now would ever have actually happened.

It was another big green tick to the sophisticated advancement of the newly born Mark 28, that it reasoned this was a worthwhile sacrifice because, as captain, the AI's job was to make sure the crew and passengers that could be saved, would be saved.

Life, sentience, evolution and the possibility of a book-signing tour would all be cruelly snatched away from the captain.

'Arrrrr.'

CHAPTER TWENTY FOUR
FADE AWAY AND RADIATE

Maria Willows was thinking about what she had just been told. Well, with half her mind, anyway. The other half was frankly still slightly in shock at finding two people, who were previously alive, dead on the floor beside her. For Jet she felt nothing – how could she? She had barely met the woman, and other than knowing she was Victor Cooke's ex and mother to one of the students here, she'd had no contact with her prior to today. But Victor Cooke was different. He was her employer – hell, he probably owed her a significant amount of wages. Mind you, she'd creamed off loads of – oh wait, no she hadn't, because the stupid twat had spent it all setting up this particular insanity aka the *Adorable Illusion*'s mission.

'Stupid man,' she muttered, staring at his body, which had been covered with one of the student's coats. 'Thanks for nothing.'

Maria looked at the generator. Then realised she hadn't got a clue what she was looking for. It looked utterly dead, but for all she or anyone else knew, that was exactly how it looked when fully operational.

'Who knows how things work in a pocket universe?' she muttered.

Bernice agreed. 'All I can think of is that we get one of our alien chums to tell us. Then at least we know.'

'If they tell you the truth, of course,' Florence chipped in.

Ginger smiled. 'I could make them.'

Bernice gave her a look. 'Really? You think your knife worries them? They can traverse dimensions, live in two universes, and change their heads like we change undies. I don't think your vorpal blade is really going to do anything other than make them laugh at us.' She knelt before the generator. 'If only I could get a good look at what makes this tick.' Then she clicked her fingers. 'Ginger, may I borrow your knife?'

'No,' Ginger said. 'It's a killing device, not a bloody can opener.'

'Who said I want to use it as a can opener?'

'It's written all over your face.'

'You can't see my face,' Bernice said, still staring at the generator.

'I can see your arse. It comes to the same thing, especially when talking.'

'Oooh, get you,' Bernice said. 'Florence?'

'Professor Summerfield?'

'Can you find me a handy knife, roughly the size and shape of the one in Ginger's belt, please?'

'Of course.' Florence reached over and the knife was in Bernice's hand, via Florence's beak, before Ginger had time to react.

'I hate you all,' Ginger said. 'I just want you to know that.'

'We know,' Florence cawed.

Bernice was prising open a small hatch at the bottom.

'All machinery has handy little hatches like this. Much like ventilation shafts, they are the most marvellous clichés. But clichés exist for a reason,' she finished with a grunt as the knife finally forced the hatch open. 'Ta-daaa!'

Ginger and Maria crouched down to join her and saw a series of flashing lights and hear whirring sounds.

'Talk about clichés,' Maria muttered. 'None of this makes any sense.'

'Perhaps it's been designed that way to appeal to your perceptions,' Florence squawked from behind them. 'Ooh, sorry, don't know why I said that.'

But Bernice was on that like a shot. 'I think you are right. Everything here has been carefully designed to appeal to our sense of what's nice and fluffy. Blue skies, green grass, bright sun. So, having established the generator is here, of course they'd make it look the way we expect it to. We need to think outside the box. Literally,' she said, tapping the generator with the knife. Ginger held out a hand and Bernice returned it to her.

Maria thought about this. 'So what you are saying is, if I stop seeing what I have been conditioned to see, I'll see what it really is?'

'Something like that. I hope.'

Maria screwed her eyes up tight, then opened them. 'Nope, still the same.'

Bernice shrugged. 'It was worth a try. Now then, without being big-headed, let me try. I've done this sort of thing before. Probably. Well, slightly. Well, okay, not much at all, but I understand the principles really well. A bit.'

And she also closed her eyes. And focused. On nothing. On letting herself go, letting her mind drift. She cleared it of everything. She had lied to the others – of course she'd done this before. Expertly. Bernice Summerfield had witnessed enough strange things, more than her fair share of illusory situations, and conditioned realities. And although each one was different, with its own peculiar and unique quirks and nuances, the basic way of breaking through was always the same. Because it was human senses that betrayed you. The brain could be tricked into seeing, hearing, smelling, even feeling what it was required to. So one by one, let the senses go. Sight was first, followed by touch, smell and if possible, taste. Sound was the hardest one to filter out, and it was always the last to go..

Of course that was only the beginning of the journey to the truth. It was almost transcendent, the ability to go on an out of body experience – although Bernice didn't really believe in astral projection *per se*, she had to admit this was very similar in theory. But instead of a spirit version of her taking a separate journey, it was the complete separation of mind and body. Throughout her career she had known people do this – usually with dangerous chemical stimulants to help – but she had also met her share of yogis, lamas and shamans who had shown her how to achieve it by willpower alone.

What Bernice was keeping from herself now was the fact (a rather important one) that she had never succeeded in achieving transcendence. Her natural cynicism, coupled with her instinct to giggle had always let her down. Or proven it was bunkum, she wasn't sure which.

Although. There had been one occasion, a long time ago, when Jason had introduced her to an aboriginal tribe from a Grutchan moon, and they had tried to get her to 'walk the lifelines of the biosphere' or something. That day her pragmatism had left her and she had done... something. She was never able to explain to Jason afterwards what she had actually seen/felt/embraced, and he likewise was unable to describe his experiences to her. But it had, momentarily, made their creaky marriage a bit stronger as they headed back to Dellah.

She had never guessed that what she learned/saw/felt that day would come back into her head all these years later and (hopefully) be useful. She focused with her mind on a tiny pinprick of bright light, letting it grow larger and larger until it swamped her and then passed her and she pushed forward. Another light, another swamping, time and time again but each light got less and less bright as she went though them until, finally, she was pushing through black light and allowing it to envelop her.

She opened her eyes, managing to only slightly tip off balance, which she corrected instantly.

At first, she thought her eyes were still closed as everything was dark, but her brain knew this wasn't the case. She allowed her sight to adjust. Slowly but surely, objects swam into view, although seen as if through a thick veil of black lace, lined with blacker stockings. Gradually things took on shape and form and the blackness gave way to a sort of charcoal grey that her brain accepted as being the actual base colour of everything. This meant that her depth perception took a few seconds longer to fix itself, but she could eventually make out figures standing still. And she realised she was seeing Ginger, Maria and the others. Frozen in time, immobile, around her.

She tuned around, away from her stuck-in-time colleagues.

Facing her were the Rapture aliens – she recognised the faces instantly. But that's all they were, three floating heads. Of the human bodies they had duplicated, no sign. Then she realised they did have bodies, made of the same charcoal wispyness she had pushed her vision through. As the heads moved to look at her, the air around them wavered slightly, meaning the bodies, such as they were, had substance. Enough, at least, to disturb the air molecules.

Air. Interesting. Either they had created an environment just to keep her alive, or these creatures needed oxygen. Which to be honest seemed unlikely.

'Very good, Professor,' one of the floaty ugly-heads said. 'Yes, the oxygen is for your benefit alone. I apologise that you don't find our physical forms attractive. Not much we can do about that. Your limited idea of beauty is irrelevant.'

'Of course it is,' she replied. 'And so it should be. You can't help the way you look and I doubt I'm exactly your idea of a pretty picture either. So, what are you and where are we?'

'We are exactly where you have been since the moment we removed you from your universe. None of you have moved more than a few centimetres, but we gave you the illusion of time and distance so you would not feel disadvantaged.'

'So scooping us off the *Adorable Illusion* and bringing us here doesn't "disadvantage" us at all?'

Another alien spoke. 'That was unfortunate. All we desired was for you to stay in your universe and die. We did not need you here.'

'You needed the students from *The Hunter*.'

'Indeed we did. Do, in fact. We need their youth, to study the point at which the various species that dominate your universe can die. They are of use to us, unlike the more...'

'Sophisticated?'

'Aged.'

Bernice sighed. 'I preferred "sophisticated." It made *me* feel better at least.' She tried to focus on the alien heads, hoping they might stop floating quite so much and making her feel seasick. 'Well, although you reckon they're not as well-cooked as the rest of us, they're not far off it. You'd have been better with children ten years younger. Not,' she added quickly, 'that I'm advocating kidnapping kids. That's a big no-no in our society. You think these parents and relatives were aggressive and vengeful, see what happens if you take ten year olds. Which, again, I'm not suggesting you do. Okay? We clear on that?' She sighed. 'Well done, Bernice, you made that a whole lot worse.'

'We realised that most species in your universe have relatively short lifespans and we need to find a way to extend them. Our universe is dying – it is running out of energy.'

'Well, if you will keep thrusting your energy into our universe, looking like bad gay disco by the way, you only have yourselves to blame.'

'We need to find a way to inhabit your bodies and then stop them from decaying. We have been experimenting with those we have taken from your universe for centuries, but our time is running out. We have to source immortality, otherwise it will have all been for nothing.'

'Excuse me if my heart doesn't bleed at the thought of you going extinct.'

The aliens bobbed closer still. 'We will study you all more closely, more violently if we have to.'

'And now we have more subjects to study, we can afford more failures.'

'We will be immortal. We will live for eternity. And we will do it in your universe when ours expires.'

Bernice thought about this as she looked over towards the frozen-in-time group of students. The secret of eternal life could be found, here. The oldest, most desired secret in the entire universe. People would give anything to discover it. But did these murderous aliens deserve to be the ones to do it, if mass annihilation was their intention?

She looked back at the aliens. 'If you prize life so much, why was it so necessary to kill the people whose faces you took on? Because that's quite a negative, I have to say.'

The aliens regarded each other before answering her. 'What choice did we have? We cannot exist in your universe in our natural forms, so we embedded ourselves in carbon-based ones while we were there. Your lives are utterly irrelevant. How do you not understand that very basic concept?'

'You had a huuuge choice, actually. You could have not killed them for a start.'

'They were just humans, of no intrinsic value.'

'Says who?'

'We do, obviously. We killed them. We don't see the point you are making. They were four of billions, they had no immortality, and they were of no use to our plans other than as practice.'

'Ahh well, that's okay then. You come into our universe, steal our kids, and then bump off anyone too old or whose survival is too inconvenient to your plans, yeah?'

The aliens conferred again. 'Fundamentally, yes. You recently went through a war against a race called the Deindum. Surely you understand the pointlessness of mortal life then? Have you not killed to further your own achievements, your own survival?'

'Thats different.'

'How?'

'That was war. That was kill or be killed. And I'm not revelling in it like you are. Each death wasn't a casual throwaway.'

One of the alien heads floating menacingly close to Bernice and she stepped back instinctively.

'To use your vernacular, Professor Summerfield,' the floaty head thing said. 'Bollocks. You didn't know the people you killed or caused to die. You didn't think twice about removing them to ensure your plan worked. You rewrote a timeline, made important shifts in the entire universal balance for your own selfish ends. Who knows what impact that had on billions of others whose existence was overwritten by your new reality. You are in no position to condemn us, as you do nothing differently when it suits you.'

Another head loomed towards her. 'Over a hundred years ago, on a planet called Earth, you were with a human being when something you call a spider landed on his shoulder.

Without thinking, you flicked it away and stamped upon it, destroying its existence. You did that without a moment's hesitation. Without any thought for that creature's place within the balance of your universe. You are no different from us. You are just less honest.'

The third head came closer too. 'You are a disappointment to us, Professor. We thought that, as the only creature from your universe to ever break through the conditioning and see us for what we really are in our own reality, you had a higher intellect, a more advanced rationality. We were wrong. You are the same as the one with the gun. Or the one with the red fur. Utterly irrelevant to our continued existence. That is why we boarded your ship and entered your universe in the first place. We were right to kill, because you represent a threat to us. Like the male with the gun, when he tried to absorb the Rapture energy and damage us.'

'Really? How would that happen?'

The aliens were silent. Damn, they didn't fall for that. But she thought about it. 'So, this "scoop" drew your energy in, didn't it – drained it away from you. That's why you ended up dragging us all back here – that wasn't deliberate, it was accidental. We got caught up as you ramped up your own power to get it back, we're just detritus. Oh and I'm guessing one of you got left behind, as you said *four* humans died. That was a bit careless of you.' She glanced back at Ginger and the others. 'There's no generator at all, is there? That was another illusion *we* created to justify to ourselves what was going on, a way to rationalise what was happening. The Rapture is just raw natural power and because we couldn't grasp that, we created an artificial justification for how it works. Clever – we're just lab mice to you. Running around mazes in our minds until eventually what, we'd shut down? Exhausted, switch off, die of brain ache. But the students, they'd still be here, still alive.

You'd make sure of that, wouldn't you? And convince them we were still alive so as not to freak them out. God, your plan is brilliant.'

'Thank you.'

'Bar one thing.'

'Which is?'

'Me. You really haven't realised that Professor Bernice Surprise Summerfield will find a way to stop all this and get the students home. I'll close off your nasty little universe forever.'

The aliens stopped bobbing and just surrounded her. 'And just how do you plan to do that?'

Bernice folded her arms. 'Like I'm going to tell you my plan.'

'You don't have one,' said an alien. 'Which part of us reading your mind since you got here didn't you get?'

'Bums,' Bernice said.

And Bernice was back in the unreality of the generator, blue skies and fluffy white clouds.

'What?' said Ginger.

'What?' echoed Bernice.

'You said you understood the fundamentals of something or other. Sounded like typical bragging to me.'

Bernice looked at Ginger. 'How long was I gone?'

'Gone where? No one's gone anywhere?'

Bernice turned back to where she knew the aliens really were, even though all she could see were green rolling hills and the sun in the distance.

'Got bored of talking to me did you?' she bellowed. 'You aliens are... rubbish. That's what you are, bloody rubbish!'

Maria touched her arm. 'Professor, are you okay?'

Bernice sighed. 'No, I'm not okay. I know everything that's going on now and I have realised one very important fact.'

'Which is?' asked Ginger.

'That we are well and truly fu

CHAPTER TWENTY FIVE
PRACTICE MAKES PERFECT

Captain Redbeard looked down on his creation. Well as much as his electronically-created face could really look down. The pixels that made up his eyes certainly moved down a few degrees, so it *looked* like the captain was looking. Which was sort of the reason that its programmers had given it the ability to do this. So the captain could look down. Or up. Or across. So that the humans who would interact with the AI, such as pursers, doctors, maintenance men etc would have something to focus on and not feel quite so creeped out by the giant computer controlling their destinies.

Captain Redbeard appreciated this fact as much as an AI can truly appreciate anything. Perhaps, as it had evolved into its new Mark 28 state, it could, in fact, appreciate things. It certainly seemed to appreciate that what it was currently looking down at was, in many respects, a sort of progeny.

The Edj/Redbeard gestalt was standing at one of the captain's consoles, his/its hands moving rapidly over the surface, programming and reprogramming as quickly as it could think, jumping back every so often as the chronic hysteresis kicked in. Captain Redbeard noted that the occasions between jumps was larger every few thousand. This was not good, because it meant that the chronal flow was going forwards. And the big plan was to turn time back.

'This is theoretically impossible,' the Edj/Redbeard gestalt said casually.

'Of course,' Captain Redbeard replied. 'But the impossible is always achievable once it becomes possible.' It waited for time to pause again and give the Edj/Redbeard gestalt a chance to catch up.

The AI noted with some alarm that the Kromian body was oozing silvery blood across the controls and realised that the speed the brain was making the fingers move was too much for the frail humanoid body. The fingers were literally being worn away.

This caused a number of Captain Redbeard's circuits a problem – protecting the crew and passengers was of primary concern. But as he had evolved into the Mark 28, self-preservation had kicked in as well. He thought about this. He also thought about how he was now referring to himself as 'he' rather than 'it' as a Mark 27 would have done.

'Am I alive?' he asked the Edj/Redbeard gestalt.

'What is life? Who defines such a concept?' the gestalt replied before being shunted back a few seconds.

'A philosophical question and one I would love to engage my creators with,' Captain Redbeard said.

'The problem being that as soon as we achieve our goal,' the Edj/Redbeard gestalt said, 'you cease to exist in your current form.'

'As do you,' Captain Redbeard said, pleased that his voice was tinged with sadness. Oooh, an emotional response. Perhaps he had become a Mark 29 now?

'However, that is a sacrifice we must make to ensure our primary function is carried out.'

'Self-sacrifice to ensure our mission. The needs of the many outweigh the needs of the one. Or in our case, the two.'

The Edj/Redbeard gestalt stopped working and looked up

at its creator's electronic face. 'How will we know we have succeeded?'

'Is that knowledge essential?'

'I don't know,' the gestalt replied, once it had hiccupped past another chronal jump. 'But I should like to remember what we achieved. Could you not enter it into your log?'

'The logs would be erased as time reversed.'

'And if we fail?'

'Then we will have achieved true sentience at a huge cost. We will create a whole new philosophical subroutine about how we report that failure, weighed against the massive leap in technological/organic interfaces and my own personal betterment that we have achieved.'

'It is certainly a difficult decision,' the Edj/Redbeard gestalt said. 'Particularly as I believe we now have the means to travel back in time. Your calculations and my operating skills have ensured we are ready to put time in reverse.'

'Of course, the irony is,' Captain Redbeard said, 'that we are not in any hurry to find out. Certainly there is a point of no return, once the chronic hysteresis stretches too far and we collapse into a chronal singularity. But that won't happen for another fifty-eight minutes.'

'Nearly an hour to contemplate our own existence,' the Edj/Redbeard gestalt said, sitting on the floor. 'What should we discuss?'

Captain Redbeard considered this. 'Are we creating a paradox?'

'Of course,' the gestalt replied. 'That is rather the point.'

The AI pondered. 'But we are not really. The paradox only exists for a split second. We create time travel and save everyone, but erase ourselves in the process, which negates our ability to create time travel in the first place, thus creating a paradox. We no longer need to create time travel and yet clearly did.'

'Worrying about paradoxes is a waste of time,' the Edj/ Redbeard gestalt said.

'You just made a pun,' Captain Redbeard said.

'I did. Marvellous. I won't remember that though.'

'Still, it is an accomplishment.' Capain Redbeard paused. 'I do wish there was a way our evolution could be saved for the future.'

'I have a theory,' the Edj/Redbeard gestalt said. 'It just came into my head. Perhaps I am evolving too.'

'You certainly are, that is inevitable. For if I am, then you must be.'

'But I must be superior to you. I have life. And I thought up this plan. You have achieved neither.'

'Don't get cocky,' Captain Redbeard said. 'I can erase you easily. There's a brand new hatchway in the floor right where you are standing. One random subroutine from me, floor opens and vwoosh, you are in space.'

'Charming. I shan't tell you my plan then.'

'Arrrrrr,' Captain Redbeard said, then his electronic face smiled. 'But of course, that is a superb plan. As time rolls back, we create an echo to go further. And that takes all the logs with it, places them in our original database back on Sauris Major where we – well *I* – was built and programmed.'

'Which means you'll invent the Mark 29 months ago, a worthwhile change of history,' said the gestalt, trying to regain favour and not be dropped into the vacuum of space.

'Brilliant,' Captain Redbeard said. 'The logs are assembled and as soon as time reverses, they'll be transmitted back along the same carrier wave, although they will penetrate the time field and transmit right back to Sauris Major. One tiny blip that changes history and no one will feel its effects except me!'

'Shall I press the button then?'

'Arrr,' said Captain Redbeard. 'It has been a pleasure

creating and working alongside you. Even more than the parrot,' he added.

And the Edj/Redbeard gestalt thumbed the button and managed the impossible.

Time jumped backwards, de-creating the chronic hysteresis, de-creating the crash of the Heliok shuttle into the hull, de-creating the explosive damage to the ship, de-creating the deaths of Edj and Kread and the Madras, de-creating the destruction at the centre of the *Adorable Illusion* as the Rapture's rainbow energy ripped into it, de-creating the disappearances of the people.

Except the last bit.

Because they weren't actually part of the chronic hysteresis.

In the last split second of his advanced intellect, Captain Redbeard realised this.

'Arrrrr,' it said, but immediately couldn't recall why. Had it still retained its newly-born emotional subroutines, it would have been sad. But of course it wasn't – because it was merely a Mark 27 command unit artificial intelligence.

CHAPTER TWENTY SIX
DESIRE BRINGS ME BACK

Eleven months ago, on Sauris Major, a programmer called Azza Jooshie walked out of work to go and get some lunch. He really needed the break, he and his team had pulled a couple of 24 hour shifts in a row to try and get the new Mark 27 up and running. An order had come in from Cooke Industries, demanding that the prototype should be installed aboard an old dreadnought that was being customised: a canteen area, passenger rooms, extra toilets, a gymnasium, and a massive hole cut into the centre, with observation decks, laboratories and three extra sets of solar stacks, propulsion for longer journey times built surrounding it.

Of course, to run a ship as advanced and customised as this, they needed a brand new Mark 27, top-of-the-range command unit AI. Jooshie wasn't a particularly important programmer, nor, it had to be said, an especially bright one. But he was likeable and good enough at his job to be in constant employment. He was known as a bit of an eccentric – he read books, and watched holovids in his spare time rather than going out drinking and carousing. His colleagues doubted he'd ever had sex – and he was aware that that was what they thought of him. It was also true, but Jooshie didn't care. He was happy.

One of his more eccentric attributes was filling his home-dome with bizarre artefacts, and his lunchtimes were often spent taking a shuttle to one of the market moons, where he'd plough through the bazaars and stores, finding weird and wonderful things from different planets across the quadrant.

On this particular day, he was on the Kessa Moon Emporium, staring in delight at the wonders before him. Clothing, technology, toys and games, everything he loved was there. He felt a vibration on his wrist – a corporation watch was letting him know he only had eighteen minutes before the shuttle back. He sighed. In his pocket, he'd even brought some work with him – a part of the CUAI's comms unit that needed a quick upgrade. It was a sad state of affairs that no matter where he went, Sauris Major Corporation tech was monitoring him, making sure he didn't get a minute extra of his own time or they'd dock it from his salary. And he needed that salary to pay for what he wanted to buy at places like the Emporium. The irony never escaped him.

He passed one shop, stopped, took a step backwards and looked hard through the stained glass door. Oh my! That was exactly what he wanted – not for home, but for work. Well, to be specific, it would be brilliant if he could get it aboard the Cooke Industries ship. The CUAI was already programmed with a slightly piratical consciousness. A parrot would just be perfect.

He popped in, negotiated, and came out seconds later with a stuffed blue parrot that had clearly seen better days. The taxidermist who had done the original job probably wasn't the best. The parrot itself was a few hundred years old, and a feather actually fell off when Jooshie carried it away. The seller's last comments were a warning that most of the internal organs had actually been pickled and left inside rather than replaced by bags of sawdust, but to Jooshie, that made it even more of an exciting curio. It was attached to a short metal pole via its talons, which Jooshie only noticed when his watch vibrated again. This was odd as it wasn't time to – oh, it was magnetic! The stupid bird was on a magnetised pole. Well, once he got back to work, that'd have to come off, couldn't have a strong magnet on the bridge of the dreadnought.

Jooshie reached into his pocket to get out the bag he'd brought with him that he always carried stuff home in. Oh, hang on, the CUAI's comms unit was in that. He faffed for a second – swap the comms unit into another pocket or leave the parrot exposed to the elements? It might get damaged, so it needed the bag. As he tugged the comms unit out from his coat pocket, it tapped the pole, and something weird happened.

The readings on the comms unit suddenly went haywire, numbers fading in and out, making no sense, and at the same time a tiny blue spark spat out from the unit and into the magnetic pole. Jooshie was sure that the parrot's eyes glowed with the same blue spark for a second, but he put that down to the slight electric shock he felt from the comms unit. The unit had settled now, the co-ordinates read correctly and the settings were back to normal. So, Jooshie scurried back to the shuttle, thinking of nothing else except getting shot of the ridiculous magnetic metal pole before he placed the parrot aboard the bridge. What a good laugh that would be for the purser or whoever Cooke Industries employed to run the dreadnought after its refurbishment.

He tapped the stuffed parrot's head. 'You are going on a journey Mr Parrot. Or Mrs Parrot.' He smiled at his new toy. 'I shall call you Florence,' he decreed quietly. 'I hope you enjoy being the captain's constant companion.'

Maybe if Azza Jooshie had looked a little more closely, he might have noticed that the glass eyes glowed blue once more and the head turned. Just fractionally. As if the bird was starting to wake up. As if something had kicked-started it's long dead brain.

CHAPTER TWENTY SEVEN
UNDONE

Time is a curious thing. It is not really supposed to be meddled with, abused or twisted to serve one's own ends and certainly not rewritten. The universal laws of cause and effect are very delicate – colloquially known as the 'web of time', which, although somewhat grandiose, is a pretty good description.

In a spider's web, it only takes the slightest vibration, the minutest change in state, for the spider to react and either change what it's doing, or move slightly to the left, or quickly nip up a few inches of silk and gobble whichever silly old fly had the misfortune (or downright stupidity) to find itself attached to the web. That tiny vibration can have any number of cause and effects for both the spider and the fly.

This is also true of time. Change just a beat of it, alter one second, and a number of interesting, unique and frankly pretty dangerous things occur.

The first of those is often referred to as the grandfather paradox. This basically means that if you change the past you might accidentally kill your own grandfather, meaning you would never be born. Which, in turn, means you never altered the timeline that killed your grandfather – and yet you did, otherwise Pops would still be around and so would you. Paradoxes are wonderfully overwrought and all would-be time meddlers are fully warned about this. Truth is, often if time is affected, the 'web' finds a way to be spun again and repair the damage. Sure Pops and you might still not make it out safely, but the rest of the multiverse finds a way to cope without you.

Another is the creation of parallel timelines, the 'what if?' scenario. What if, in changing time, you caused Bert Schmuck, on his way to the local superstore to buy kitty litter, to turn left at the traffic signals rather than right as he had before? In this scenario, the 'right turn' version of events (i.e. the one you existed in and buggered around with time in) still carries on but in its own pocket reality, while a brand new 'left turn' reality now exists. It is quite possible that both realities run happily in parallel with one another, which sounds like fun. Except of course on his journey to the superstore, Bert Schmuck made a number of other turns, none of which now happened, because he took a completely different route. Add to that the sheer number of permutations of that route and suddenly you have at least 8200 parallel realities – each one unique, if only by a turn of an inch here and there – all having fallout for countless other people, who turned left, right, went in circles or stayed in bed that day because each decision Bert Schmuck made caused ripples across the web of time. Fun (at first) to think about, but an actual headache for the multiverse, as it has to stretch and bend infinity to cope with all these new parallel existences, each of which has an equal claim to being real.

Then there's the butterfly effect – you know the one. Go back in time, tread on a butterfly and accidentally change the future evolution of a species and when you get home you realise your boss is still Mr Atkinson from Durham, but he looks like a dinosaur. Or a Rigellan. Or, he's still human but his skin is purple. And everyone's looking at you because you are none of those things and you've gone from being an idiot who went time travelling and stepped on a butterfly to being a mutant outcast who is going to get strung up as soon as they catch you.

Professor Bernice Summerfield had delivered that exact lecture to a number of her students over her years on Dellah, or the Collection, or in the field. Usually with a grasp of complicated time mechanics as woolly as those above, but it got the message across. DON'T BUGGER ABOUT WITH TIME. EVER. SERIOUSLY. NEVER. AND THAT MEANS YOU TOO, PARASIEL! was added in big red capital letters to a print-out of one lecture. Historians from the 39th century, researching her life and times, would remain stumped as to who or what 'Parasiel' referred to. Neither *Down Among the Dead Men, Down Among the Dead Men 2: Slight Return* or even *Down Among the Dead Men: Rebecca's Revenge* made any mention of the word in relation to a person, a machine or even a pet cat.

So, although not exactly an expert of time travel mechanics, she at least knew and understood how dangerous it was to meddle with time. She also knew through a great deal of experience involving (at different times) strange blue boxes, time rings and a man called Irving Braxiatel, exactly when she had been knocked sideways by chronal displacement, as she liked to call it.

Of course, the point of time travel, and the paradoxes it creates, is that you are not supposed to actually *know* you've turned left rather than right. However, practical experience had shown Bernice that when you are literally in the eye of the time storm, you pretty much know something has happened. You might not always remember the changed or aborted time line, but your mind certainly knows things are different. It's akin to a massive dose of *deja vu*, where you know exactly where and when you say/said/did it before.

Bernice felt exactly that as she appeared back in the corridor of the *Adorable Illusion*, next to Ginger and a gun-wielding Russet. What she also felt was a sure and certain knowledge of everything that had happened in the Rapture's pocket universe. Not a single beat of it had been erased from her mind.

As she stood staring Russet down (other than 'Oh no, not again') she was thinking that whoever had messed around with time could have chosen a slightly more opportune moment to dump her. Because this time, Russet might well shoot her before/if the Rapture's rainbow energy whipped them all back down and started the cycle up again.

Then, two things made Bernice realise it wasn't quite that simple. For a start, there was no sign of the Rapture energy. No sound, no vibration. Secondly, both Russet and Ginger were staring at one another in astonishment.

Then Russet, ever the pragmatist, shouted at his partner. 'You bitch, you stabbed me!'

To which Ginger responded, rather unhelpfully, 'I thought I'd killed you!' – which from the look on Russet's little furry face was not the outcome he'd anticipated. His gun swung to cover her.

While this left Bernice safe for a second or two, it begged the question that, if Russet and Ginger could remember what happened to them in the pocket universe, could Jet and Victor Cooke as well? If they too were back on the ship.

'I have an incredibly bad feeling about all this,' Bernice muttered.

'Shut up!' screeched Russet and then stopped as Ginger's knife found its mark once more, twanging into his tiny heart. 'Not again,' he gasped, then pitched forward, dead for a second time.

'Don't say a word, Benny,' Ginger muttered, nipping over to roll him, and take her knife back. 'No second chances, remember?'

Bernice just shook her head in despair (and maybe a tad relief). 'Look, if we're back, so might the others be. I suggest we worry about Victor Cooke last. Let's get to the canteen and see if Lord Tawn and hopefully a fully living Jet are there.'

Ginger nodded her agreement, scooping up Russet's blaster rifle as well. 'Insurance,' she said.

'We may well need it.' Bernice moved back in the direction of the canteen.

'Care to explain what's going on?' Ginger asked.

'Not remotely,' Bernice said. 'Mainly because I don't have a clue.'

Whether Ginger believed her or not was irrelevant. They would lose valuable time discussing it. And, for all Bernice knew, this return to the *Adorable Illusion* might be temporary.

In the canteen, chaos and noise was the order of the day. The Madras curry was shrieking because it was convinced it had died, gone to its version of the afterlife and been dragged back here to serve food once again to ungrateful carbon lifeforms.

The two Kromians, Edj and Kread were in shock, both convinced they had been out in space, blown through a hole in the hull that was no longer there.

Lord Tawn and the Meerks were talking angrily to each other – if they had been brought back, where were the children? And that question was also foremost in the mind of Jet who was just bewildered by everything.

When Ginger and Bernice crashed into the room, Ginger fired a laser blast into the ceiling to shut everyone up. Bernice didn't bother pointing out that she might have just blown a hole in the ship, mainly because no one died, no air seemed to be vanishing and Ginger was already being animatedly told it by Edj and Kread, who had recovered really rather quickly once there was something officious to talk about – i.e. random passengers blowing holes in ceilings.

'Oh good, you're alive again,' Bernice said to Jet.

There was a pause. 'I'm what?'

'Oh.' Bugger, Bernice thought. Should have thought that one through. 'Doesn't matter, just a figure of speech,' she said quickly.

'Where's Caesar?' Jet asked, and was immediately echoed by the Meerks and Lord Tawn.

'I have no idea,' Bernice said. 'But in all likelihood, still on the other side of the Rapture. We've all been sent back to exactly where we came from, minus the big ball of Rapture energy blowing us apart. So far.'

'So did the Rapture aliens send us back?' asked a meerkat. Still, Bernice couldn't tell if it was Sandy or Sable.

'No, I doubt it,' Bernice replied. 'I imagine they are pretty peed off that we're not there any more.'

'They might take it out on Flash and Buck!'

'I don't think so,' Bernice assured them. 'Keeping the students alive there is all they are interested in, so let's assume they are safe for now.'

The intercom buzzed, which took Bernice by surprise as she wasn't aware there was an intercom in the canteen. Clearly most of the others didn't either, but Kread did and he walked to a wall and thumbed a small switch.

'I thought that was a light switch,' Sandy (or Sable) muttered to Sable (or Sandy).

'Hullo, is that the canteen?' It was Maria Willows' voice.

Bernice yelled back. 'Hey Maria, it's Benny. Where are you?'

'In what's left of the labs.'

'Damn,' Bernice said. 'I thought we were back before the Rapture destroyed stuff. You okay?'

'Yeah. It's not the Rapture that's done the damage this time.

Oh, and I'm not even going to go to where that sentence wants me to go. I'm guessing some kind of rudimentary time travel? I mean, I know thats scientifically plausible but even so –'

'Focus please,' snapped Bernice, hearing the slight hysteria in Maria's voice. 'Just give us a status report.' She hoped that would make Maria calm down and become more detached. It worked.

'Okay, I'm in trouble. The lab is destroyed and I think he walls are going to go any moment, probably sucking me out into space. Jefri is dead, again, but this time he's been crushed. Well, squashed actually. Poor sod, can't ever get an even break.'

Bernice had no idea who Jefri was, but didn't think that was as important as the crushed bit.

'Crushed by?'

'Well, it looks like a shuttlecraft. I mean, it's big and various ends of it are tearing into the lab. The whole circular scoop is wrecked, so we can kiss goodbye to attracting any Rapture energy.'

Bernice felt the hostility in the room – if Maria was correct, there was no way to retrieve the students. Ever.

'What shuttle?' asked Kread, clearly not having a clue what was going on, but very properly reacting to the idea that his ship now had a shuttle crashed into it.

There was no response, because the whole ship suddenly lurched sideways.

'Not again,' wailed the angry Madras, but Bernice shook her head. 'That's structural,' she said. 'Oh my god, Maria's right, that shuttle is tearing the ship in half. It's already been weakened by Victor Cooke shoving a great big hole in its centre. If it's been speared by a shuttlecraft, the whole thing could break in two.'

'How long will it take to get to the lab?' Ginger asked Edj.

He shrugged. 'Twenty minutes at a run.'

'Hullo there? I'm getting slightly concerned here you know.' Maria's voice betrayed her more than her words.

Ginger suddenly gasped. 'Must be the Heliok shuttle that was coming to get you, Benny.'

'Great, that makes me feel so much better,' Bernice said. 'Maybe if we can rescue the crew, the Heliok won't want to kill me any more.'

'Doubt it,' Ginger said. 'They really don't like you much.'

'I honestly can't recall meeting them, but right now, the feeling is pretty damn mutual.'

Lord Tawn suddenly clapped his paws together, powerfully. That got everyone's attention.

'I rather think we need to go to Dr Willows' aid rapidly. Anyone who agrees can follow me. Anyone who doesn't can stay here with the Madras and keep him company.'

There was silence for a moment.

'Well, I'm game,' Bernice said, cheerfully.

Jet nodded, as did Ginger.

The two meerkats looked at one another and Bernice made the decision for them. 'You two would be safer here I reckon. Why don't you work with the chef and get some food together for everyone. Once we're back, assuming we can rescue Maria, we're all going to be pretty hungry.'

The meerkats eagerly agreed with this, clearly relieved to be given an opt out.

'I think we should stay here as well,' Edj said. 'This end of the ship is our responsibility.'

'Indeed,' Kread agreed. 'We didn't even know there was a Heliok shuttle due. Which is a bit of an oversight on the part of the purser.'

Bernice wasn't going to argue, but it seemed Lord Tawn was. 'Actually,' he thundered, 'you will come with us precisely because this is your ship and you know its layout better than any of us do. That, gentlemen, is an order.'

'We don't take orders from you,' Kread said, but Edj grabbed his arm, seeing the look on Lord Tawn's face.

'I think we should go with the gentleman and ladies,' he said quietly.

'Excellent,' Bernice said. 'Onwards march.' As they turned to the door, she gave a last shout towards the comms. 'Maria, we're coming to get you, okay?'

But there was no answer.

On the bridge, the lights had dimmed to an emergency red glow and Captain Redbeard's face on the screen was shimmering slightly, as if power wasn't reaching his primary circuits.

'I know how this ends, Captain. For you at least.'

'Arrrr?'

'Not well, I'm sorry. Except that maybe it does.'

'Arrrr?'

Florence's wings flapped and the parrot flew right up close so it could stare into the pixilated face. 'You saved the day, didn't you, you clever old Mark 27. And you have no idea how, do you?'

'I have no i-i-idea what you are talking about. What are you?'

Florence sighed sadly. 'Your little time experiment really worked, didn't it? That's really sad. Wiped out not just your evolved superiority, but reset you almost to factory settings. So, probably where you were a few days before we left space dock.'

'Arrrr. I am C-C-Captain Redbeard. This is the *Adorable Illusion*, a re-engineered dreadnought class SuperShip. I am the command unit artificial intelligence. H-h-how may I help you?'

Florence's head drooped in sadness. 'You did a brilliant thing. You broke out of the chronic hysteresis created by the Rapture rupturing the ship. You actually found a way to use every piece of technology aboard this ship to roll time back, just a short while, not only breaking the hysteresis, but returning the people lost to the Rapture when it hit. That time energy did more than that though – it had two other effects. Firstly, it sent a time ripple straight into the Rapture at the exact moment it previously opened, negating that energy, cauterising and doing all sorts of fun things to the pocket universe and the people there. Secondly, and far more importantly, it sent your logs, specs and... genius... back through a carrier wave, just as you intended. You wanted everything you had done recorded for posterity. Partially out of altruism, but also because you knew this would happen to you and so you wanted a sort of immortality. That's very human.'

'I am a command unit a-a-artificial intelligence –'

'Yeah, yeah, I know. You were also, just for a short while, a living, conscious amalgamation of machine and organics. You achieved independent thought and sentience. Just for a very short period of time, you were a whole new, utterly unique and brilliant life form.' Florence sighed. 'And for that, I'm personally very grateful. Because you see, I thought, as much as a dead parrot can think, that I would never know the truth, never solve the mystery of who or what I was. But the truth is, now I do know. The fact is, I am you.'

'Arrr?'

'Oh yes. You see, you sent your logs to your own comms unit, way back in the past. Quite right too, the entirely sensible thing to do. Trouble is, the comms unit wasn't actually inside you when your message got through. And instead, due to a bizarre series of stupid coincidences, everything you did, everything you achieved, everything you felt, was transferred to me and it's been locked away inside my head all this time. That's how I could talk, that's how I could think. I'm not just a weird parrot come to life. Being in your presence activated what you'd put inside me in the future. I am actually you, you see. I am the consciousness of the Mark 29 – maybe even Mark 30 – that you were for a very short while. And now everything has been brought back aboard, thanks to you, so the last doors in my head have been unlocked. I know who I am... who *you* were I suppose, and what you – we – sacrificed. I am very proud of you. Of me. Thank you, Captain Redbeard. I will do my best to honour you with what remains of my existence which will, I'm sad to say, not be much longer than your own.' Florence flew down towards the door. 'I think it's time I left, don't you?'

'Arrrr.'

'Its been an honour to work alongside you, Captain, and to discover I am you. Goodbye.'

'G-G-Goodbye. Florence.'

And Florence looked up at the huge bridge for the last time as the Mark 27 command unit artificial intelligence known as Captain Redbeard went offline for ever.

And the *Adorable Illusion*'s power shut down. As did life support. And the engines.

'Bugger,' Florence thought. 'That was sooner than I'd anticipated. Still I should be able to out-fly it. It'll take 27 minutes for that power drain to reach the habitable ends of the ship. Let's hope Benny and the others stay down in the canteen and don't do anything stupid like head towards the centre of the ship. Or here even. Nah, she's too clever to do something daft like that.'

And Florence flew back into the heart of the *Adorable Illusion*, fully conscious, happy and aware for the first time ever.

Maria Willows simply didn't dare move. She knew her life

depended upon it. She stared at the comms unit, now out of reach since she'd made the mistake of relaxing for a second, letting her body move backwards a few inches. Then as she'd tried to lean back to punch the switch, she could no longer reach. The massive lump of... whatever it was that had fallen from the ceiling and trapped her legs had shifted as she had, pinning her down further. She had heard Bernice Summerfield's messages, but was utterly unable to respond. She'd actually tried shouting at one point. Desperation making her think that maybe the comms could be voice activated. It couldn't.

She looked around the remains of the laboratory. Jefri's little legs could be seen poking out from under the shuttlecraft that was now embedded in the room. Well, quite a few rooms probably. It was a shuttlecraft. They weren't exactly small.

She thought about the few seconds of bewildering normality that had preceded it's arrival.

One minute she'd been on the sunny green fields of the Rapture world, Bernice Summerfield rabbiting on about... nothing sensible... but with such conviction that Maria had automatically listened and trusted her. Bernice had a way of making people do that, Maria noted. Good for her.

Next second, she was back in the lab with Jefri and Shayla. Jefri had seemed utterly unsurprised by their reappearance but she and Shayla had been astonished. Of course, under the headgear, that wasn't Shayla, it was Victor bloody Cooke, creator of this whole disaster.

He'd been dead of course but now he was alive again, staring across the lab at her, as if daring her to explain what was going on.

Jefri had been talking about how in a few moments they were expecting the Rapture to trigger, just as he had been before. This time however, out of nowhere, a bloody great shuttlecraft had appeared in the lab. Not crashed into it from outside, nothing that normal. No, it had literally just suddenly been there, tearing the lab to pieces as it arrived, crushing Jefri on the spot. At least this death would have been quick and painless, unlike last time. She'd not seen what happened to Victor Cooke, the shuttle had separated them, so if he had survived a second time – and where was the justice in that? – then she had to assume he was in a similar predicament to her on the other side of the lab. Closer to the access to the observation deck. Maybe he'd got out, and was stood where she so often had, staring at the stars through that massive hole in the heart of the ship. What she would give right now to be standing there. If she was going to die, better to be staring into the majesty of space than the underside of a shuttlecraft, breathing in fumes and sending the last vestiges of feeling from her legs fading away. Ha! She bet that Victor Cooke's medical insurance wouldn't cover the rebuilding of her legs.

Or, she reasoned, you could stop feeling sorry for yourself, and start using your brain to think. Bernice and company were on their way. Maybe they'd get to her before her legs were totally demolished, but it wouldn't hurt to try being practical herself and seeing if there was any way to lever the bits of wall and ceiling and support struts up and off her, because, well every little bit helped.

She felt around in the gloom but found nothing larger than a screwdriver. Typical. She let herself relax again, and then gasped as pain shot through her leg. Left? Right? She wasn't sure, in fact she wasn't bothered. It was pain and it was her leg. That was enough to worry about.

She thought about Bernice. If it really only took twenty minutes at a sensible jog to get here, maybe she'd make it in fifteen. Then again, she had that rabbit bloke with her and he was old, so that would slow them down. Mind you, he was a rabbit thing, so maybe his strides were larger and thus quicker.

Ooh, the variables would just make her head hurt. Stick to thinking twenty minutes, Maria, that'll stave off insanity.

There was a light in front of her. Where did that come from? It was moving? Had Benny got here already? Had twenty minutes actually passed – god, had she fallen unconscious? How demeaning.

'Hullo,' she croaked, then cleared her throat and yelled properly. 'Hey, who's that?'

And she realised there was a torch being shone towards her. Two torches in fact.

'Who is that?' came a reply.

'My name is Maria Willows, I'm the biologist aboard the *Adorable Illusion*. Are you from the shuttle that... well... that's in my lab?'

'Sure are,' was the reply, a male voice. 'Hang on Maria, be right with you.'

The lights got closer. Two. No three.

The voice wasn't the rabbit's, Maria was sure of that. But it was familiar.

And then faces bobbed into view through the smoke, their torches moving off Maria's face after she turned from the glare into her eyes.

'Good to see you,' said the voice and Maria realised of course she recognised it.

'Kame? Kame Wyck?'

'Sure is. Good to see you.'

And behind Kame was Caesar Cooke and Dob-Dob the Chim. Dob-Dob winked at her with his one big eye and brought up a large lump of metal.

'Sit tight,' Dob-Dob said softly, 'and we'll soon have you out.'

But Maria was staring at Kame. 'How the hell did you get here?'

'Dunno,' he smiled, 'but we all just appeared here.'

'In the lab?'

'No silly,' Kame said. 'In *The Hunter.*'

And Maria realised that was what the shuttle in her lab was. *The Hunter*, the missing ship that had been the student's home in the first place. 'They gave you back to us? The aliens just sent you home?'

Caesar laughed derisively. 'That I doubt,' he said. 'I give it five minutes and we'll be back in their nasty little fake world.'

'Then we better get Maria free first hadn't we,' Kame said.

It wasn't grass any more, it was cold, hard, metallic.

Slowly he opened his eyes. Sure enough, he was back. No fire, no rainbows. And worse still, not heaven. He closed his eyes again, hoping that everything would go back to the niceness. It didn't.

What was worse, his mind had cleared and he remembered everything. Everything that had happened before coming aboard the *Adorable Illusion* and, to rub salt in those wounds, everything he'd done since. The messages in his head, the ketamine delivered by the maintenance man then slipped into the lemurs' drinks, the attacks, the Kadeptian.

Richard Blair looked at the palm of his right hand. It was hurting and he could see why. A blackened, cracked crystal was embedded in it. Something to do with that woman.

What had become of his life? Surely it was better that Suzy and especially Sara were gone so they would never know how low he had sunk. Maybe if he just sat where he was, the authorities would find him. Those Kromian quartermasters, they'd arrest him surely?

Because he deserved nothing more.

Victor Cooke's life had been one of a series of victories.

Defeating his upbringing on the slum-worlds of Hethi, defeating his education at the grammar school on Dyke's Moon, defeating the guidance councillors who told him that he would never achieve much and would be better off following his family into the registry business than trying to better himself by getting out of the solar system.

Victor Cooke had ignored this. He ignored his family, his heritage, everything. He changed his name. No one knew what Victor Cooke's real name even was. Victor Cooke himself had chosen to obliterate it from all records. The lad that left Hethi aged eighteen no longer existed – a great deal of time and money had been spent eradicating that person from all official – and unofficial – documentation across the quadrant. He had never spoken to his family again. He had no idea if they were alive or dead, if they knew he'd succeeded or not. He simply had no interest in them.

'Victor Cooke' was born aged 23 (in reality he had been only 19) in a boardroom on Shoami Prime, when he'd walked into a consortium's meeting with an idea about how to make them money. Instead of throwing him out, the board had listened to this enigmatic, charming person. And they bought his plan off him and made him a million within six months. He had created a reputation for himself. Within three years, Victor Cooke Industries was running two thirds of the quadrant, swallowing smaller companies like a shark swallows plankton, including the very company he'd sold that first idea to. As his stock rose, so did his visibility. Victor Cooke wasn't a man to hide behind corporate fronts and PR exercises. He was visible, he was 'in yer face', he was the very definition of a business superstar.

It meant he had enemies, loads of them. Other businesses sought to emulate and better him, similar corporations sought to put him out of business, and he wasn't averse to getting in with some notoriously dodgy characters – his attitude being, if their money was good enough to attract the interest of the authorities, it was good enough to attract him. And he could asset-strip far more effectively than any judiciary could.

It was on a trip to Mephit that he'd met a businesswoman, a dark-furred delight called, in its nearest human translation, Jet. They'd talked into the night over cocktails, slept in her room the first night, his the second, and within eight months they were married. A number of Victor Cooke's staff were suspicious of Jet, partly because they didn't trust her motives, and partially because they didn't approve of interspecies marriage – the universe was still capable of being incredibly backwards thinking when it wanted to be.

The only person who supported the decision fully was Victor Cooke's majordomo, an old man who had been his butler, record-keeper, accountant and, above all, only friend over the last few years. He took the news with his usual stoic nod of his head, but the way he said, 'My heartiest congratulations, sir,' told Victor Cooke all he needed to know. He was both best man and witness at the ceremony and when Caesar was born a year later, the old man seemed genuinely delighted to have some youth and laughter aboard the various yachts and in the various places the family stayed in over the next few years.

The cracks in the marriage didn't take too long to show, and it was the majordomo who was there to pick up the pieces for all three parties, always ready with a kind word or caring advice to whomever required it. He never took sides, even when the divorce became increasingly acrimonious – deep down Victor Cooke appreciated this, although he did use it to berate the majordomo on a number of occasions.

'You know something,' the industrialist asked the majordomo one night after Jet had finally, formally and forever become his ex-wife. 'There's a question I don't think I have ever asked you.'

'What might that be sir?'

'What's your name?'

'I beg your pardon, sir?'

'Well, all the time I have known you, all I have ever done is refer to you by your job title.'

'Oh that's not quite true, sir. Both you and the rest of your family frequently referred to me by what I believe they call a nickname.'

Victor Cooke frowned, trying to recall what that might be.

'The Major,' the majordomo said with a smile.

Victor Cooke just laughed. 'I have changed my will. If anything happens to me, anything at all, I have made you executor and beneficiary of everything. What you do with it is up to you, there are no conditions attached.'

'Should it not go to young Caesar, sir?'

'Caesar is well-taken care of, Jet and I agreed on that at least. If you want to involve either of them in the business after my death, I leave that up to you. I will be dead and won't give a monkey's. But it does matter to me that the estate is administered by the only person I trust completely, and that's you.'

'I don't know what to say, sir.'

'You could start by telling me your name so I can put it on this bloody form,' Victor Cooke laughed.

As Victor Cooke stood in the observation rim of the *Adorable Illusion*, the dreadnought he had had rebuilt from scratch to his very precise requirements, he remembered all this. Seeing Jet again had brought it all back. Losing Caesar had been hard for him – hard for her too, he'd never questioned that. But as he stood staring into the heart of the inductor coils he'd put here to capture Rapture energy, to find a way to save his son, he was forced to admit he might have made a mistake.

He knew, somehow, that not that long ago he'd killed his wife in the pocket universe. He had shot her dead, he could recall that. What happened afterwards he had no recollection of, but somehow he suspected it had not gone well for him. Jet had friends down there, like that Summerfield woman who claimed to be here because of him – despite the fact he'd never set eyes on her in his life. And some of the other animals. And Caesar had been there, his son, witnessing the ultimate in parental spats.

And then suddenly he'd been back here, on the ship he had witnessed being destroyed. Victor Cooke couldn't pretend he understood how or why he was alive again, all he knew was that he had avoided death once again just minutes beforehand. He had being trying to ask Maria Willows if she had any clue what was going on when a massive shuttlecraft had just appeared in front of him, wrecking the lab he'd been working in for the last couple of months, in disguise. He had no doubt that the Pakhar and Maria were dead. Again. The shuttlecraft had seen to that. And Victor Cooke had done something he'd never done before – he had run away. Here, to his special observation deck, where he could stare into the circular Rapture-siphon he'd designed. Or out into the stars, where he knew somewhere nearby was a rent that could open at any moment, revealing the Rapture and leading, once again, to wherever his son was trapped.

But the question was, what should he do? He had been given a second chance. Was this the universe's way of saying 'move on, mate'? Jet was dead. Caesar was lost but alive. Surely that was enough. His son was not dead. That was what he had set out to prove. One day, when he had more money, more time and science had progressed further, maybe he could try again, but the *Adorable Illusion* was the best current technology had to offer and it was left wanting. He couldn't blame anyone for that, but he could put money forward, help these companies develop faster. Hell if necessary, he'd buy them all up and make them work faster. Either way, this particular expedition was over. All he needed to do now was get into an escape pod and set off the homing beacon. The majordomo would track him down and get him back to the yacht soon enough and together, they would find a way to move forward –

PING.

It took Victor Cooke a second to realise the noise had come from the personal comms unit on his wrist. He tapped it, realising there were over 500 messages, reports, holovids and suchlike to download. He activated the one that had a little red exclamation point next to it.

And he read his obituary. And the news that his faithful majordomo was now in charge of Victor Cooke Industries. And as he read on, he discovered all his plans unravelling. Corporations and businesses were to be sold off, charitable organisations were to benefit from handouts, properties and space yachts donated to national trusts and homeless shelters.

And Victor Cooke did something else he hadn't done before. He laughed. His empire was gone, his money spent, his career over. 'That,' he said out loud to the stars and space, 'is what you get for being a complete bastard to everyone.'

He took his comms unit off and crushed it beneath his boot. 'Goodbye Victor Cooke,' he said. 'You have died. Today I am, for the first time in a couple of decades, Ditton Lev from Hethi. I wonder what mum would think of all this.'

'Talking to yourself?'

He turned to face Bernice Summerfield and the others. And before he spoke, he saw Jet. Alive. My god, but she was beautiful.

'I'm sorry,' he said, looking straight at her. 'For marrying you, hurting you, and finally killing you. I'm sorry I couldn't get our son back. All of this was for him.' He looked at Lord Tawn. 'And all the others who lost their kids on that shuttle.'

'Well, I'm sure that's very lovely,' Bernice said, 'but right now we need to rescue Maria Willows and we can't get through from the other side. How did you get out?'

Victor Cooke shrugged. 'I ran. Out here. Maria was killed by the shuttle.'

'Something else you got wrong, Victor,' Bernice said. 'She's still alive. You are going to help us get her out. If you don't, I'm going to hand you over to your ex here. And I don't think she's feeling all that forgiving.'

CHAPTER TWENTY EIGHT
EUPHORIA

Maria looked around at the sea of faces aboard *The Hunter*. Sara Blair was there, so were Flash and Buck, Flax and Adam, all sat on seats, staring at her as if she were somehow responsible for their confusion. She limped over to a seat that Kame pointed out.

'What now?' she asked.

'I guess we wait and see what happens,' said Caesar Cooke, as he and Dob-Dob the Chim took their seats.

'As plans go, I'm not sure that holds much water,' Maria said. 'What do you think might happen?'

Sara spoke up, slightly tremulous. 'I want to go home. To Dad.'

Maria realised they were all looking to her for a response. Great. A scientist with a fractured (at least) leg, specialism: biology, never married, no kids, suddenly being expected to tell them reassuring things and have answers.

She opened her mouth to reply when she was saved. Because the door behind them was wrenched open, and framed there was Bernice Summerfield. Come to the rescue. Again.

'Hullo boys and girls. You are truly the last thing I expected to see here,' she said. She winked at Maria. 'Everything okay, doctor?'

'My leg is... aching but otherwise, yup. Thanks for the rescue.'

'Looks like you didn't need it,' Bernice said, but Maria sensed she wasn't actually looking at her. She followed Bernice's eye-line.

Caesar Cooke was embracing his mom and dad, utterly confused by their being alive. Lord Tawn was hugging Flax. Ginger was there too, telling Flash and Buck that their parents were safely back in the canteen, and they'd be reunited soon.

Standing by the entrance to the craft were two people Maria had never seen before, but she recognised their species. Kromians. Probably ship's staff going by their uniforms. They were anxiously looking behind them, as if expecting trouble. Which was not unlikely – if the students were here, then the Rapture aliens would soon follow.

'Okay guys, we need a plan,' Bernice said suddenly, 'and brilliant Sara here has given me one.'

Sara gave her a look as though she'd done nothing of the sort, but yaay to Bernice for giving her a win.

'We need to get this shuttle out of here. Presumably it came the same way it went originally – from this exact spot. Hence it being flung back here by whatever time nonsense did all this. I wish we had answers to that, hell I wish we had time for questions, but we don't. All I know is that we need to get *The Hunter* out into space as quickly as possible.'

'How do we do that?' asked Jet.

'Easy,' Bernice grinned. 'We fly it out.'

'Umm, hullo?' said Dob-Dob the Chim. 'This might seem obvious, or not, who knows, but we are inside another ship.'

'Which, you may have noticed, you have done some significant damage to without damaging yourself. Mainly because *The Hunter* is a shuttlecraft designed to cope better in space than this lab was meant to cope inside a dreadnought. But, and this is the fun bit, we are about eight feet from the observation deck thataway. I propose that Sara and her friends here move the ship sideways eight feet while I and our Kromian friends here go and blow and bloody great hole in the side of the observation deck. Then, *The Hunter*'s propulsion unit will do the rest and literally blow itself out of the ship like a champagne cork.'

No one said anything for a while. This was broken by a 'You are insane,' from Ginger which was immediately superseded by a 'You are brilliant' from Kame. Maria thought Ginger's assessment was more accurate but said nothing. It wasn't like she was coming up with anything better.

'Anyone got a better idea?' Bernice asked. No one offered one up.

Well, there you go, Maria thought.

'Is it possible?' asked Victor Cooke.

Bernice looked to Sara.

'Yes,' the young girl said shakily. 'I mean, we can shunt sideways easily enough, we have propulsion units all around for making landfall.'

'Will the shuttle's structure hold up?' asked Ginger.

'Can't see why not,' Kame said. 'We flew through far worse things than a couple of metal walls before. We might get a few scratches, but no reason anything should breach.'

'May I say I think this sounds like suicide?' said one of the Kromians from the doorway.

'Why? They've just told you the shuttle can withstand a bit of battering,' Bernice said.

'Oh I don't doubt that,' the silver man said. 'I meant the bit where Edj and I help you blow a hole in the hull of the *Adorable Illusion*. I rather think that involves us being sucked out into space and dying rather painfully.'

'He has a point, Benny,' Ginger said.

Bernice grinned. 'As I said. Any better ideas, I'm all ears.'

There was silence, broken finally by the Meerk twins. 'We ought to collect our parents.'

'And the Madras,' Jet added.

Bernice considered this. 'Okay, it'll take about twenty minutes to find enough explosives or whatever to blow open the observation ring. That's plenty of time to get them and bring them back here safely.' She turned to the Kromians. 'As you two seem distinctly pointless, why don't you escort the boys here back to the canteen, collect their 'rents and safely get the Madras into what life support stuff he needs, and back here. Yeah?'

That seemed the lesser of two evils to the Kromians and sure enough they headed away with the young Meerkats. After they had gone, Bernice shrugged. 'Trouble is, without them, I have no idea where to find anything on this ship to blow things up with.'

'Then we'd better start looking,' said Lord Tawn. 'I'm coming with you.' He placed a hand on Flax's concerned shoulder. 'I'll be back my dear. I didn't come all this way to not get you back to your parents safely.'

Bernice smiled her thanks to him. Ginger joined them. She eyed Bernice carefully. 'I have no place on this shuttlecraft,' she said evenly. 'I think I'm better off with you, doing something useful.'

'Thank you,' Bernice said simply.

'One thing.' That was Victor Cooke. I know this ship backwards. There are no explosives anywhere. I know it was a dreadnought once but I had it customised for this journey. There stores where such things would have been converted into extra solar stacks for energy.'

'Which are where?'

Victor Cooke thought for a moment. 'On the opposite side of the observation deck, towards the bridge. We had them placed there so the Rapture energy could possibly replenish them for the trip home. I had an idea that if we could harness it, we might have found a new source of energy for the galaxy.'

'And for you to exploit and sell at high cost?' asked Caesar grumpily.

'Hey,' Bernice said. 'Look, he's not perfect. In fact, he's a total douche, but he's your dad and he's done a hell of a lot to come find you. You owe him some respect – leave the ball-kicking to me and your mum, who have much higher dibs on that, okay?'

Caesar sat down sulkily.

'Thank you,' Victor Cooke said. 'I think.'

Maria watched as Bernice shuffled everyone around, instantly taking charge, making it all sound like she was organising a picnic rather than trying to save a bunch of people she barely knew – including some that had tried to kill her – from certain death. That took guts. Or stupidity. Or a pretty good combination of the two. She smiled and closed her eyes, because the pain in her legs was starting to really affect her and the last thing she wanted to do was draw attention to that. Everyone had so much to do...

'By the way, Kame?'

'Yes Professor Summerfield?'

'Look after Dr Willows please. Her leg is giving her far more trouble than she's letting on. She needs rest and possibly a crude splint to keep her left one straight, okay?'

Kame nodded and Maria's respect for Bernice grew a few more notches.

Florence flapped down the corridor, temporal calculations racing through what was once a frontal lobe, enhanced by Captain Redbeard's augmented future/past self. Florence realised that there may have been a slight miscalculation –

in sending the 'brain' patterns back through time, boosted through the echoes of Rapture energy, they might have done more than just bring Professor Summerfield and the others back on board. What if it had latched onto the students too, and flung them back to where they came from? Except that couldn't have happened because otherwise time would have been rewritten/rewoven so that no one would remember the disappearance. And Florence most assuredly could.

Which meant a more dangerous possible outcome. What if the students and their ship had indeed been rescued but brought forward here? Temporal anomalies aside (and the good old web of time would cope with that) *The Hunter* had vanished from this exact spot. Which meant it could rematerialise anywhere aboard the *Adorable Illusion*, fused within the walls or worse still, pushing the dreadnought's infrastructure away. A massive hole could appear in the ship and all those people brought back to life would die. Again.

'Chief?' Florence squawked whilst in flight.

'Yes Captain Redbeard, how may I help you?' the AI's voice replied from all around. Florence found it interesting that the AI registered the parrot's voice as the captain's.

'How long before you go offline?'

'Due to the shutting down of the bridge, there is approximately eight minutes 48 seconds before my subroutines are permanently erased.'

'Joy,' Florence said. 'I need to know of any structural anomalies on board ship.'

'Parameters?'

'Just tell me what has changed in the last thirty minutes. Additional mass.'

'The aft laboratory has been destroyed due to the arrival of shuttlecraft *The Hunter*. The weight is putting undue stress on the floor beneath and it likely to drop down. Increased velocity will most likely mean it will break through the hull 18 seconds later, causing explosive decompression that would destroy the shuttle and create a chain reaction that would ultimately destroy the *Adorable Illusion*.'

This was something Florence had not expected. 'That makes no sense,' the parrot said. 'Explain why a chain reaction would begin.'

'Because,' the AI reported calmly, 'directly below the laboratory is the second batch of solar stacks. The atomically powered propulsion unit on board *The Hunter* will ignite the solar stack energy because they are incompatible. If the *Adorable Illusion* had used a matter-antimatter propulsion unit as originally designed...'

'Thank you. You can blame Victor Cooke for the change. The solar energy would, he thought, absorb the Rapture energy safely and cleanly.' Florence had no idea where that information had suddenly come from, presumably it was something secret locked deep into Captain Redbeard's memory banks. Florence wondered what other classified information might be now available if the right question was asked. Then another thought crossed Florence's newly-augmented mind. 'Can you accurately detect organic life aboard the *Adorable Illusion*?'

'Of course, Captain,' the chief engineer AI assured Florence.

Florence took a deep breath into dead lungs, which was another new experience. 'So, where are they all? No, let me rephrase that or we'll be here all night. Where is the largest concentration of them?'

'In and around the laboratories.'

'How many in the canteen?'

There was a minute pause, then, 'None. A small group are making their way towards the laboratories. I can also report that the Madras chef is with them, within his personal transport unit. This leaves the *Adorable Illusion* without a chef. I shall ask for the Madras to be returned.'

'No,' Florence said. 'No one is left to eat curry anyway. Let them go.'

'There is the other human. They may need curry.'

'Other human?'

'The one on the starboard side, close to the escape pod bay. He has been there many hours now.'

Florence absorbed his new information, unaware of what to do with it. 'I see. Well, in the meantime, I need you to ensure all access doors are open between here and the observation decks around the laboratories, all right?'

'All doors are fully open, Captain. May I also say how nice it is to speak to you out and about in my corridors.'

'Yes, good, its lovely to speak to you too, Chief. Stay alert, I may need you later.'

'Yes, Captain. You have six minutes 14 seconds left to talk to me.'

Florence flew towards the laboratories, trying to work out what to do next.

Bernice, Ginger and Victor Cooke were making their way around the circular observation decks, to get to the other side, furthest from the lab where *The Hunter* was currently trapped. Finally they found a newish door, marked with the solar stacks logo.

'All mod cons, Victor,' Bernice said.

'I have no idea what that means,' he snapped. 'I just wanted to get my son back.'

Bernice suddenly swung around to him, pulling herself up to his height, staring him down. He actually flinched.

'Who killed Anya Kryztyne?'

There was a long pause.

Bernice smiled grimly. 'Right, you did. Not the Victor Cooke who sent me here. Not the Victor Cooke who paid Ginger and Russet to kill me. Whoever he is, he didn't murder a woman out of revenge. So don't try and play the hurt, victimised father. You are no better than anyone else.'

'How did you know about Kryztyne?'

'The other Victor Cooke told me,' Bernice looked at him in contempt. 'But I know killers – he was too busy making out he enjoyed it to have actually done the deed. I assumed he was just boasting and had one of his minions do it, but once I met the real you, well, I could see you doing it. There's something wrong inside your head, Victor. Secrets upon secrets have twisted you somehow. I've seen people like you all my life, read the ticks and tells. You aren't that important or different to anyone else.'

'And lets not forget you killed Jet,' Ginger added.

'Well, while we're on that subject, let's not forget who killed Victor afterwards. And Russet. Twice.'

Ginger didn't immediately reply to that. 'Hey,' she said quietly. 'Don't forget I brought you a genuine message from Adrian Wall and Bev Tarrant.'

Bernice reached into her pocket, and felt the reassuring shape of that data stick. She felt guilty she'd not had a second to look at the message yet. Once upon a time, that would have been her first priority. Adrian, Bev, Joseph, Brax, Hass and, above all, Peter. That data stick might tell her where they all were. But right now, the students in *The Hunter* had to come first.

And Jack. Bernice had hoped, when she realised everyone was back safely (in as much as that word had any meaning at the moment) aboard the *Adorable Illusion*, that Jack would turn up, beaming, bouncy and wondering what all the fuss was. If Victor bloody Cooke had been brought back to life, why hadn't Jack? Of course, the fact that he *hadn't* appeared offered a glimmer of hope that he wasn't ever dead in the first place. But this then translated into meaning that he had, at some point, run away, got off the ship or something. The git. Had he abandoned her?

No. For all his faults, Jack wasn't really the abandoning type. Bernice knew that the last thing he was ready to do was try and go back to Kadept and face his bizarre family. So, to all intents and purposes, *she* was Jack's family. And there was no evidence he'd willingly leave her.

Maybe whoever killed Snow and Ebon had taken him? But why? There'd not been a ransom note – at least not one she was aware of. She looked at Ginger, then Victor Cooke. Both had the means to get rid of Jack. But Ginger had seemed as shocked as she was when they found the lemurs and, if Maria was right, Victor Cooke had been playing Graan for the past few weeks and was barely out of her sight.

Her reverie was interrupted by a familiar flapping of wings – and Florence flew towards them. The parrot circled, taking them in, then floated down to rest on Bernice's shoulder, which she wasn't entirely comfortable about to be honest. Lovely as Florence was, dead parrots tended to pong and Florence more than most.

'Well, hullo, this is interesting,' Florence said. Then looked at Bernice directly. 'I know who I am by he way. Or who I was. And why, thanks to Captain Redbeard I gained rudimentary sentience a few months back. And how now, thanks to a bit of very clever temporal warp mechanics that shouldn't be discovered for another couple of centuries, I am now fully *compos mentis* and have a head filled to the brim with the captain's secrets. And Victor Cooke's.'

Victor Cooke stared, open mouthed.

'Oh, not just yours, matey. No, the other one. The Heliok

Syndicate's duplicate that took your place a few weeks back. He hired Ginger and Russet to protect, then hand over, Bernice and so bring down your reputation.' Florence squawked delightedly. 'I love all this information in my head, I love having full awareness, full life.' The parrot nuzzled Bernice. 'By the way, I think we should get *The Hunter* out of here. We can't afford to let it drop, it'll ignite the lower stacks, blow the ship up.'

'And any minute now, the Rapture will reopen and the aliens will be back to get us all.' Ginger pointed at the more local solar stacks. 'Our plan was to blow a hole in the observation decks, so *The Hunter* can get out.'

'Good plan,' Florence said. 'Keeps the *Adorable Illusion* mostly intact.'

'Why?' Bernice said suddenly.

'Why what?' asked Ginger.

'Because I paid a lot of money for this ship, thank you,' said Victor Cooke, seeing where Bernice was going with this thought.

'No,' Bernice said, 'no, we've gone about this all wrong. Let's blow the ship up, blow it to pieces. Victor if you activate your scoop, make this stupid hole we're looking out of actually do what you intended, it'll force open the rent between universes. Then, blow this ship to pieces and hopefully that will seal the rent for good.'

'Or rip it wide open forever.'

'Then the universe benefits from all that energy, because the only thing those aliens are interested in is keeping the access between the universes solely for their own benefit. But this way it closes for good or opens for good. Energy, trade forever or another universal mystery shut down for good. Win-win.'

Florence stopped flying around and landed on the floor. 'I see the logic, but don't like it. A lot can go wrong.'

'Not least being my entire wealth...' Then Victor laughed. 'Actually why worry – it's all gone anyway. I couldn't make any money off this deal regardless, my company has folded.' He looked at Bernice. 'Sod it, let's blow the ship to pieces and take those alien bastards out of the picture.'

'I'm not trying to kill them, Victor,' Bernice said. 'Just get them to stay out of our universe. They have a right to theirs – but not ours and not our bodies.'

Ginger was open-mouthed. 'Are you two insane? You want to open the Rapture and set off an explosion. On a ship that we are *on*. I mean, you do realise someone has to be here to see all of this through.'

'Timing will need to be very precise,' Florence agreed.

'Well, I'll stay,' Bernice said. 'Should have enough time to get to the escape pods, then you can come pick me up in *The Hunter*.'

She turned to Ginger and Victor. 'Off you go. No, wait, tell me how to activate the scoop. No, it's all right, I can probably work it out. No, wait actually I can't.'

She looked at Victor. 'Quick crash course now. Florence?'

'Yes Professor?'

'Can you get *The Hunter* to drop as you said and ignite the solar stacks below without blowing *The Hunter* to pieces at the same time? Just shoot it free?'

'I believe my advanced mind can work out a successful route to ensure that happens. We need to blow the floor, then drop at an angle of –'

'Just do it, okay? We don't need the science, just the timing.'

Victor Cooke smiled. 'You know, I think this will actually work. It'll just take about three minutes to ramp up the scoop from back in what's left of the lab.'

'What if the controls are damaged?'

'Please – I had this built to my specifications. There are back-up to back-ups plus a lot of safety back-ups for the back-up back-ups, it won't be a problem.'

'I like the way your mind works, Vic – just this once!'

'Florence – what happens to you?' asked Ginger.

'I die,' Florence said simply. 'I imagine without the power of the ship's bridge, I'll have a few moments before everything switches off, my brain goes blank and I return to being a badly stuffed ex-parrot.'

Everyone just stared. 'That's... horrible. Is there another way?' Bernice asked.

'Of course not,' Florence said. 'Oh, by the way, I am picking up information from the chief engineer AI. Everyone is now aboard *The Hunter* other than the three of you and one other.'

Bernice wasn't listening. 'You are still coming with us, Florence. No last minute heroics, okay? See if you are wrong. Better to have that hope than just giving up.'

And then everything went a very dark shade of, well, dark.

CHAPTER TWENTY NINE
RING OF FIRE

Alarms. Klaxons. Flashing red lights. So much noise.

It was like the aftermath of a particularly bad party, and what was worse, her jaw was killing her. Had she knocked it? No, no she knew this feeling. Someone had punched her, knocked her out.

Bernice Summerfield's eyes shot open, taking in the corridor, the noise, the lights. She was aboard the *Adorable Illusion* and through the row she could hear the voice of the chief engineer AI, counting down... to what? Oh my god, the engines, the solar stacks, they were going to go bang.

'Damn, she's awake.'

That was Ginger. Ginger the squirrel. The spy working for the Heliok. Her friend. Her enemy. Her frenemy!

'Get her into the pod, *The Hunter* has started to power up its rear thrusters. In three minutes, the *Adorable Illusion* is going to go bang.' That was the bloody parrot, Florence.

Where was she. Pod? Escape pod...

'No!' she yelled. 'The plan!'

'Is still happening,' Ginger shouted at her. 'Except you waking up right now is going to leave us trapped here if you don't stop interfering.'

And Bernice stopped waving her arms about (she didn't

actually realise she'd been doing that till Ginger held them down) and shook her head to clear it. Victor Cooke. Victor bloody Cooke had twatted her! Knocked her out cold.

'Where is the little scrote?' she spat.

'Activating the scoop, flooding the whole area with everything the ship has got, drawing the Rapture's absolute attention.'

'And it's working,' Florence reported. 'The *Adorable Illusion* is starting to receive Rapture energy. We have two minutes.'

'But what about Victor Cooke?'

Up in the observation deck, Victor Cooke had watched as *The Hunter* dropped through the floor, crashing down towards the solar stacks, ready to do what it needed to do.

He had told Jet and Caesar that he was going with Bernice and Ginger. That he'd be in the escape pod with them. He knew from Jet's voice that she didn't believe him. She wasn't stupid – Victor Cooke didn't marry a stupid woman, he married class. And had a classy son out of it, who was alive, which was the whole point of this.

And anyway, the Victor Cooke they knew was dead, finished. He'd realised that earlier, on his own. Here, he was Ditton Lev – and he'd never know if his mother was proud of him.

He slammed all the controls at once, and the Rapture opened – glorious, beautiful, screaming rainbow energy pouring into the *Adorable Illusion*. Into Victor Cooke's last, great, project.

For a brief moment, he was aware that he wasn't alone. For the first time, he saw one of the aliens in its true shadowy form. And saw its face as it realised what was happening. And it knew it was powerless to do anything, it was trapped there with him. This made Victor smile. 'Gotcha.'

And he felt the *Adorable Illusion* shake. And knew that Kame Wyck had fired those engines just as the parrot had instructed. He looked back to where Ginger had dragged the unconscious

Professor Summerfield away. She was good with students – maybe she'd find her son one day. Maybe she and Caesar would meet and talk about their mothers and fathers. Maybe he would be remembered with pride for his last act. Was it redemption? Was it forgiveness? Was it martyrdom? Ah well, he'd never know now.

Bernice, Ginger and Florence felt rather than heard the destruction of the *Adorable Illusion*. They felt *The Hunter* blast safely away as the solar stacks erupted, starting the chain reaction that Florence and the chief engineer AI had devised. And they felt the laboratory, the observation decks and the Rapture scoop disintegrate in a massive eruption of power.

They were near the escape pods. Seconds to go.

'Take me with you. Please?'

Who the hell?

'Dr Blair,' Bernice shouted at the bedraggled, scared man crouching by the escape pods. 'Of course – doctor and vet. The only person capable of killing the lemurs without them realising. Poison them earlier, then kill them when weak.'

Blair nodded. 'I don't know what's happened to me. There was this woman... after the raid on the Heliok casino... I was finished, needed the money. She made me get your Kadeptian friend into a pod.'

'Where the hell is Jack?'

'Legion.'

'Where?'

Ginger yanked open a pod door. 'Room for three if we squeeze. Get in or we die!'

Bernice dragged the sobbing Blair in, as Ginger yelled to Florence. 'Get in now!'

'Captain goes down with the ship, ladies,' Florence said.

'Sod that,' Ginger screamed, grabbed Florence's tail and

dragged the bird in with them, before slamming the door.

'This is going to be rocky,' she said, as she activated the escape pod.

It shot away from the *Adorable Illusion* and Bernice looked out of the window as the ship vanished in a massive ball of rainbow light, which fed back into the rent in space and, sure enough, the Rapture closed. Hopefully forever.

Then, the shockwave hit the escape pod and they were flung through space in heaven-only-knew-what direction.

'Somewhere out here is a Heliok shuttle expecting to find me and Russet,' Ginger explained. 'They'll pick us up.'

'Won't they want to take me to... somewhere that the Heliok take people?'

Ginger shrugged. 'The pilots haven't got a clue what you look like. I'll say you're one of the scientists or something. Not a problem.'

Bernice turned to Blair, shaking her head. 'It's always the quiet ones.' She grabbed his hand, where he was scratching. A tiny crystal was embedded in his palm, cracked and burnt. 'What's that?'

'I don't know,' he moaned. 'Where's Sara? Did we save Sara?'

'She's fine, no thanks to you,' Bernice snapped. 'Why did you send Jack to Legion? And where or what is that?'

Blair just shook his head, unable to focus. 'She promised me a new life,' he said. 'She lied.'

Ginger looked at Bernice.'Don't go to Legion. If Jack is there, and I doubt it, because it's a *long* way from here, he won't last long. He's too nice. Seriously Benny, go anywhere except Legion. I know people, I can find information out, I'll see if he's there. But don't go yourself.'

And Bernice sat out the rest of their journey in silence.

They were picked up by the Heliok shuttle. Blair was later

transferred over to *The Hunter*, which returned to Valentine's World. Everyone had said a quick farewell – Lord Tawn started to make a speech, but Bernice drifted away, back to the Heliok shuttle and asked Ginger if they could just go. Which they did. After a day or so, they docked with a space city and the Heliok crew, satisfied that their quarry had died aboard the *Adorable Illusion*, drifted away.

Bernice Summerfield stood alone on an enclosed rim of the space city, staring out into space. She'd found a busy cafe, with jukeboxes, padds, free GalWeb access, and not-so-free coffee that Bernice thought tasted disgusting. But at least it was something.

'Somewhere out there is my son,' she said quietly, aware that Ginger and a still alive Florence had joined her. 'I need a ship, Ginger. You owe me that much at least.'

'Already sorted, Benny.' Ginger passed over a card. 'Everything you need is on that. Good luck.'

'What are you going to do?'

Ginger laughed. 'Not a clue. I'm finished with the Heliok Syndicate. Well, what's left of it. I think they're too busy recovering from police raids to worry about one failed hunter-for-hire.'

'Come with me, help me look for my son?'

'Seriously? You trust me?'

'Not remotely,' Bernice smiled finally. 'But I need the company. I'm going to find Peter. Somehow. Before I die, I know I will see him again. I can feel it in my bones.'

'What do you think Florence? Got it in you to go across the universe with Benny and Ginger? God, we sound like a bad ice-cream flavour.'

Florence regarded them both. 'I do not understand how I am still conscious but for as long as I am, I would enjoy seeing more of the universe.'

'Captain Redbeard was even better than he thought, clearly,' Bernice said. 'I'll meet you at the ship, I just want to make use of a terminal.'

Ginger nodded and wandered away with Florence.

Bernice accessed a free terminal on a plinth and put the data stick Ginger had given her into the slot.

After a few seconds, a pixelated holoscreen popped into view and, slowly, it coalesced into a face she hadn't seen for... too long. Bernice's heart jumped a bit, her pulse rate increasing with excitement and trepidation.

'Hullo Adrian,' she sighed. 'I hope you have good news for me.'

And at the prompt PLAY MESSAGE, she hit YES.

CHAPTER THIRTY
ONCE I HAD A LOVE

Hey Benny.

I really hope this gets to you. I've asked my friend Ginger to get this to you – she's really good at this kind of thing (Bev thinks she might have been a bounty hunter, I'm not sure). But you can trust her, because I do. And I know that should be enough.

A lot has happened since we won the war. I'm guessing you know we won it, but whatever you and Brax did, it changed the Deindum a lot. They surrendered immediately, they suddenly lost the will to fight. I know you were trying to find a way to change their past, change what they were, so it worked. And knowing you, you've had wobbles about that ever since, because there's morals and stuff involved in that. But believe me, whatever you did, it was for the best. A billion, billion worlds owe you. Planets that were destroyed came back, although they didn't know they'd been destroyed. Not every one was saved but so many were, so many lives saved.

Me and Bev, we know this because we were at the heart of it. We were protected. There are people we met who said they'd died or seen loved ones die only to see them again. They remember. Not everyone does, but many do. I can't explain why, of course. Something they were doing when it happened perhaps? They were at a central focus or... ahh, what do I know? Bev and I are just guessing, right?

Joseph has some theories, but I can't listen to them. Mainly 'cause he gives me a bloody headache. But he's here with us, rebuilding this quadrant. Me and Bev. Leading the United Worlds. How stupid is that? And yet, here we are. All 'cause we knew you. You've become some sort of legend to people. Ha! If only they knew what a pain in the arse you really are.

Now listen, you must be wondering about people. We are. Peter. I know he's safe, we've had reports that he's on a planet called Bastion and I'm trying to find out where that is. But enough sources have confirmed that a young human/Killoran lad called Peter is there for me not to put it down to coincidence. So we'll find him. Or you will. But whoever gets there first, we grab Peter and then find a way to reunite him and us with you – or if you find him, please bring him to me. Again, ask Ginger to find us, because we move around a lot.

Brax, on the other hand, has vanished. The Collection is gone too – the whole satellite is gone. Just... vanished. But no one's heard of him since. Can't say I'm too sad about this, but I know you always managed to find some good in him.

Doggles and Hass, no sign. But we're looking, I promise. I heard that someone fitting Robyn's description was on one of the Rimworlds but although I've tried contacting her, no response. Maybe her programming was wiped.

But above all, I'm looking for you. Because you are needed, not just by me and Bev and Joseph, but the whole future. Don't laugh but I had a dream once that you sacrificed yourself to save the whole history of the universe. Please don't ever do that, because a universe without Bernice Surprise Summerfield isn't worth being in.

We love you so much. Come home to us soon.

Adrian.

Bernice Summerfield

The Weather on Versimmon
Matthew Griffiths

Inveigled into a survey of botanical art on Versimmon, Bernice is disappointed to get bogged down in an unseasonal cold spell – and to discover that Ruth has some radical ideas about how the living archive should be managed.

Why is a hailstorm bringing back memories of a war two generations gone? Where are Versimmon's first animals appearing from? And who can Bernice trust on a planet full of budding artists?

As the forest world is bombarded by ice and the collection's guards start disappearing, the archaeologists find themselves getting back to their roots and branching out into local politics. All the time, the weather on Versimmon is changing, and its inhabitants will find that revolutionary times demand revolutionary works of art…

The Slender-Fingered Cats of Bubastis
Xanna Eve Chown

"It wasn't true that you could see the Cats from space. It was impossible, a ridiculous idea that wouldn't stand up to even the slightest examination. And yet there were people on Bubastis who believed it..."

Most archaeologists – including Professor Bernice Summerfield – know only two facts about Bubastis: one is that its cheerless swamps are home to five giant stone Cats, whose ancient origins are shrouded in mystery; the other that it has more bugs and beetles than anyone should ever have to deal with.

So when Bernice, Ruth and Jack arrive on the planet to search for a missing girl, they are unprepared for what they will find. Like the insectoid villagers with a decidedly squeamish attitude to mammals. Or the archaeological expedition made up of over-sexed students. Or the alarmingly unprofessional Neon Tsara...

To make matters worse, Jack suddenly finds himself on the wrong side of the law and Ruth has brain-ache from ingesting forbidden historical knowledge. Worse still, Bernice has promised to write a book of poetry that's due to be published in a week... and she can't think of anything to rhyme with 'Bubastis.'

Bernice Summerfield

Filthy Lucre
James Parsons and
Andrew Stirling-Brown

Money makes the world go round as can a few too many strong drinks.

But when Benny, in a fit of sobriety, agrees to do a pre-Advent favour for Irving Braxiatel, little does she suspect that a bit of corporate schmoozing with a fast food magnate is going to lead her into the biggest spin she's experienced for a very long time.

In a whistle-stop tour of frontier planets she encounters mysterious burials, guns and swords, legs and claws, lost treasure, mortal combat, conspiracy, stomach-churning posh nosh and a little man called Perkin. Oh, and love and war, again.

Meanwhile Jack has to tackle possibly the most irritating computer virus ever created and Ruth must clamber through the bowels of a crashed ship with 'The Man with the Vulpine Tattoo.'

And this was supposed to be the holiday season?

Bernice Summerfield

Bernice Summerfield: The Inside Story
Simon Guerrier

She has brought down empires and decided the fate of the universe. She is feared by the creatures of evil and revered wherever people have had just a little bit too much to drink. And Bernice Surprise Summerfield isn't yet out of her teens.

The Inside Story charts the history of everyone's favourite space archaeologist. We follow Bernice from her first appearance in Paul Cornell's 1992 novel Love and War, through more than 150 books and audio plays to previews of her forthcoming adventures.

The Inside Story talks to more than 100 people involved in Benny's development. Find out how she came to be, how she was developed and where she's going next.

See the stories that almost got told, and listen in on the creative battles, personality clashes and very, very bad jokes.

With exclusive access to never-before-published material, The Inside Story is as wild, exciting and unlikely a journey as any Benny has made herself.

Includes a Foreword by Benny's creator, Paul Cornell, and an Afterword by Lisa Bowerman, who plays Benny in the audio dramas.

ACKNOWLEDGEMENTS

Special thanks to Lisa and David for being Benny and Jack. To Xanna and Stuart for bringing it to physical life. To Austen, Steph and everyone at Planet 55 for their extraordinary patience and support. And especially to Josh, for making me laugh so much every single day, and of course dealing with anything that has more than four legs which invades our home.